DATE DUE

MAY 1 4 2010		
JUN 08 2010		
JUL 0 6 2015		

Demco

FREEZE FRAME

HEIDI AYARBE

LAURA GERINGER BOOKS
HARPERTEEN
An Imprint of HarperCollins *Publishers*

Library of Congress Cataloging-in-Publication Data
Ayarbe, Heidi.
Freeze frame / by Heidi Ayarbe. — 1st ed.
    p.   cm.
Summary: Fifteen-year-old Kyle believes he does not deserve to live after
accidentally shooting and killing his best friend.
    ISBN 978-0-06-135173-0 (trade bdg.)
    [1. Firearms—Fiction. 2. Violence—Fiction. 3. Death—Fiction. 4. Best
friends—Fiction. 5. Friendship—Fiction.] I. Title.
PZ7.A9618Fr 2008   2007049645
[Fic]—dc22   CIP
                                                              AC
Typography by Carla Weise
09 10 11 12 13 LP/RRDB 10 9 8 7 6 5
❖
First Edition

For my big sister, Carrie, and husband, César.
Thank you for believing.

Gray slats of light slipped between the bars, only to be swallowed by blackness. I shivered and pulled the colorless blanket around me, squeezing my eyes shut, holding my breath until the pain swelled and exploded in my chest. I exhaled and counted. Each breath took me farther away from where I wanted to be. But I had to go back. I had to change it.

Almost all of yesterday played like a movie in my head. I could start it, rewind, stop, fast-forward, and replay scenes—except for one. That scene never came clear. It was as if the film from the reel had been exposed to sunlight and gotten blotchy.

In some scenes, I even thought about making changes, doing a director's cut.

Melanie, go back and flip your hair to the other side.

When I thought about it like that, I felt like I had control, like it was a Quentin Tarantino movie, all out of order. I could change anything. But then I would remember. No matter how much changed inside my head, it was the same everywhere else.

October 8, 8:52 A.M., Scene One, Take One

We got up from the table because Jason had used all the syrup. The guy really poured it on. Dad ran down to the store to stock up, as if he knew I needed breakfast to be perfect.

Mom ordered us to get ready for the homecoming game and scooted us out of the kitchen. "You can eat in a couple of minutes."

"Sorry about the syrup, Mrs. Caroll," Jason said.

I shook my head. "My pancakes are gonna get cold. You could've saved a drop."

"Big deal, Kyle." Melanie flipped her hair. "God, Mom, he can be such a dumbass."

"Mel, watch your language." Mom glared.

Jason swallowed a laugh. In his house, he'd be nailed for saying *dumbass*. "Sorry, man. I like a lot of syrup."

"I guess so." I rolled my eyes. "Pig."

"You shouldn't insult your *guest*," Melanie huffed. "Grow up, Kyle."

Jason wasn't a "guest." You can't consider your best friend since kindergarten a guest, even if he hasn't been around for a while.

I glared at Mel. "It sure wouldn't have hurt you to save some either." I puffed out my cheeks and gut. "If I were you and had to wear that cheerleading skirt, I definitely wouldn't be eating pancakes—and especially not with syrup."

"Mom!" Melanie yelled. "Did you hear what he just said?"

Mom shot me her you're-a-step-from-deep-shit look.

"What?" I asked. "I didn't do anything. I swear!" But by that time Mom was after me with a spatula, and Jason and I ran out the kitchen door before she began screaming too.

"Oh, man," I grumbled, standing barefoot out on the frostbitten grass. I danced from one foot to the other. The cold burned my toes.

"Things don't change around here, huh?" Jason's teeth chattered. "It's cold, man. I'm, like, still in my pajamas." He looked around. "Remember when we decided to go snow camping out here after watching *Vertical Limit*?"

We'd thought it'd be pretty easy, pretend like we were mountaineers or something. Eat beef jerky for breakfast. We didn't even last an hour. We might've lasted longer if Jase hadn't insisted that he had frostbite. And I didn't want to have to explain to his mom why his toes fell off.

I laughed. "Maybe the coast is clear. Let's go back inside."

Jason and I peeked in the kitchen window. We saw Melanie blabbering away at Mom. Mom pushed a plate of half-eaten pancakes in front of her.

"It doesn't look good. Mel's pretty pissed." Jason turned toward me. "You might not get to go to the game."

"Nah." I shook my head. "You think?" I was standing on my toes, trying to keep my feet from freezing off.

"Yeah, man. That's the kind of shit that gets me sent to Pastor Pretzer."

Jason's family was really churchy, and he always had to talk to his minister when he got in trouble. Whenever we did something wrong at his house, Mrs. Bishop quoted something from the Bible. Her favorite was "Do unto others as you would have them do unto you."

When we were in ninth grade, I asked Mrs. Bishop if that meant we could do unto Kayla Griffin as we would have her do unto us, and she sent me home. I didn't think Mrs. Bishop would get so worked up. It's not like we were twelve or anything, and it *was* pretty funny.

Mom told me I was being disrespectful. I had to write a letter of apology to Mrs. Bishop and was put on Jason's "probation friend" list. After nine years of being best friends, I became a probation friend. Only Mrs. Bishop could think of crap like that.

"Well, I wouldn't have called her fat if she really was," I told Jason. "I'm not *that* big of an asshole." I looked back in the window. "Plus, when did our sisters become such freak shows? I mean, Mel used to be pretty cool before all the cheerleading and diets and shit."

Jason shrugged. "I dunno. So, what's next?"

"Let's hang in the shed until things cool down, unless you want to go around through the front door."

"Our feet would freeze off before we got there."

We crossed the backyard to Dad's work shed. The dew soaked my pajama pants. The door was locked, but I knew where Dad kept the key and grabbed it from the ledge. The shed had metal doors, kind of rusty; they screeched when we opened them.

"*Shhhh,*" Jason said. "Keep it down."

The shed smelled like a mixture of oil, fertilizer, and wood shavings.

If I were a director, I could change everything. Jason and I could've gone into the garage and waited. We could've sucked up the cold and snuck in the front door. We could've gone down the street to his house. Maybe I wouldn't have told Mel she was fat. As a director, I had so many choices.

That's why this movie in my head sucked. It didn't change. Nothing was under my control.

I shoved the palms of my hands into my eyes, pushing so hard, I could feel the thumping in the back of my brain. I heard the *tick, tick, tick* of the seconds marking the time in my head.

I smelled burning.

October 8, 9:03 A.M., Scene Two, Take One

Jason and I sat on the workbench. Light filtered through the grimy windows; everything looked distorted and gray.

"It's not much warmer in here than outside, Jase." I shivered.

"Yeah, but it's all right. We should come in here more often. We could call Alex and the guys over. There's a lot of cool stuff." Jason got up and started to look around.

The hair bristled on the back of my neck. "Last time we got busted."

"Well, we wouldn't have if you hadn't set the wood shavings on fire. Your dad and mom just about shit when they saw the flames."

"I didn't really think I could do it with a string and stick like they do in the movies. It was kinda cool, though."

Jason rolled his eyes. "Yeah."

Mom and Dad had acted as if we'd set the whole state on fire. They came running out with the fire extinguisher, screaming and hollering. The side of the shed turned black.

And Jason and I had to go to a fire safety course at the community center.

"What's your dad do in here, anyway?" Jason opened some drawers.

I shrugged. "Stuff, I guess." I looked around. Shelves sagged with the weight of paint cans, tools, tattered boxes, and unfinished projects. "I think he likes it because he doesn't have to clean it up. Mom doesn't even come in here."

"Check *this* out." Jason handed me a huge pair of curved, rusty scissors. They looked like a medieval torture tool.

"Let's see what else there is." I jumped off the bench and started going through drawers and boxes. "Hey, look!" I pulled down Grandpa's old 8 mm film projector. "I'd forgotten about this." A box of home movies was tucked behind it. I pulled out some reels and blew off the dust. The film still looked pretty clean. "Maybe we can set it up later, huh?"

Jase didn't answer. He was distracted.

"Whatcha got, Jase?"

Jason jimmied the lock on a metal box. He whistled. "Check this baby out."

I put the movies down. Jason's find was much better.

I opened my eyes. The tiny cell was bright. The sun had risen, but I wished it hadn't. I didn't know how long I was going to have to stay here or what I was supposed to do. It wasn't like Mom and Dad had sent me there as a punishment.

I could just hear how stupid that would've sounded. *Kyle, you really messed up this time. We're locking you up.*

Yesterday nobody said anything at all. It was how they looked that made me sick.

I lay back down on the cot.

Footsteps echoed down the hallway. The door slid open.

"Hey, kid!"

I didn't answer.

"Kid, um . . ." He shuffled some papers. "Kyle Caroll? You sleeping?"

I opened my mouth, but no words came out.

"Caroll, you got visitors here. You gotta get dressed and come out. They're not gonna wait all day."

I looked at the cop. I thought about the next scene of the movie. Everything got blurry then and went black. But that was the moment that everybody wanted to hear about. Over and over again. What could I say? I didn't know what had happened.

I thought about it again. The air smelled like iron and fire. I saw gray powder and heard a thundering boom. But I couldn't see.

One time Jase and I rented a movie called *Groundhog Day*, where the guy woke up every day on the same day. He had to get the day perfect, because if he didn't, he'd wake up on the same day again.

I kept wishing that would happen to me.

I looked at the cop standing at the door. I wondered how fast he could run. Sometimes these guys seemed a little too thick around the middle to catch anyone.

"There's a lot of people with a lot of questions, kid. You need to get ready."

He didn't look too tough. He looked kind of bored, actually. I wondered if he had been up all night. His face looked scruffy. My face never looked scruffy, but I shaved anyway, just 'cause the other guys did. My razors usually lasted about five or six weeks unless I forgot to take them out of the shower and they got all rusty. They lasted way longer than Mel's. It kinda sucked to have a sister hairier than me. Once I asked Jase if Brooke was hairier than he was. "I won't dignify that with a response," he said.

Dumb question. Jason was one of the hairiest guys in tenth grade.

"I don't have any answers." I turned my back to the cop.

October 8, 9:16 A.M., Scene Four, Take One

There was a terrible noise. And a smell like burned matches. Hundreds of them. I choked. Then everything got quiet except for a sharp ringing in my ears—like one of those emergency broadcast tests.

"Oh, shit, Jason. Shit, shit, shit, shit, shit. Mom and Dad are gonna shit." I looked around the shed. "Did anything break?"

But Jason didn't move.

"Jesus, Jason, help me out, man. We're in deep."

Jason was slumped against Dad's workbench.

He didn't say anything. I couldn't hear much anyway, but I would've at least seen his mouth move if he had said something, like in one of those silent films. It was all wrong. He just looked at me funny.

"Jason, don't be an asshole. Help me out. Jason?"

At that moment, I felt like somebody had drained all my blood. Why the hell was he doubled over that way?

The shed door screeched open. Mom blocked out all the light.

"What's going on, Kyle? What was that noise?" Mom

looked at me, at Jason. "Oh my God, Kyle, what happened?"

I stood there.

Mom pushed me out of the way and ran over to Jason. "Mel! Mel, call nine-one-one!"

Mel stood in the doorway, gaping.

We were all stuck, like somebody had hit the pause button, only Mom didn't pause. Mel stood. Jason slumped. I froze. And Mom moved, flittered, vibrated.

"Jesus, Mel. Get out of the way, then." Mom ran out of the shed and into the house. I could hear the hinge of the kitchen door. It squeaked and stayed ajar. Dad needed to fix the door. Mom came back with a blanket and sat on the shed floor. She held Jason's head in her lap.

Mom whispered something to Jason. It was a deep chant—humming, murmuring, rocking back and forth.

The cop came closer. "Kyle Caroll? Kid, you hafta get up now."

I had to stay still. I had to stop time. Freeze frame. Pause.

"You've got some lawyer, your PO, and your folks here."

The film wasn't pausing.

"PO?"

"Yeah, kid, Mark Grimes, your parole officer. He was

here last night with you."

"Oh, yeah, that's right."

"Get up."

I couldn't see my parents. I shook my head.

He leaned over me. "Get up and get dressed. C'mon, kid."

I looked around the cell. They'd told me it was a holding cell—someplace I'd be for only a night or two until they figured out what to do with me.

I turned to the cop. His nametag said BYERS. "What's the date?"

"October ninth." He scowled. "Let's go, kid. They're waiting."

I looked at him. How was it possible to keep moving forward when everything had stopped yesterday?

The same two officers from yesterday were in a cramped room with a smudgy plastic clock hanging crooked on the wall. I looked down at my wrist. They had taken my watch the night before.

The cops were drinking their coffee black. The fatso cop drank in slurps, steam fogging up his glasses. He had to take them off and wipe them. The glasses, thick and heavy, left red indentations on the bridge of his Silly Putty nose.

Mom hugged me—too tight. "We're going to figure this out, Kyle."

I shuddered. It didn't seem like there was a lot of figuring out to do. They pulled out a chair for me.

"Michael, we need to ask your son some questions,"

said the fatso cop. They knew Dad. I don't know how or why, but they did.

Dad nodded.

I sat between Dad and our lawyer—Mr. Allison, who Dad golfed with every Thursday afternoon. I guess Dad had called in a favor.

Mark held out his hand and introduced himself. "I'm Mark Grimes, the parole officer assigned to Kyle's case. We have a detention hearing tomorrow during which I will recommend that Kyle be left in custody until all his psych evaluations are complete and I can better assess the situation."

Mark crossed his arms. He wore a blindingly white shirt that showed his muscles. His head glistened—the perfect kind of bald and tan that you only see on Harley guys. There was a tattoo on his wrist of some Chinese writing or something.

Mark had come to the detention center when they processed me the day before. "Everything is just procedure," he said. "Follow the directions of the detention staff when they're booking you."

They photographed, fingerprinted, and strip-searched me.

When they finished, Mark was waiting. He looked me up and down. "Basically, kid, you belong to the state of Nevada. I work for the state, so now you belong to me."

"Yes, sir."

"We're going to be spending lots of time together until things get worked out around here, so you might as well call me Mark."

I nodded. "Okay."

They took a mug shot. If Jason had ever had to get a mug shot, Pastor Pretzer would have sent him to hell or something. Maybe I could get him a copy. I was about to ask Mark for my one phone call when I remembered. My stomach lurched and I almost threw up. I leaned my head against a cool brick wall.

"Kid, you okay?"

I nodded.

"It's late. You'd better get some sleep. We have a big day tomorrow. Any questions?"

"Um, is my mom okay?" The lump returned to my throat when I thought about how Mom had looked in the hospital parking lot.

"Your family is fine. You'll see them tomorrow. Get some rest." Mark clapped me on the back, closing the door to the tiny room.

I hadn't realized how tired I was until then. I couldn't sleep, though. My mind replayed the day over and over again, always getting stuck at that one scene. A black screen faded to forms of gray, as if the shed had been dipped in murky fog. Jason's body was blurred, lying in a black pool. Then the screen became red.

"Kyle, are you ready?" Mr. Allison asked. "We need you to focus now."

"Oh, yeah. Sure." I nodded, looking around the small room.

The skinny cop stared at me with buggy eyes. He reminded me of Gollum from *The Lord of the Rings*. Fatty, on the other hand, looked more like Igor. It was like *Clash of the Movie Tools*.

> "Igor, bring me the brain."
>
> "Yes, master." Igor rubs his hands together and hobbles down the dark corridor to the deep freeze.
>
> "My precious. My precious," Gollum says, limping after him.
>
> "Rubbish, Smeagol. Bloody fool," Dr. Frankenstein mutters. "You'd think he could find something appropriate to wear over those putrid rags." He pinches his nose and sneers down the hall after the receding shadows. He flips through a thick medical book, then looks over his spectacles at the body, prone on the metal slab.
>
> The sky flashes with streaks of lightning. For a split second light illuminates the corpse's pasty face.

I jerked my head sideways and gasped. Everybody in the room stared at me. Dad's hand was on my shoulder.

"Do you need me to repeat the question?" Gollum leaned back in his chair. "Can you take me through what happened yesterday, step by step?"

Both of the officers pulled out their little notebooks at the same time. It looked like one of those choreographed moves in Bollywood. I wondered if one of them would get up on the table and sing. They looked at me in the way adults look at kids on those after-school specials before the kid admits to having tried beer at a party. Do directors tell them to make those faces?

I looked at Dad.

Dad nodded.

I told them everything I knew, up until the blurry scene. Their pencils whirred. They flipped the pages and scratched more.

"We need to know what happened next. Do you remember pointing the gun? Squeezing the trigger? Anything like that?" Gollum leaned in.

"I don't know." I shook my head. Scene Three was gone—a snippet of the film cut and thrown out. I'd seen a movie called *The Final Cut* where people had these implants in their brains that recorded their entire lives. After people died, cutters would edit their lives and present the recordings to the dead people's friends and family in the form of a movie. It was like my scenes had already been edited.

Igor looked up over his glasses. "Hmm . . . ," he grunted.

"Okay, let's skip to what happened next. We'll go back to that part later. What do you remember after that?"

October 8, 9:18 A.M., Scene Four, Take One, Continued

Mel and I watched Mom and Jason.

I heard Dad's car drive up. "Dad's back with the syrup, Mom." Now we could have our pancakes and go back to our regular day. I remembered I hadn't eaten yet. I wondered if we'd have time to eat before the game. I felt hungry—starved.

"Mel, get yourself together and go get Dad." Mom held Jason's head in her arms. She still rocked back and forth. "Now, Mel. *Go!*"

Mel moved in slow motion. She rested her hand on the doorframe and stepped back out of the shed.

"Hurry!" Mom shouted.

Mom changed at that moment—she became a still image. Everything in the shed lost the illusion of motion, as if the film had slipped off the reel.

Freeze frame.

Fast-forward . . . Pause . . . But there was no rewind.

Play.

"Hurry!" Mom hollered again, the film spinning back on the reel.

Mel jerked into action. Her ponytail bobbed up and down with each step. The kitchen door slammed shut. I heard distant shouts and hollers.

Jason and I were the only ones left on pause. Stuck. I started to worry we'd never catch up.

Come on, Jason. Get up, get up, get up, get up, get up.

Dad got to the shed in three strides. Mel ran behind him. Dad wrenched the shed doors open all the way. The rusty metal and hinges moaned. Light streamed in. The gray disappeared and I felt relieved, squinting in the bright October light. Maybe the dream was over.

"Oh, Jesus, Kyle." Dad gripped my shoulders and slipped the gun out of my hand. The gun was hot, burning through my palm. When it was gone, I felt like I could step away. Rewind everything and start again. But the rewind button was jammed, and we just moved forward—without direction, without a script.

This wasn't supposed to happen.

"God, Maggie, what's going on?" Dad held his fingers to Jason's neck. "Jesus Christ, oh Jesus," he whispered.

"I've called the ambulance. There's a lot of blood. I, I—" Mom's chin wrinkled and her voice wavered. "Michael, you need to go get Gail and Jim."

Why did Dad have to go get Mr. and Mrs. Bishop?

I glared at Mom. I knew they'd be pissed. But they never said *pissed* at the Bishop household. So they'd probably be "totally disappointed."

Jason was just messing around. He was gonna get up soon. I waited for him to say something.

"Kyle, come on." Dad pulled me out of the shed. Mel stood outside, shivering. "Melanie, get a coat. You need to wait out front for the ambulance. I'm going to get the Bishops."

Mel nodded dumbly, and Dad left me standing outside the shed in the wet grass. By then, I couldn't feel my toes. I couldn't feel anything.

5

Gollum scratched his pointy chin. He looked at Dad, at Igor. "Michael, are you the legal owner of the gun?"

Dad nodded.

"Can you tell us why you had the gun?"

"Yeah. Ray, my brother; he had a pawnshop in Reno." Dad cleared his throat. "He had some problems, so I bought him the gun."

The officers exchanged a look. There's something about the word *pawnshop* that makes people get weird, like they're embarrassed about it.

"When he closed the shop, he returned it to me." Dad's voice got real quiet. "I didn't even remember. It was so long ago."

"We need to get your registration and permit. Can

you get that for us?"

"Of course. Certainly. I brought it with me. Yesterday . . ." Dad's voice trailed off. "I couldn't seem to find anything."

The cops wrote furiously. Dad's hands trembled, handing over the registration and permit. I felt like my sense of time was off again.

I wanted it all to be over. I wanted the policemen to leave everybody alone. I wanted the sick feeling to leave my stomach. I wanted to stop smelling the burn. I wanted the movie to stop.

"Kyle." Gollum leaned in. "I really need you to take us back to yesterday."

The rewind didn't work. Didn't he know that?

"Can you do that?" His eyes widened, the lids peeling back.

I rubbed my eyes. My throat tightened. It was hard to swallow. "But," I stammered, "but the movie. It's missing a scene."

October 8, 9:24 A.M., Scene Five, Take One

Mrs. Bishop brushed by me. "Maggie, what happened?" she asked. She dropped to the floor. "No, my baby! Hold on, hold on, hold on." Her words barely made it through her tears.

Mr. Bishop came right behind the men with the stretcher. They pushed Mom and Mrs. Bishop out of the way. They talked fast into walkie-talkies, hoisting Jason onto the stretcher.

"Gunshot wound to the chest."

"Fifteen-year-old boy."

"Nine millimeter."

"Massive blood loss."

"How long ago did this happen?" They looked at me. "Kid, can you remember?"

I shook my head. "I don't know." How long ago did what happen?

Mom stepped forward. "We heard a loud noise around nine fifteen. I ran out, saw what had happened, and called nine-one-one."

The blanket dripped black with blood. A crimson pool formed on the floor.

Jason blinked every once in a while. I could hear him gasping. He made a terrible, wheezing, choking sound, worse than anything I'd ever heard.

Stop it. Stop making those noises. Say something.

His eyelids fluttered.

I reached out to touch his arm, but the EMTs pushed me away.

The Bishops ran behind the stretcher. Mrs. Bishop heaved herself into the back of the ambulance and sat next

24

to Jason. The paramedics turned on the lights and siren and peeled out of the driveway. Mr. Bishop and Dad followed the ambulance.

"Mom, you need to change," Mel said. I looked at Mom's shirt, then down at my pajamas, stained with the same red-black color. I felt splatters on my face and started to scratch at the dried blood spots.

"And the pancakes are burning," Mel said.

Was that the terrible burning smell?

Mom pushed me to Mel. "I've got the pancakes. You help Kyle."

Mel nodded. She steered me through the kitchen door and upstairs. "Christ, Kyle, *snap out of it!*" Mel looked nervous. She threw some clothes at me. "Get dressed. Wash your face. We have to get to the hospital."

My toes were blue—the same blue as Mel's cheerleading uniform, as Mom's eyes, as Jason's lips. Why were his lips so blue? I pulled my socks on and shoved my feet into my orange sneakers.

"Come on, Kyle. We need to get going." Mel yanked my sweatshirt over my head. She took a cold washcloth and scrubbed at my face. She jerked back when she touched my hair and gagged. "Put on a baseball cap." Her voice quaked.

"I didn't—" I couldn't finish the sentence. "He isn't—?"

Mel wiped her cheeks. "Come on. We've gotta go."

We rushed downstairs. In the kitchen, Mom held on to

an old towel and wiped her hands, over and over again. The pancakes were burned and the kitchen looked as disastrous as the morning I bet Jase he couldn't eat seventeen pancakes. I never thought he'd actually go through with it. I ended up losing out on an entire semester of Twinkies from my lunch for that bet.

Jase was the biggest sophomore in all of Carson City. At Carson High School, all the coaches drooled over him. Jase liked sports enough. He just had other shit he wanted to do more. They didn't get that. I did.

Mom led me to the garage. "Kyle, get in the car. Mel, go over to the Bishops' and get Brooke and Chase. We're going to the hospital."

I climbed into the very back of the Suburban. I pulled my knees in tight and tried to squeeze the pain out of my stomach.

Mel came back with Brooke and Chase. Brooke and Mel cried all the way to the hospital. Chase didn't say anything.

He passed his Jack Sack from one hand to the other. *Swish, swish, swish, swish.* I could tell he was scared. Even though he was only eight, he did everything with Jason and me. He was a great kid. Chase unbuckled his seat belt and turned around. His head popped over the seat back, and he held out his hand.

I took it in mine.

"Kyle, is that what you remember?" Gollum smiled.

"Yeah, those Jack Sacks *swish* when you pass them back and forth. You know what I mean? All those little pieces of sand—tiny, tiny pieces of sand, trapped in that leather cover. They *swish*."

"I do. I do." Gollum nodded.

He was lying. He probably didn't even know what a Jack Sack was.

"Can you remember anything else? Besides the sounds of the Jack Sack, of course?" Igor looked nervous. Sweat rings soaked through his gray shirt. He paced back and forth and wiped his forehead with a coffee-stained handkerchief. Maybe he was hungry. I hoped they had more bagels for him in the other room.

"You know Chase can say every word, line for line, from the X-Men movies?" I shook my head. "Every damn word."

Thinking about Chase made everything much worse. I chewed on my lip. I wondered how they'd explain all this to him. Who'd tell him?

"Okay, Kyle. We need to get back to what happened yesterday." Gollum and Igor exchanged a look. Igor rolled his shoulders back in circles and moved his head side to side. "Let's talk about what came next."

"I don't know. I guess. The hospital. Yeah, we waited at the hospital."

I looked over at Dad. He nodded, like I was doing okay, like I should keep going. He tried to smile, but his eyes looked like the Nevada road map—red lines and dark circles. He hadn't shaved and his shoulders curved in. Dad shrank that day. And it was all my fault.

6

October 8, 9:39 A.M., Scene Six, Take One

Dad waited for us at the emergency room entrance. He held a cotton ball to the crook in his arm. He threw his heavy coat over his shoulder. "Maggie, we're donating blood. He needs blood. Melanie and Brooke can go too."

"Why can't we?" Chase stepped forward, holding my hand.

The emergency room doors opened and shut. People hurried in and out. Doctors and nurses rushed up and down the hallways. Cushioned footsteps echoed on the linoleum floor. I listened to the crinkle of cheap hospital gowns being put on and clothes dropping to the floor with soft thuds.

It smelled like sterile plastic, a kind of sickly new smell.

I'd come here two years earlier when Jason bet me the Fourth of July sparklers his grandma brought him from Mexico that I couldn't jump from the roof onto the porch. I missed the porch and landed in the hedges, breaking my ankle. I had to wear a cast for ten weeks and then do another five of physical therapy. We both got in big trouble for that one. Jase shared his sparklers with me anyway, just because he felt so bad. But I didn't remember the hospital being so loud.

"Mr. Caroll, I want to give my blood, too." Chase looked up at Dad. He pulled on Dad's sleeve.

"You're too young, Chase. You need to be bigger." Dad took us into the waiting room. "You can help by sitting with your parents."

Mr. and Mrs. Bishop sat in the far corner, holding tightly on to each other. Chase tugged on my arm. "C'mon, Kyle."

The Bishops looked up at Dad and me. They had these empty, expressionless eyes. Mrs. Bishop held a Bible.

Dad put his coat on. "Let's give them some space. We'll wait outside."

Chase let go of my arm. He ran over to Mr. and Mrs. Bishop.

"Is he okay?" Chase asked. "What happened?"

Dad led me outside. I felt better in the bitter October cold. The wind chafed my cheeks, and my fingers turned numb again. I didn't move closer to the building.

I didn't want protection.

Mel and Mom joined us. Mel pulled her jacket up high and hugged herself. She was still wearing her cheerleading uniform. The four of us stood in the cold silence. The doors whirred open and shut with each patient coming and going.

We waited.

October 8, 10:02 A.M., *Scene Seven, Take One*

Dad and Mom didn't speak. Mom chewed her nails. She went to the hospital chapel. She lit candles. She brought back cheap vending-machine cocoa for all of us. I singed my tongue and the skin peeled back, raw and burned. I liked the feel of the burn. It was the first thing I'd felt all morning.

We waited.

I peeked through the windows and my breath fogged the glass. The Bishops sat huddled together. From the outside, they looked like a normal family, just sitting in an ugly room. Grandma and Grandpa Bishop had come. Every now and then, Grandpa Bishop would walk outside and light his pipe. He'd nod at us, puff on his pipe, and return to the warmth of the waiting room.

Inside, the machines beeped and footsteps padded down the hallways. Telephones rang. Children cried. When the doors zipped open, the sounds amplified by thousands, but then the doors would shut again.

"That's his ER doctor." Dad's words shattered the underwater silence that surrounded us.

I didn't want the waiting to be over.

Please be okay. Please, please, please be okay. Please. I clenched my fists.

"Should we go in?" Mom asked. She stepped toward the door.

"Maggie." Dad shook his head. He pulled her into his arms. The four of us pressed our noses against the cold glass. My heart accelerated. I bit my burned tongue.

October 8, 10:46 A.M., Scene Seven, Take One, Continued

The doctor approached the Bishops. He shook his head. He didn't say anything. He didn't have to.

I looked at my watch: 10:46.

10:46.

I yanked out the winder. The hands froze.

We didn't have to wait anymore.

Dad's shoulders slumped. He struggled to catch his breath. Mom leaned into him, clutching his shirt. Mel threw up right outside the ER doors. My heart stopped.

I hadn't even seen the cops until then. I didn't pay attention to the tapping on my shoulder. I kept staring into

the waiting room, hoping that everything was a mistake—
a horrible mistake. We needed to do another take of the
scene. Throw out this script. Write another one.

Time of death: 10:46.

Mom looked really confused. She grabbed my shoulders and shook her head. She looked right through me,
eyes wild.

Nobody made any sense. Everything moved in slow
motion and everybody had warped kidnapper voices.

Dad shouted something and threw his coat over my
shoulders. Mel puked again. The officers talked to me.
They pushed me toward their car. But the sound track I
heard was the quiet gurgling noise Jason had made earlier.

Cold metal handcuffs tightened on my wrists. I felt
thankful for the warmth of the police car, but I couldn't
stop shaking.

I saw Mom holding on to Dad; Mel's hand was on her
stomach; Dad slouched around both of them. They looked
like they were drowning out there. My head pounded. I
watched through the back window as the car turned a
corner and my family faded out, disappearing from the
screen.

October 8, 10:46

The End

7

Gollum and Igor cleared their throats.

"Kyle," asked Gollum, "how long had you known about your dad's gun in the shed?"

"I—I don't know."

Dad shifted in his chair. Mom dropped her head.

"We're just trying to clear a few things up, okay?" Igor dabbed sweat off his forehead with a yellowed handkerchief, took off his glasses, and rubbed his eyes.

"Kyle," continued Gollum, "whose idea was it to look for the gun?"

My chest constricted. "I don't know. I don't know."

"Did you point the gun at Jason knowing it was loaded?"

"I don't, I don't remember." I closed my eyes, but all I saw was the gun in my hand, like the camera had zoomed in for a close-up.

"Who taught you how to shoot a gun?" They looked at Dad, and the camera zoomed out: an aerial view of us sitting around a wobbly table, the steam of the coffee curling up, fogging the lens, blurring the scene.

Igor raised his left eyebrow. "Did you aim the gun at Jason?"

Did I? Did I point and aim and shoot and kill? I squeezed my eyes shut, only to see the red lens and a pool of blood.

"Can you tell us who taught you how to shoot a gun?" Gollum smiled. His lips stretched thin across yellowed teeth.

"I—I—I never—" I stuttered. "I don't know." I didn't even know I *had* shot the gun.

"Please help us out here. We just need to get some answers." Igor paced back and forth. He drummed his fingers on his fat belly.

"Kyle," Gollum said, his eyes boring holes through me, "had you and Jason been getting along all right lately? Did you have any fights or disagreements you'd like to tell me about? Maybe some things happened at school?"

I thought back.

"Hey, Jase! Where're you heading?" I had caught up to him leaving the building after science.

35

"Hey, I looked for you by your locker. Me 'n' the guys are going to Taco Bell."

"Again?" It slipped out. I cleared my throat. "Cool."

"There's room, man. C'mon."

We'd joined up with Alex, Pinky, and Troy as we made our way to the parking lot. Alex rolled his eyes and said, "Yeah, Shadow, there's room. You don't take up much space."

Jason laughed. "C'mon, Kyle." He lowered his voice. "Dude, they just mess around like that. They're pretty cool when you give them a chance. Plus, *yo quiero Taco Bell.*" The perfect Taco Bell Chihuahua impersonation. "I'm dying for one of those triple-bean burritos."

"What, so you can drop a bomb in math?" I cracked up, picturing Mr. Rivera running around the room frantically to open all air vents and windows before we met our demise from Jason's toxic gas.

Alex exchanged a look with Pinky and Troy. "Real mature." Pinky and Troy grunted.

I shrugged.

Jason looked back at Alex and rolled his eyes. So now Jase didn't even laugh at fart jokes?

Alex laughed. Then Pinky and Troy did. It was like Alex was the brain for the three. One brain. Three heads.

"C'mon, Kyle."

"Nah. Brown-bagging it today. Got some homework to do before math."

"Okay then. See ya after lunch."

"Yeah, see ya." It felt like somebody had just punched me in the stomach.

I watched them walk to Alex's new four-door truck. Alex was one of the only tenth graders with a driver's license. And for his sixteenth, his parents had given him a sweet cherry red truck.

Jason turned around and shouted, "I'll bring you something back. We're still cool for after school, right?"

I smiled. "Yeah, we're cool."

Igor cleared his throat. I came back to the same small room with the stench of sweat. "You remember anything at all, kid? Anything we should know about?"

I thought about Jase and the guys and felt the sting of tears. I shook my head. Jesus, I was such a tool.

"Did you and Jason struggle in the shed? Did you fight?"

"No." My chest felt like Igor was sitting on top of it. "I know we didn't fight. We never fight."

"Fought," Igor corrected me.

"Yeah," I whispered.

Mr. Allison stood up. "I'd like to know where this line of questioning is going. We're talking about a fifteen-year-old boy here and his best friend." Mr. Allison clenched his jaw.

"We're talking about a fifteen-year-old corpse, okay?" Igor snapped back.

Mom gasped.

Dad stood up. "We've talked to you enough today. My son, m-my son . . ." He stammered. He kicked his chair out of the way and paced the room. "I just went to the store for more syrup, okay. That's all they wanted that morning—maple syrup."

Fucking maple syrup.

"Let's settle down, everybody—take it step-by-step," Gollum said in a soft voice. He hummed his words like music.

Mr. Allison stood up. "What are you trying to do here?"

Everything started to sound scripted, like in *The Truman Show*. I half expected Igor to hold up his pen, grin, and say, *It's a good thing we have these brand-new Swick permanent marking pens to write down this boy's statement— the only kind of pens the Carson City police department uses.*

Then Gollum would pipe up, *Oh, and these bagels from the Kaufmann Bagel Shop, all natural, all kosher, using only the finest ingredients purchased from local farmers, are de-e-e-e-licious.*

I listened for a catchy jingle. Mr. Allison pulled me

back to the room by squeezing my shoulder.

Gollum stood up. "We're trying to find the truth, Mr. Allison—what really happened in that shed yesterday morning. We think that the Bishops deserve at least that much."

The room spun. The officers cleared their throats and scribbled in their notepads. Mr. Allison looked angry. Mom buried her face in her hands.

"Don't even start to play that power game with me." Mr. Allison's eyes narrowed. His comb-over flopped the wrong way.

We'd gotten to that part in the movie where the innocent guy tells everything or the guilty one lawyers up. But I didn't know which guy I was.

"Like we said, we're just looking for the truth." Igor gnawed on a toothpick. The clock ticked, rattling the walls. Louder. Louder. Deafening.

Then Gollum snapped his notebook closed and put his pen away in his breast pocket. "Mark," he said, looking at my PO. "He's all yours."

Mark finally spoke. Until then he'd looked like he was meditating. Or napping. This all had to be pretty routine to the guy. "Tomorrow morning, at eight A.M., you will stand before the juvenile master. Kyle, that's the kind of judge who handles cases like yours. But as I said, until I have the full psych evaluation, Kyle will not be going home." Mark uncrossed his arms and snapped his gum.

"Mr. and Mrs. Caroll, we appreciate your time." Gollum held out his fingers and wrapped them around Mom's small hand. "We hope to resolve this quickly."

How can you resolve a dead body? Dead is dead, right?

The two policemen left. Mr. Allison stood up. "Michael, call me if you have any questions. We'll figure this out."

"Thanks, Bob. We really appreciate it." Dad shook his hand. Mom hugged him.

"Kyle." Mr. Allison came over to me. I looked right through him. I wanted him to disappear too. "I'm real sorry about Jason. I know he was your best friend."

I'm sorry, too.

My throat constricted and everything went out of focus. Fade to black.

Mr. Allison left with Mom and Dad. They took me back to my holding cell to wait for Mark. I counted the seconds and a scene flashed through my mind, then stuck there.

I tried to erase it, because it scared me. I had never thought about death like that before. I had never wished for it to come and get me.

8

Mark and I walked down a hallway. We passed by other cells and a social room. Everyone wore the same blue-gray jumpsuits, like the kind auto mechanics use. There were some kids lying down on bunk beds playing cards. A skinny girl lay on a cot facing a concrete wall. Her shoulders jerked up and down like she was crying.

"What's wrong with her?" I asked.

Mark looked at her, then back at me. "Not my case."

"Are there a lot of us?"

"What do you mean?"

"Cases? A lot of cases?"

Mark nodded. "Too many, I'm afraid."

"Oh." My sneakers squeaked on the linoleum. I was glad they had let me keep my orange sneakers. It was this pair of knockoff Vans I'd won when I went to the International Chili Cookoff with the Bishops last spring. I was the only one who could eat the whole bowl of Tasmanian Devil–Breath Chili from Down Under without asking for a glass of water. After winning, I couldn't feel my mouth, and I guess my lips and tongue looked pretty swollen, because the Bishops rushed me to the emergency room. Jason was pretty pissed.

"I didn't even get a chance to eat my Indian fry bread."

"Thanks for your concern, asshole."

"Man, Kyle, you did this for a pair of butt-ugly shoes."

"They're not ugly. They're tight." I was sucking on ice, so when I spoke, drool dripped down my chin.

"They're orange."

"So. Orange is tight."

"You'll never wear 'em."

"Yeah, I will." I pulled off my high-tops and put on the orange chili shoes.

"You'll never wear 'em in public."

"Wanna bet?" By that time, a tingling numb feeling had crept into my throat. Blisters popped out on my lips. I have to admit I was a little worried. I chomped on the ice and let it trickle down my throat.

"Yeah. I bet you won't wear 'em."

"I'll wear 'em. Every day."

"For how long? A weekend?"

"A year. I'll be the fashion trendsetter this year."

"Yeah, right."

"Bet your 1948 Captain Marvel Adventures number eighty-one."

Jason paused. "And if I win?"

"You get any film collection I have."

"Any?"

"Yep."

"You're not gonna stick me with that Bollywood shit."

"Like I said. Your pick."

"Okay. I want your David Lynch collection, including *Twin Peaks*."

I paused. This was big.

"What? Stakes too high?"

"Deal."

"You're on." Jason grinned.

I looked down. The orange sneakers contrasted with the gray jumpsuit thing. They were pretty dirty. So far I'd worn them for 170 days straight.

"Kyle!"

I turned around and saw Mark standing in the middle of the corridor, fifty feet away.

"Have you been listening to me?"

I shook my head. "Sorry." I looked down at my shoes. "I was just thinking."

Mark nodded. "Come on. Dr. Matthews is going to help you work through some things now. She'll be good to talk to."

It was better to think about my shoes.

"You seem like a pretty good kid, Kyle." Mark clapped me on the back. He liked back clapping. I guessed it was the manliest way he could hug a guy. "You're going to be okay," he said.

Who cares if I'm okay? What about Jason? What about Chase? What about Mom? It was like the world had taken a freaky turn and I'd ended up with all cameras focused on me.

We arrived at a dinky office at the end of a long hall-way. It didn't have the doctor's name on it or anything, so I kind of figured she just came every now and again. I peeked in the window.

Dr. Matthews's matted hair was swept up into a knot on the back of her head. It actually looked like a spider-webby doorknob from a 1930s horror flick—like in an old Boris Karloff film. Wisps of gray around a rubber band, smack in the middle of her head. She wore a shapeless dress with bright colors and jungle prints. She jingled when she walked because of the loads of jewelry that covered her body, head to toe. The office smelled like burned cinnamon.

I looked at Mark. "She's the one who's going to

decide if I'm sane?"

Mark pushed me through the door and introduced me to Dr. Matthews. "I'll be waiting for you when you're done."

"You'll have to excuse the makeshift office. I'm getting mine redecorated. It should be done sometime next week." Dr. Matthews smiled, and lines webbed from the corners of her eyes to her temples.

She cocked her head to the side and said, "We have a lot to talk about. Why don't we just jump right in."

Jump.

"Jump!"

That's what Jase and I shouted to Mel and Brooke when we went barreling down Elm Street in Dad's rickety firewood wagon. We were in fourth grade and thought it would be fun to tear down the street. We just never thought about the steering part. Or the stopping part. Jason took the helm, and just as we hit the turn going onto Richmond, Jase shouted "Jump!" He knew we'd never make the turn, and a wall of rosebushes was straight ahead. Jase and I jumped, but Mel and Brooke didn't. They catapulted forward into the rosebushes, and it took about three hours for Mom to dethorn them. That time neither of us was too bugged about getting busted because it was worth a lifetime of laughs to watch them fly into the bushes—a classic Buster Keaton moment. But I kind of think Brooke still holds a grudge because of some lame-ass scar she has on her forehead.

They should've jumped.

"Jump," I whispered, and shook my head. "Jump."

"Kyle?" Dr. Matthews raised her right eyebrow. "Would you like to take a seat?"

She sat on a colorful couch and leaned against the pillows. I sat on the far end of the same couch. There was nowhere else to go.

"Can you tell me how you're feeling right now?"

I looked down at my sneakers. God, I was glad to have those orange sneakers.

"Okay. Maybe you could walk me through what happened yesterday."

So I told her the same stuff I'd told the police. She just listened and nodded. When I finished, she didn't say anything for a long time. I kinda thought she was asleep until she sighed. It wasn't a regular sigh. It had kind of a hum to it. Maybe it was a hum and not a sigh. I really couldn't tell. She might've just had some kind of respiratory problem.

"Can you remember anything at all between finding the gun and Jason being shot?"

Scene Three. All I saw were split-second images, like in the old days when the movies flashed subliminal messages of popcorn and Coke on the screen. Nobody saw the popcorn or Coke images—they just got really hungry. That's what I saw when I tried to remember Scene Three. Flashes that I couldn't splice together to make the scene whole. And it made me feel sick.

I shifted on the couch. "I'm trying." I picked at a callus.

She laid her hand on my arm. "That's okay. You'll remember."

But what if I don't want to? What if I really did it? On purpose? What if I'm a killer?

"I'm here to help you fill in the blanks—put the pieces of that day back together."

I looked up at her and clenched my jaw.

"Why don't you tell me how you feel about what happened?"

Everybody wanted explanations. Everybody wanted to "get" it. Get me. I never had to explain myself to Jase. He got that on Tuesdays I'd always be late showing up to his house to go to school because I had to watch the first five minutes of the re-reruns of *The X Files* to make sure it wasn't episode 6X07, "Rain King," where Mulder is almost killed by a cow that's dropped into his hotel room—the only one I haven't seen in all nine seasons. A fucking cow, of all things.

Most people would just think I should rent it and get it over with. But Jason understood. He knew that renting it would be like giving up. He just got stuff. Or he used to.

Dr. Matthews cleared her throat. "Can you tell me how you feel about yesterday?"

It's like I hit the fucking delete button. *Zap!* He's gone. How was I supposed to feel about that? I looked at Dr. Matthews and shook my head.

"Okay, let's try this. What's the first thing that comes to your mind as we speak?"

Sorry.

"It doesn't have to be anything you think I want to hear. Feel free to let your mind wander and grab onto the very first thought you have."

Sorry.

I started to feel pretty hot in that closed-in office. It was about the size of Grandma Nancy's linen closet—with a lumpy couch and schoolroom desk squashed into it. There were no windows, just the one that was on the aluminum door. Sweat stung my eyes, and I wiped it off my forehead.

Dr. Matthews cocked her head to the side. "Are you okay?"

No. I mopped the sweat off my forehead and stared at my shoes.

Then we sat quietly until Dr. Matthews said, "We'll have a chance to get to know each other better. If you need to see me, even when it's not your appointment time, you can always ask for me. Do you have any questions?"

How long will it take the state to build up the case so they can put me away forever? What will it be like to live in prison? Did I do it? Did I kill Jason on purpose?

She had a kitchen timer on the desk. She picked it up and slipped it into her pocket. "Our time's up for now, Kyle."

Mark knocked on the door. Dr. Matthews invited him in. Some kid stood in the hallway with a brown-uniformed cop. The kid had piercing holes all over his face: eyebrows, lips, nose, chin. He stuck out his tongue—split down the middle like a snake's to match the tattoo that coiled up his neck to his ear. He glared at me.

"I'll be right with you, Simon." Dr. Matthews smiled a tired smile.

Simon? Talk about the wrong name. A kid like that should be named something meaner, tougher, like Damian. But then again, Arnold Schwarzenegger doesn't look much like an Arnold.

Dr. Matthews closed the door behind Mark.

"It's my turn, you mad cow! It's my hour! The judge said." Simon had a high, piercing voice, like it had never gotten around to cracking. The door didn't do much to muffle his shouts.

Dr. Matthews winced and sighed. She turned to Mark. "Please take a seat."

Mark looked really uncomfortable sitting behind the small desk.

49

"We need more time," she said. "I want to see him every day."

Mark looked at me. I shrugged. I kinda figured that Simon could use more Dr. Matthews time than me; he was a human colander, for God's sake.

"Kyle's not quite ready to talk." She smiled at me. "The mind is a wonderful thing. It has a way of protecting us from the truth sometimes."

Why can't I remember?

I dunno.

Dude, do you remember?

I'm the dead one.

So dead people don't have memories?

I haven't really thought about it.

Some help you are.

You could cut me some slack here. I am the dead one.

Yeah. You mentioned that.

Dr. Matthews stood up. She looked like a prism; her body shattered into thousands of colors. If she were one of Jase's superheroes, she'd be Mega Matthews, the huge psychiatrist who wraps her enemies in straitjackets, then poisons them with cinnamon incense, erasing their memories.

"Kyle, are you listening?" Dr. Matthews asked.

I looked up and shook my head. I had forgotten where I was for a moment and squinted. Dr. Matthews was pretty "mega."

God, I'm such an asshole.

"I'm going to give you some medication for a few days to keep you on an even keel. It's nothing to worry about. Just standard procedure, okay?" Dr. Matthews swayed in the middle of the room, and I focused, pulling all the color back together to make her whole again.

"Okay. Sure. Standard procedure."

She squeezed my arm. "We'll talk tomorrow."

Great. Mega Matthews, take two. How many takes would I need to get it right? I guessed as long as the state wanted to pay for it.

Mark led me back to my cell. "I'll see you tomorrow morning. We have the detention hearing first thing. I'll come for you at seven forty-five."

Tick, tick, tick.

Everything kept moving forward.

Stop. Just push the stop button.

But Mark's lips moved. People walked by us in the hallway. The afternoon light grew dim. And I was stuck on play.

That night they gave me Dr. Matthews's pills with my food. My world lost its colors. The brightness turned to shades of gray and forms lost their edge. But my dreams were filled with red, black, and deep purple. Veins, tendons, arteries, muscles, and blood, pumping, flowing, and then clotting and stopping. I woke up when the room was so black, I couldn't even see my own hand. I stayed awake and listened to some girl cry down the hall. Another kid tapped a pencil or something against the wall.

I counted backward, wondering if I could turn everything around if I concentrated hard enough, but I couldn't. The sun rose, and I was two days away—farther from Jason than I ever thought I'd be.

9

The courtroom smelled like lemon furniture polish and old men's cologne. It was too small for a jury. And the judge was a surprise. You always think judges are gonna be some balding fat guys with mustaches or something, but not this one. Jason and I used to talk about what jobs would be good for meeting hot women. Judge would've been one of them.

"You know what would be cool?" Jason said one day when we were in seventh grade, out of nowhere. We were just hanging out in Jase's room. "Teaching."

I looked at Jason. "Teaching what?"

"Art . . . or something."

"C'mon! That's so lame. What teacher have we ever had that's hot?"

Jason shrugged. "I dunno. I think Miss Simpson isn't too bad. And Mrs. Carmichael is a pretty good-lookin' old bird."

"Mrs. Carmichael? She's gotta be at least thirty-five! And way far away from being Hooters-hot. You need a job where you meet Hooters-hot chicks. Like a cop or fireman. Think *Backdraft*, not *Stand and Deliver*. Plus, when I get picked for Carson City's hottest firemen calendar, the chicks will be all over me."

"Hottest firemen calendar?" Jason shook his head and cracked up. "Whatever, Mr. December."

"Dude, why not?" I did my Mr. Universe pose.

"You're hopeless."

I punched him, and he put me in a headlock. "C'mon, Jase." I tried to break free, but he had me tight. "It's way better than playing school with Miss Simpson in her plaid vests."

He let me go. "Okay, seriously. Have you ever thought about what you wanted to do? I mean for real?"

"Not Mr. December?"

"Kyle, I'm serious."

I thought for a while. "Not really. It just seems so far away. Plus, all I like are movies. And I don't think having a managerial position at Blockbuster is a babe-magnet kind of job." I shrugged. "What about you?"

"An artist."

"An artist? Like painting and art galleries and shit?"

"More like graphic design and comics. Grandma Peters

is teaching me to draw with charcoal. She said I had to get the basics first. It's pretty cool."

"Dude, so that's what you've been doing. I mean, when you say you're busy and don't want to watch old movies."

Jason nodded.

"Will you show me your stuff?"

"It's not any good."

"C'mon, just show me."

"Don't laugh." Jason pulled out a notebook of chalky black drawings. At first they weren't so great, but then by mid notebook, the apples really looked like apples. He had even drawn a picture of an old tennis shoe with the toe worn through. "Check these out." He had a separate notebook filled with Marvel comic characters.

"*You* drew these?"

He nodded. I flipped through the pages and started noticing familiar faces. "Dude, that's me."

Jason cracked up. "Yeah, I drew you as a movie director."

I whistled. "And check out the actresses. Nice, Jase."

He grinned. "I thought you'd like that."

"You know, you could draw those caricatures of people—like they do at Disneyland."

Jason shrugged. "Maybe."

"Definitely. These are good."

"You think?"

"Shit, Jase. You're going to be the hottest new name on the comic-book market." I already pictured his stuff in a series. Or maybe he'd even have drawings hanging up in some kind of cool New York art show with people milling around eating cheese and crackers off silver platters.

"Grandma Peters signed me up for art classes after school this year, three nights a week. Dad's pretty bummed I won't be playing basketball or anything. His oldest son, an art pansy."

"Drawing superheroes is definitely not pansy. It's cool, Jase. Really. When are your classes?"

"Mondays, Wednesdays, and Fridays."

I felt a twinge of sadness. What would happen to our Friday Night Flicks club? "Then you *really* must like this."

"Yeah, I guess so."

Before Jason closed up the book, he tore out the sketch of the movie director. "Here." He handed it to me. "Only if you want it." He scuffed his shoes against the wall, leaving a black smudge.

"Yeah, I want it. This will be worth a mint someday." I still have it hanging up on my bulletin board. He never signed it, though.

The judge cleared her throat. "What do we have on the agenda today?"

A lady tapped things on a black machine, and a man

sat in a little box next to the judge. He handed her a file. She flipped it open.

Mark stood up. "Juvenile Master Brown, at this time I don't think we need to remand Kyle to West Hills Hospital because I don't believe he is a suicide risk. I do, however, request that he be placed in the juvenile detention center until I can better assess the situation."

"Where's the jury?" I asked.

Mr. Allison leaned in. "There is no jury. You're in juvenile court. You will have a disposition before Juvenile Master Brown in the next two weeks. She'll review your case and then determine your . . ." His voice faded. "Your sentence. Do you understand?"

I nodded. Twenty to life without the possibility of parole. I tried to remember how the defendants acted in all those movies when they're sent away. Most of them don't even cry. They're just stone-faced.

How will I react?

I looked at all the people crowded into the small courtroom.

"Do you have any problem with that, Mr. Wiley?" the judge asked the other lawyer across the room.

"No, Juvenile Master Brown, I don't. When should we meet again?" Mr. Wiley shuffled his papers and nodded at me. He wore a much nicer suit than Mr. Allison.

"Can we meet Wednesday afternoon or Thursday

morning?" Mark said, looking at his calendar.

"So soon?" Judge Brown raised her eyebrows.

"The Carolls, from what I've seen so far, are good people. My main concern is the psychological welfare of Kyle, and I don't think that the juvenile detention center can offer him more support than his family. I do, however, want to take the time I need to visit the home and make sure there is no longer a risk factor."

"Mr. Wiley?" Judge Brown looked over her glasses at the other lawyer.

"That's fine. Thursday morning?"

The man who sat next to the judge said, "We will meet here Thursday at ten-thirty A.M."

"Good. Next." The judge didn't even have a gavel to pound on her desk.

Mr. Allison patted me on the back. "See, it's going to be okay," he whispered.

I glared at him. How was it possible that things would ever be okay after what I had done? I needed to edit that day. It didn't matter about Jase and the guys. We didn't have to hang out anymore. I just needed to go back and edit that one day—one scene. Scene Three.

But how could I edit what I couldn't remember?

Mom and Dad rushed over to me. "We'll get you home Thursday."

Mark was waiting for me outside the holding room. "Let's go," he said. "Back to Dr. Matthews."

10

I walked to Dr. Matthews's office. She had a stack of pictures on top of the small desk. A guitar leaned against some boxes in the corner. "Hi, Kyle."

"Hi."

She smiled and motioned me to sit at the other end of the couch.

Then we had one of those weird silences that Jason told me happen a lot on first dates. Dr. Matthews wasn't a date, of course, but just sitting with her like that on the couch made me as nervous as hell.

"I like your couch."

She smiled. "I've had it since my college days."

"A long time, then, huh?"

She raised her eyebrows.

"Sorry, Dr. Matthews. I, um, didn't mean it like that."

She laughed. "Pretty long, actually."

I nodded. I wondered if she'd ever changed the upholstery or anything, because it looked pretty ratty. I picked at a loose string and unraveled part of a faded purple flower.

"Can you tell me what happened last Saturday?"

"Again?"

"This time, I want you to close your eyes and talk about everything you remember—the color of your clothes, the smell of the grass—everything."

I closed my eyes. The images came back to me in flashes—like I was looking at film negatives—and ended with the red-black pool of blood and the blue of Jason's lips. All I could smell was the burn. All I could hear was the ringing in my ears. I opened my eyes and shook my head. I gave her the abbreviated version—like a movie preview.

"Jason and I were cold. We went to the shed. Now Jason's dead. End of story."

She laced her fingers together and sighed. I traced a bumpy leaf with my finger. I wished she'd say something; instead we sat there in that cramped office, listening to the ticks of the kitchen timer.

"Kyle, this is a place where you can say anything that's on your mind."

I'm sorry. I'm sorry. I'm sorry. My lip quivered and I took a deep breath.

"Or nothing, too. That's okay."

Nothing. That was better.

Dr. Matthews looked at the time. She stood up and stretched a little. "I still want you to take your medication. It will help you feel better."

"Okay."

"I'll see you tomorrow, Kyle."

"Sure, um, see you tomorrow."

Mark wasn't waiting for me in the hall that time. Some guy in a brown uniform took me back to my room. "Where's Mark?"

"He'll be here tomorrow. Some of the kids are going to play checkers and Parcheesi in the common room. You game?"

"No, thanks, sir." I couldn't imagine playing Parcheesi with Colander.

I counted the bricks that lined the cell door until it got too dark to see. The next couple of days were gray. Everything seemed blurred, like in those old 8 mm home movies Mom and Dad had from when they were kids, the ones I had found in the shed. No sound. Just the snap of the film spinning around the reel.

When I was little, Dad once showed me his record collection. We sat and listened to music in the den. The sound was crackly, and one record got stuck. Just when I thought the song would continue, it moved back to the same spot.

"It's scratched here, you see?" Dad shook his head and pulled the needle off the black disc. He showed me the record, and I ran my fingers across smooth vinyl and felt a hairlike scratch. It didn't feel like anything big at all, but it was because of that tiny little mark that the song just wouldn't go on.

"Can't we fix it?"

"I don't think so." Dad gently held the record in his hands. "Maybe I'll bring some records to the café. What do you think?"

It was the first time Dad had ever asked me what I thought about his café, The Hub. I imagined how cool it would be to have The Hub packed with people, listening to the crackly music. "I think it would be great, Dad."

Dad smiled.

October 8 was the place where my needle got stuck. There was no way to go on. And it couldn't be fixed.

That Thursday, I stood before the judge again. Mark requested that I be put on house arrest and released to my parents until the disposition. I had to continue psychological counseling and was given a prescription for the gray pills. Dr. Matthews explained they didn't want me to have severe spikes and drops in my moods. The pills would level me.

But I hadn't felt anything but emptiness since October 8. And the pills didn't fill the hole in my stomach. They just made the days gray, my nights black-red.

I had to check out of the Kit Carson Juvenile Detention Center like it was the Ritz. They made sure I didn't swipe any of the stained sheets or anything. At the counter, they handed me a list of my stuff: one PEDRO FOR PRESIDENT T-shirt, one pair of jeans, one pair of socks, one gray Wolfpack baseball cap, one navy blue Carson High sweatshirt, one watch. Beside the word *watch*, somebody had written "broken."

I pulled all the items out of the yellow plastic bag, one at a time. Everything smelled burned. The cap still had splotches of brown blood on the inside. The watch was at the bottom of the bag.

October 8, 10:46.

"Everything there, Kyle?"

I held the watch in my hands. The brown smudges flaked off.

10:46.

I wished I had set it at 10:45—at 10:45 Jason was still alive. I rubbed the face of the watch, smearing the brown spots with my sweaty thumb.

"Is there a problem?" Mark looked at the inventory and the clothes that I had pulled out of the bag. "Kyle?"

"No." I shoved the stuff back into the bag and put the watch into my pocket. Mom had brought me fresh clothes to wear.

Mark shook my hand. "We have a week before your

disposition, where I'll be making a sentencing recommendation. As long as you're doing what you need to be doing, you and I won't have problems."

I nodded. But I didn't know what I was supposed to be doing. Maybe not killing any more friends. Everything else, though, was pretty vague.

When we got home, Mel ran up to her room, closed the door, and turned on the radio full blast. I went upstairs, too. Everything looked the same. My *Attack of the Killer Tomatoes!* poster hung on the door, taped together from the time I had torn it up after my cine club had failed in eighth grade.

"Kyle, that's a cool poster, and you just ruined it." Jason shook his head.

"Nobody else seems to think it was cool. Nobody even came."

"I was there."

"That makes two of us, then."

"Dude, most kids want to see *The Lord of the Rings* or something. It was pretty out there to debut with *Attack of the Killer Tomatoes!*"

I threw the scraps of the poster in the trash. "Whatever. I just wanted to try something different."

"Nobody knows how good that movie was. You're just a visionary, man."

"A visionary, huh?" I bit my lip, not wanting to cry in front of Jason. Not all guys would be so cool about their best friend being a total loser. "Want a tomato?" I had bought twenty pounds of cherry tomatoes to sell during the movie instead of popcorn.

Jason laughed. "Dude, let's tape this up." He picked up the pieces of the poster out of the trash.

The poster got all hazy and I pushed the memory away. How come I could remember that but not the shed?

I shoved the yellow plastic bag of clothes from the detention center into my dresser, put the watch on, and went downstairs. Five days of unread *Nevada Appeals* were piled on the coffee table.

I flipped through them until I saw Jason's picture on the front page of Tuesday's paper. "C-11" was printed under his picture. The headline read "Tragedy Puts Carson City on the Map: Is Any Community Immune from Gun Violence?"

My hands trembled as I opened to page C-11.

Obituaries.

The words blurred on the page.

You're dead. You're really dead.

Yeah. Big surprise?

It's here. In writing.

Well, you can't believe everything you read.

I tore out his obituary, crumpling it up and shoving it into my wallet.

"Kyle?" Mom hollered from the kitchen.

Stay cool. It's just the fucking newspaper. Keep your voice steady. I walked into the kitchen, wiping my sweaty hands on my jeans. "How come Mel's not at school?"

"We thought we could all take a break this week."

I slumped into a chair. Maybe they all hoped that things would change if we stopped our lives, too. But the same Carson High was there with the same teachers, same students, same secretaries—same, same, same. All except for Jason. None of us could escape that.

Dad went out to the shed. I sat in the kitchen while Mom worked.

"Do you want to help me out?" She passed me a bowl.

I squished the ricotta cheese and eggs between my fingers. Mom had made two lasagnas and was starting her second pie and a batch of cookies by midafternoon.

Melanie slumped into the kitchen. "Is there anything to eat? I skipped lunch."

"I don't have anything prepared. You'll have to get something on your own." Sweat trickled down Mom's temple. She concentrated on her egg whites.

Melanie looked at the table, heavy with food. "Where's Dad?"

"He's in the shed." I stirred the chocolate chips into the

dough. Dad had spent the whole day there since we got back from the courthouse. He'd taken a bucket and bleach. The police had taken all the photos they needed and said Dad could clean it up.

Mel sat next to me. I handed her the bag of chips.

"Thanks," she whispered. "I'm kinda hungry."

"Me, too." It felt strange to want to eat something. Wrong.

We heard the shed doors screech closed. Dad put a padlock on the outside and snapped it shut; then he stood and stared. He held a bucket of water in his hands. Bloody rags hung over the side. Dad looked like a frame still. He didn't even move.

"Mel." Mom's sharp voice interrupted my trance. "Come with me. We're going to take this food over to the Bishops'."

Mel looked at Mom. "What am I supposed to say to Brooke?"

Mom paused. "I don't know, Mel." She shook her head. "We need to take things one day at a time."

I remembered how when I was little, Mom and Dad had the answers to everything. Or maybe I just thought they did.

It was easier being little.

Mel and Mom left with two baskets filled with food. I tried imagining the conversation on the Bishops' porch. I watched out the front window as Mom and Mel walked down the street, slowly, deliberately. They returned fast. Mel ran up to her room, crying. Mom put the still filled baskets down on the table and dished out lasagna.

She knocked on Mel's door, screaming over the latest boy band's music, "Mel, turn that down! Come out and eat some lasagna!"

"I'm never leaving my room again." Mel had said this millions of times before, but this time I believed her.

Mom came back downstairs. She went to the door and hollered at Dad. "Michael, come inside! It's late. It's cold. You and Kyle need to eat."

I looked at the wavy noodles, doused in tomato sauce and melted cheese. "I don't know, Mom."

Mom sat across from me, dark circles ringing her eyes. "I love you. We love you. You need to know that."

Dad came inside from the backyard and stood behind Mom.

I shrugged and took my lasagna into the front room. I looked down the block at Jason's house. It seemed so weird that just yesterday . . . no, not yesterday, but—I counted on my fingers—five days ago . . .

Dong, dong, dong, dong. Four o'clock. Too much time had passed. I ran upstairs to the grandfather clock and held the pendulum in my fingers, watching the hands come to a halt.

STOP. I needed to stop time.

11

I returned to my plate of cold lasagna and watched the cars line up in front of Jason's house. People streamed in and out.

They looked down the street. Some pointed. A couple of high school kids tried to get into our backyard. Dad hollered at them and threatened to call the police. The phone rang nonstop. Dad finally unplugged it.

Streetlights blinked on. I went out and sat on the porch. It was really cold for October. Colder than the morning Jase died. I hid in the shadows and listened to the slow crunch and scuffle of sad footsteps on chewed-up asphalt. People walk differently after somebody dies. They speak in whispers.

It's not like you're gonna wake the guy up, I thought. *Man, you couldn't even wake Jason up when he was alive.*

I bit my lip and clenched my fists. I hadn't realized how hard it was to be alive. Since it had happened, I'd been in a cell, going through the motions. But here I was, looking at Jason's house, breathing, living. And it hurt. It was wrong. Jason's life had stopped. So should mine.

It wouldn't be long before they sent me away again, though. "I don't remember" is about as lame a defense as anybody can present. And Mr. Allison was no Atticus Finch. At least from a prison cell I wouldn't have to look at the Bishops' house. In prison, I was just as good as dead.

In eighth grade, when Jason's grandma died, I spent the day with him. He was pretty down. Grandma Peters wasn't a blue-haired kind of grandma. She took country-western dance classes, wore leather pants, and sometimes smoked cigars. And she taught Jason how to draw. She always said stuff like "I wonder how the hell I got a Bible-thumping daughter" when we were about to say grace at the table. Grandma Peters seemed too young to have a stroke like that.

Jason and I watched everybody come in with those same plates of cream-colored food—something Grandma Peters would *never* have served in her life. We called it "dead food" and wondered why, when somebody died, people didn't bring pizza. Or at least that person's favorite food. Maybe it had too much color. Pizza was way better than some chicken hot dish made with cream of mushroom soup baked dry in somebody's oven. Even Mom's soupy lasagna was better than that.

That day, I couldn't get a smile out of Jason until I bet him my new Swatch that I could drink seven Cokes and hold out on going to the bathroom longer than he could. I got to the point that my sinuses burned from holding it. I ran to Jason's bathroom, but his old aunt pattered up behind, tapped me on the shoulder, and stepped ahead of me.

I couldn't wait, ran out back, and peed right on Mrs. Bishop's rosebushes—two seconds before Jason joined me. *Two seconds.*

"Dude, I thought you'd never go. I was dying."

I sighed. "Two seconds. Two seconds, man. That sucks."

Jason laughed. "Yeah, but how much would two *Matrix* seconds cost? You're getting off easy."

"Yeah, but I was thinking more along the lines of two *Brick* seconds."

"You and your movies. Is there a movie you haven't seen? " Jason held out his hand.

"Plenty," I muttered, unclasping my Swatch. Jason unhooked his cheapo Dimex and we traded.

"It looks good on me." Jason whistled. He stuck out his wrist and did his victory dance—the same dance he'd been doing since we were five.

Later that evening, I helped the Bishops clean up. We sat down to watch *The Amazing Race* when Mom called. I heard Mrs. Bishop laugh and say, "I've got three, what's one more? No. No. You know, Maggie. They're like brothers. Yep. He's on his way." Then she hung up.

"Time to go." Mrs. Bishop got my coat. "Thanks for your help."

"No problem, Mrs. B."

Jase walked me to the front door. "Hey, Kyle, um, it was a shitty day. Thanks for hanging out. I mean, I feel better."

I raised my eyebrows. "Dude, Jase. Are we having a greeting-card moment?"

"Forget it, man." Jason shook his head and laughed.

I started to leave but then turned back around. "You're welcome," I said.

He grinned. "Okay, Hallmark. See you tomorrow."

"See you."

I looked at the Dimex on my wrist: 10:46. I was glad to have it—something of his.

Jason would be bummed to think everybody, even my mom, was bringing dead food to the house because of him—because of me. Maybe next week I'd have pizza sent over there—Jason's favorite. Pan-crust five-meat supreme with extra cheese. Maybe Dad would spot me some cash.

My breath came out in cloudy puffs. I didn't realize I was shivering until Dad sat down next to me on the porch and threw his jacket over my shoulders. He fidgeted. Then he lit a cigarette and puffed. I kind of wished I could smoke. I wondered if it made him feel better.

"You haven't smoked for a long time."

He exhaled gray smoke. "Some things might change, you know. A lot of things, actually." The cigarette glowed.

I nodded.

"I don't blame you. But sometimes, when things happen, people want to blame someone." He looked at me and inhaled, deep and long. The ashes burned crimson and crept toward Dad's fingers.

"The Bishops have the opportunity to talk at your disposition. They might say some things you don't want to hear." Dad snubbed out the cigarette. His breath smelled burned. Everything smelled black. "It's cold, Kyle. It's late. Let's go inside. We can talk tomorrow." We went back indoors.

I wanted to tell him not to worry. I wanted to show Dad I could be a man and handle being sent away to prison. The words caught in my throat.

"Tomorrow is school," I said. I thought about walking in through those same front doors as if nothing had changed. I wasn't supposed to be here. Not like this. My stomach churned.

"We're all going to take a few days off." Dad squeezed my shoulder.

He gave me one of Dr. Matthews's pills, but I spit it out after he left. My mind raced. I closed my eyes and tried to remember everything, but all I saw were pools of blood and Jason's blue lips. I got up to go to the bathroom. That's when I heard them.

"You forgot about it? You *forgot* about it? Jesus Christ, Michael. It's a gun, not a goddamned dental appointment." Mom was sobbing.

"I don't understand why we have to go over this every night. You don't think I've asked myself this? You don't think that's the first thing I thought about?" Dad sounded like he was crying, too. "Blame me. Blame me for everything, because I already blame myself."

"That's not fair."

"Our son shot his best friend with *my loaded gun*. He will be sentenced in a week, and we don't know what will happen to him. *That's* not fair."

I heard someone rummaging around the room. "Where are you going?"

"Out. I need some space right now. I need to clear my head."

"Michael, don't."

"I need space."

I slipped back into my bedroom and closed the door,

putting on my headphones and pumping my stereo up as loud as I could stand. I ripped my clock from the wall; its red numbers blinked and faded to gray. I crushed it under my foot.

Jason's watch glared at me from my bedside table.

10:46.

I'd stop, too, once they locked me away. Freeze frame. Just like Jase.

12

"There isn't one clock working in this house, Michael." Mom rushed down the stairs, tugging on some pantyhose, holding Dad's jacket and two ties in her hands. She came back up. "How come the stove is the only . . . Never mind."

Dad came out of the bathroom with a mouth full of toothpaste. "What time is it?"

"It's eight thirty-two. We can't be late," Mom said.

"We won't. Okay?" he replied.

Mom handed me the jacket of Dad's suit she was making me wear and held out a retro, tie-dyed, seventies tie in one hand. "Kyle, you need to wear a tie. Pick one." The tie in her other hand looked like something Mr. Hammons would wear on parent-teacher night—blue with diagonal rusty-brown stripes. Jason and I cracked up when we saw

Mr. Hammons in a button-up shirt and tie, because he always wore jeans and SAVE TAHOE T-shirts. Funny how he thought wearing a tacky tie and an old suit might impress parents more than his SAVE TAHOE stuff.

"Kyle? Kyle! Listen to me. We don't have time for your dawdling. Which tie do you want?" Mom held them up against my shirt.

"This one's fine." I grabbed the retro tie.

"I don't know if I can do this. I haven't even talked to Brooke yet. What are we supposed to do?" Mel came out with curlers in her hair. She was stuffed into a tight black miniskirt and a tube top. Charcoal black paint lined her eyes.

Mom took a deep breath. "You're not going to wear that. You're going to wash off the clown face and put on your dark green dress."

"Maggie," Dad whispered.

"And Kyle," Mom added, "you're *not* going to wear those filthy orange shoes with your dad's suit."

"Why do you even give a damn about what anyone's wearing on a day like today?" yelled Mel. "Are you worried we'll attract too much attention? I might be wearing an outfit you don't like, but, Jesus, Mom, Kyle *killed* Jason."

She did have a point. I had killed Jason.

Dad winced. Mom turned crimson. I really thought she was going to smack Mel. But she didn't. After all, Mel had only said what we all wanted to pretend wasn't true.

"Melanie Ann, calm down. Everybody is upset today. We just need to get it together as a family and be there for the Bishops, okay? This isn't about you. It's about Jason and the Bishop family." Dad turned Mel around and walked with her to her room. I held Dad's tie in my hands.

"Dad will knot that for you in the car. I need to get ready. Why don't you wait downstairs?"

I hoped Mom's face would lose the bright red color before we got to the church. At least Mel's scene was a good distraction from my sneakers. They peeked out from under my pinned-up pant legs. I hoped Mom wouldn't notice them at the funeral.

176 days down, 189 to go. A bet's a bet.

We had to walk four blocks to get to the church. Mel tripped all the way in her new high heels. When we finally got there, we could only find room in the far back corner. *Everybody* from Carson City was there. I think I even saw Jack, the guy who mows the Bishops' lawn.

I used to be invisible. Jason's friend, the skinny kid, the shadow, the tagalong. But now they all looked at me. They stared. They hummed and clicked their tongues.

My eyes burned when I saw the shiny wooden coffin draped with white flowers and green grassy stuff. Purple light slanted through stained-glass windows, giving everything an eerie glow.

I didn't see the Bishops anywhere. I didn't see Chase. There were two rows of empty pews right next to Jason.

"Kyle, stand over here." Mom motioned me back into the corner.

People crowded in, pushing, trying to get a spot, craning their necks to see above everyone's head. The air reeked of perfume, incense, and funeral flowers. I pushed my way to the very back corner of the church to get more air. My chest felt tight.

Don't lose it.

Mom's tiny hand closed around my wrist. She pulled me over and put her arm around my shoulder. I could still see the coffin. I couldn't believe Jason was in there. I wondered what Mrs. Bishop had made him wear.

Does it matter what he wears now?

I bet Mrs. Bishop hadn't put on the Swatch. She said gambling was a sin and wouldn't let Jase wear it after she found out where he got it. But he'd earned it. By two seconds. He'd earned it, even if they wouldn't let him wear it. I should've called her and said to put it on. He really liked that watch. But I didn't call. I didn't do anything.

One by one, people went up, looked inside, and left something by the coffin. Even Sarah McGraw brought something. She never even talked to Jase at school.

I tried to loosen Dad's tie but couldn't figure out how to slip the knot down.

"Kyle," Mom whispered. "Would you like to go up?"

I hadn't seen Jason since Saturday. It was almost like he was on one of his family vacations—just gone for a while.

I swallowed hard and nodded.

"We'll go together." Dad and Mel walked ahead of Mom and me.

People stared and then looked away. It was like a bad TV movie, the kind they air on all major networks the same night at the same time.

ABC: *Killing Jason—The Kyle Caroll Story*

NBC: *The Murder of a High School Student*

CBS: *Kyle the Killer*

I had turned Jase into the movie of the week.

"Come on." Mom pushed me along.

Mel clutched Dad. My legs felt weak, and I had to stop several times to catch my breath—it came in short bursts. I grabbed my chest to make sure my heart still worked. A numb feeling spread through my body.

Why did I, Kyle Caroll, Mr. Nobody, live, when Jason died? It should've been the other way around. The main character never dies in the movies. It's always his sidekick. This movie was definitely fucked up.

It took forever to get to the front of that church. The

coffin hadn't looked so far away a few minutes before.

Melanie sobbed when she saw Jason. She teetered and started blubbering, "I'm so sorry. I'm so sorry." Dad held Mel in his arms, and they walked to the back of the church.

I'm sorry. It sounded so hollow, echoing off the church's bare walls.

Mom and I got to the coffin, and I looked in. It was Jason. But it wasn't. Mom started to pull me away, but I had to stand there for a while. It didn't make any sense.

His eyes were closed. His hands were crossed in front of his stomach.

They had cut his hair. He had been growing it out since December. He wanted to look like a real artist, and *they cut his hair.*

He wore a blue suit I had never seen, with the sleeves so long, they covered his wrists. I touched Jason's hand to check for the watch and recoiled from the waxy skin. This wasn't Jason. It couldn't be.

I couldn't have done this. I couldn't have killed my best friend.

I leaned into the coffin and put my head on his chest, listening, hoping that somehow this was a sick joke. Like when your parents really want you to learn your lesson the hard way, so they help you pack your bag to run away. But they fill it with all sorts of stuff, so you drag it halfway down the block and you realize you can't go any farther because the suitcase is too damned heavy.

Maybe somebody would say, *See, you shouldn't play with guns.* And all of Carson City was in on it. Like in that movie *The Game*—a total setup. We'd laugh, feel relieved, and eat cake or something while listening to some police guy talk about gun safety.

But Jason didn't move. I grasped his suit, my tears staining his starchy white shirt. "Wake up. Please, Jason. Get up. I can't . . ." The words were icicles in my throat.

There was a powdery, lavender smell in the coffin that itched my nose, like an old-grandma smell. Definitely not a Jason smell. Everything was wrong, out of place. He wasn't wearing the watch.

"You can't be dead," I whispered.

But he was.

Mom pulled at my scarecrow suit. "Kyle, let's go."

I stood back, fighting to catch my breath. My heart stopped. I know it did. It stopped pumping blood throughout my body. I gasped for air and yanked on my tie.

How could I say good-bye?

I was ready to walk away with Mom when I turned back and leaned toward Jason one more time. His face looked weird. "Dude, are you wearing makeup?" I'm not the most brilliant guy in Carson City, but I know dead people can't have pink cheeks. I'd seen Jason. He was gray in the shed. Blue-gray, and he hadn't even died yet.

I wiped my hand across Jason's pink cheeks. Powdery blush and brown stuff rubbed off on my fingers. They cut his hair. They blew off the watch. They put makeup on him. I pulled out Dad's old handkerchief and tried to clean it off.

I wiped and wiped, but it was like the makeup was applied with some kind of freakish permanent spray. I had to get it off, though. Nothing else mattered.

Then I felt a heavy hand on my shoulder that ripped me around. Mr. Bishop towered over me. The Bishop family stood behind him. "What do you think you're doing? To my son?"

I held the limp handkerchief in my hand. Nothing made sense—none of it.

"My son is dead. You and your family have no right to be here. *You* have no right." Mr. Bishop shook. "You have no right," he whispered, clenching his jaw.

People got quiet. They moved around in their seats. Papers rustled.

"Kyle." Mom pulled on my arm. "Honey, we need to go sit down." Dad had turned around and started walking back toward us.

"Kyle," Dad said, coming up to me, "let's go sit."

I couldn't move. It was like in the shed. Freeze frame. Pause.

"Get out of here." Mr. Bishop came closer. My hands

were still stuck on the coffin.

"Enough!" Dad stepped between us. He pried my fingers from the glossy wood. "Let go of it, Kyle. Just let go."

"We're going to sit down," he said to Mr. Bishop, his voice cracking. "We loved Jason."

I looked away. I hated to see Dad cry.

Play.

Everything started to spin around me like weird special-effects lighting. Blackness crept through my brain, turning the church blotchy gray with pinpricks of white light. My knees buckled, and I grasped onto the front rail. My body shivered and icy sweat dripped down my back.

Pulling myself up, I stumbled down the aisle, past my parents and the Bishops. I tried to breathe without inhaling the sickening church smells. I yanked at my tie and ripped off the suit jacket. The exit looked so far away. Everybody's faces were blurred and distorted. Dizzying light streamed through the stained-glass windows. Squinting, I kept my eyes on the heavy wooden doors, ignoring the whispers. I rushed outside, tripped down the concrete steps, and collapsed on the lawn behind the dried-up rosebushes. My body heaved and hiccuped until all that came out of me was acidic yellow bile.

I lay on the dead grass and gasped for breath. My head throbbed. The deeper I inhaled, the less air I got.

I'm gonna die. Please let me die.

"Take it easy. Slow your breathing." Mom's cheeks were wet with tears. She held a paper bag to my mouth and nose.

The world stopped spinning, and everything came back into focus. Dad and Mel stood over me. "You okay?" Dad asked.

No.

I nodded.

Dad helped me up. "Let's go home."

We walked slowly to the car. "I didn't say good-bye," I whispered.

I listened as the organ played "Amazing Grace" from behind the heavy church doors. I wondered what other music they would play. What would Jason have liked?

I looked back. Mr. Bishop was right. I had no right. I had no right to be there. I had no right to be.

13

"**K**yle! Kyle, wake up!" Mel leaned over and shook my shoulders.

I sat up and grabbed her. "I can't," I gasped, struggling to steady my breathing. Nightmare images came back to me: choking, the inside of a coffin, being buried alive.

"You're okay." She sat down next to me.

I held her tighter.

She circled her arms around me. "I was walking to the bathroom when I heard you."

I nodded, still hanging on to her pajamas.

"I still kinda need to go."

"Go where?"

"To the bathroom."

"Oh. Oh yeah. Sorry." I didn't let go.

"Kyle?"

I let the fabric slip from my fingers. "Yeah, thanks. Sorry about that."

"G'night."

She closed the door and I was blanketed in darkness. I grabbed my pillow and waited until the first purple shades of dawn seeped through my window before I closed my eyes.

"You look tired today." Dr. Matthews handed me a glass of water. "Did you sleep well?"

"Sure."

Mom and Dad had called an emergency Matthews session. "We're going to try something called association. When I show you a picture, I just want you to tell me the first thing that comes to mind." She held out an ink-stained picture. "What do you see?"

"A stain."

She raised her eyebrows. "A stain of what?"

"Black ink."

She scowled. "And this one?"

"A bigger stain."

She did one of those hum-sighs. "Think of it like cloud watching. Have you ever done that? Looked up at clouds and found figures?"

<><><><><>

Chase, Jason, and I had done it all the time. With stars, though, instead of clouds. We named our own constellations. Chase's favorite constellation was the *Taraxacum officinale*—the dandelion. He said it was a very misunderstood flower. At first I thought he was shitting me, but the kid actually found the same group of stars every night. One year for Chase's birthday, Jason and I bought him a star and named it Dandelion because we couldn't remember the scientific name. We thought he'd like it, but he said, "How can you buy something that belongs to everybody?"

We tried to return it, but we couldn't. I kinda felt like shit after that.

Dr. Matthews cleared her throat. "You know what I mean, Kyle, about the cloud watching?"

"No. I've never watched clouds," I said.

Dr. Matthews put the cards away. "Can you tell me about the funeral yesterday?"

I bit my lip.

"Can you tell me about the makeup?"

Trying to save my best friend from an eternity of lip gloss and blush didn't seem so unreasonable to me. I didn't know what the big deal was. Everybody'd just flipped out.

"Did you read Jason's obituary?" she asked. It was as if she knew I'd torn it out the week before and carried it around, too afraid to read the words. "What did you think about it? The obituary?"

"I didn't read it."

"Why not?"

I bit my lip harder, until I tasted metal. I looked away, out the tiny door window.

"Would you like to read it?" She handed me a fresh version of the clipping I had crumpled in my wallet.

I blinked, hoping that everything would disappear, that the words would morph like they did in that movie *The Butterfly Effect*. All he had to do was look down at his notebook to change the words, and he'd change the past.

I concentrated on the obituary, but the print stayed the same. The words didn't change.

> ### JASON GABRIEL BISHOP
>
> *Jason Gabriel Bishop, 15, of Carson City, Nev., died from a gunshot wound on October 8, 2008. He was born July 17, 1993, to Gail and Jim Bishop in Dayton, Nev.*
>
> *Jason was an accomplished student at Carson High School, and first in his class. He belonged to several school clubs. He was an active member of his youth group at the Foursquare Church and a mentor to younger church members.*
>
> *Among his survivors are his parents, Gail*

and Jim; paternal grandparents, Jacob and
Marlene; and two siblings, Brooke and Chase.

Services will be held Saturday, October 15,
at 10 A.M. at the Foursquare Church, followed
by a reception. The Meyers Crematorium and
Funeral Home is in charge of arrangements.

The obituary depressed the hell out of me. What does any of that say about Jason? Nothing. All it talked about was his church and his mentoring. But what about who Jason really was for the other 163 hours of the week? What about the Jason who was the next Marvel comics artist? What about the Jason who was the best big brother to Chase? What about the Jason who would make a bet on just about anything—and win? What about the Jason I knew—not some made-up, Bible-toting, preachy mentor Jason? It seemed so sad that Jason's parents didn't even know him, like they were missing somebody who wasn't even real.

"What do you think?" Dr. Matthews urged.

Having it in print made it feel cheap—nothing more than headline news. All *Nevada Appeal* subscribers would have read this and thought, "Oh, too bad." Maybe over coffee they'd *tsk-tsk* and talk about the dangers of Carson City, sorry about the churchy dead kid. Then they'd go on with their regular day because, to them, it was just words on a page.

I handed the obituary back to Dr. Matthews. "I think they didn't know Jason."

Dr. Matthews nodded. "And you did?"

"Well, yeah. He was my best friend."

"Would you have written something different?"

I would've written about the first time Jason and I got to go camping on our own, up at Marlette Lake. We hiked the five miles up from our families' campground and hung out the whole afternoon, swimming, fishing, and skipping rocks. We started a campfire and ate sizzling, charred hot dogs off sticks that tasted like pine, then bet on who would see the most falling stars. We hadn't even set up camp. We weren't gonna because we wanted to sleep outside, under the stars.

Then it started to pour, one of those Nevada rains that come out of nowhere. We hadn't seen a cloud before the first drop pelted us. We ran like mad to get the tent up when I realized I had forgotten the poles. We ended up scrambling five miles down to our families' camp in sheets of rain, up to our ankles in mud.

Most guys would've been pissed. Jase just said, "Yeah. I could've brought them, too. Whatever."

That's the kind of stuff I would've written about. It says a lot more about a person than being on the honor roll.

"What would you have written, Kyle?"

"Something else. Something real."

Then we had another one of those awkward silences when Dr. Matthews waited for me to keep talking but I didn't.

She cleared her throat. "Your hearing is coming up soon. What are you feeling about that?"

Maybe it would be easier for everybody not to see me anymore. I shrugged. "It's not really up to me. After what I did and all, I guess it depends on the laws."

"What do you hope the outcome will be?"

I deserve to be sent away. My life needs to be put on pause.

"I guess I don't hope for anything, you know? Just waiting."

"Waiting is hard."

"I guess so," I said.

"It might help to fill in the blanks on that day."

It doesn't matter anymore. Jason is dead, so whatever happened in the shed doesn't matter.

Scene Three.

Erased.

Jason.

Erased.

Now it's my turn to fade out.

When I got home from Dr. Matthews's, Mark and Mr. Allison were waiting for me.

"I'm here. I'm not happy. Remember what I said?" Mark asked.

"Um, not really."

"As long as you stay in line, you and I won't have problems. Your performance at the funeral yesterday isn't what I consider staying in line." Mark snapped his gum. A blue vein bulged across his temple every time he clenched his jaw. *Snap,* bulge, *pop . . . snap,* bulge, *pop.*

"Kyle, Mr. Grimes is talking to you. Please look at him." Mom brought out a pot of coffee for everyone. Dad had picked up a dozen donuts. Grease seeped through the box.

"We need to talk about your behavior." Mark sat down.

Eight days had gone by. Eight days of meetings with Mark, Mr. Allison, Gollum, and Igor. Eight days of Dr. Matthews and gray pills. Eight days of nothing but *tick, tick, tick.* And we had finally gotten to Sunday morning.

Mr. Allison paced back and forth. "Kyle, we need to talk about everything. Tuesday we stand before the court and Juvenile Master Brown. This is your future—your life."

Some life.

"You know that the Bishops can speak at your disposition. They have the right to address the juvenile master," Mark continued. "This can be good or bad. I don't know the Bishops very well, but after the stunt you pulled yesterday at the funeral, I don't suppose they're going to talk very favorably."

"Kyle, this is really important," Dad said, sitting next to me.

Snap, bulge, *pop* . . . *snap*, bulge, *pop*. Mark spit his gum out into a napkin and took a bite out of a greasy donut. Glaze stuck to the corners of his mouth. "A homebound teacher will be with Kyle until after the disposition. I don't see how it would do any good for him, at this time, to go to school. My recommendation will be probation—no time served—until he is eighteen years old. This probation, though, can be successful only if he has heavy psychological counseling. I don't see why Kyle should go to a detention center."

How can I not be sent away?

"So he'll be able to come home? For sure?" Mom asked. She had chewed her nails down to nothing.

"It's ultimately up to the juvenile master—the judge— after she reads through all statements. Usually, she'll sway toward the PO and psychiatrist's recommendations. But there are times when things don't necessarily go the way we believe they should. That could happen, for instance, if the DA and the Bishops put forth compelling reasons why Kyle should serve time."

"Oh, God." Dad's voice was just a whisper.

It was like I had broken something inside him.

"Let's not even go there for now." Mark clapped Dad on the back. God, he had to get this back clapping under control. "I have faith in the system," he said. Obviously

Mark hadn't seen *The Shawshank Redemption* or *The Count of Monte Cristo*.

"These things happen," Mark said.

These things happen.

"But what about college? Getting a job? Voting? Will Kyle be a felon?" Dad rubbed his temples.

Voting? Dad's worried about me voting?

"Juvenile records are sealed. No future employer will have access to Kyle's past. What happened here stays here."

Buried with Jason.

Dad sighed. *Relieved, I suppose. Good thing murder won't get in the way of a college education.*

"Okay, then," Mark said. "I'd like to have a little time with Kyle."

Everybody went to the kitchen. Mark and I sat in the living room, the box of donuts between us. "This is your one chance. I'm doing my best to help you, but you've gotta help yourself. And what you did yesterday doesn't help. All of this can count against you. Everything you do from here on out will be put under a microscope, analyzed, and dissected. You've got to shape up."

I nodded.

Mark scratched the back of his head. "I'll be coming by to help you prep for the disposition. A lot of us here are working hard for you, but your future is in your hands."

So was Jason's future. In my hands.

Mark said good-bye to Mom and Dad. He put on his black leather coat. "We'll talk soon."

And then they all disappeared, one by one—Mark, Mr. Allison, even Mom, Dad, and Mel—leaving me alone, staring outside at the Bishops' house.

Neighborhood kids ran up and down the street, playing football like it was a regular Sunday. Like nothing had happened.

Only eight days had passed. Jason was already forgotten.

I figured I knew, then, what death felt like. Nothing at all.

For the disposition, Mom wore the blue dress she saved for teacher conferences. Dad wore the suit I'd borrowed for the funeral. They had bought me a new shirt and tie and a pair of gray slacks. Not like it mattered.

Mr. and Mrs. Bishop came in. They shuffled into the back row. Mrs. Bishop strained to keep her head up and ended up resting it on Mr. Bishop's shoulder. He had black circles under his eyes and fidgeted with his wristwatch. I never really knew what sadness looked like until then.

The judge had declared it a closed hearing, open only to family. That was good. I didn't want anybody bugging Mom and Dad. They had enough shit to deal with.

The lawyer at the other table shuffled papers. Mr. Allison whispered things to Dad. Mel sniffled and blew her nose. Mom leaned over and straightened my tie. "Things are going to be okay."

She had been saying that the past ten days, like some kind of mantra.

But they weren't.

I looked down at Jason's watch and rubbed its face. I almost felt relieved. Soon it would all be over. The end. My end. Roll the credits.

Judge Brown came in, and we stood up. She turned to the lawyer standing across from Mr. Allison and me. "Mr. Wiley, I've reviewed the case. Would anybody for the prosecution like to make a statement?"

We all turned to the Bishops. Mrs. Bishop held a crinkled handkerchief and dabbed at her eyes. Mr. Bishop sat with his arms crossed in front of him, a roll of skin bulging over the top of his shirt collar.

The courtroom was silent.

Say something, I thought. *Tell her about what I did; about the "probation friend" list; about Jason's new friends. TELL HER.*

Mr. Wiley shook his head. "No, Your Honor, the Bishops don't wish to make any statement. You have everything before you."

"Would you like to say anything to the court?" Judge Brown looked at me.

I took a sip of water and looked back at the Bishops.

Mr. Allison and Mark had prepped me the past week about what I should say. They said it's really important to show remorse. "Look sorry," they'd said. "You really need to look sorry in court."

What does *sorry* look like? Does it have a color? A shape? Is it dark or light? I knew what it felt like, but what did it look like?

"Mr. Caroll, would you like to address the court?" Judge Brown asked. She leaned on her desk.

Mrs. Bishop stared at her lap, her head too heavy to hold up. Mr. Bishop's eyes darted back and forth from the judge to the stenographer. Mom's knuckles turned white from squeezing Dad's leg so tight. Dad wrapped his arm around Mel, and she leaned into his shoulder. I looked at Mr. Allison.

"Go ahead," he urged.

I'm sorry.

Mr. and Mrs. Bishop looked up at me. Mrs. Bishop didn't even try to wipe her tears.

"I—" I cleared my throat. "I, *um*—"

I remembered Mr. Bishop trembling in the church, saying, "You have no right . . . you have no right." I heard Brooke's sobs and Chase asking if Jason was going to be all right. I saw splatters of blood all over Dad's shed and the burning flesh. I saw Jason's body doubled over, lying in a pool of blood.

Jason would never graduate from Carson High or go to college. He'd never get to backpack around Europe. He'd never have a fancy New York art show.

I had no right.

If I didn't look sorry, they'd have to send me away. Judge Brown would see that I deserved to go to a detention center.

I turned from the Bishops and shook my head. "No."

"Just a moment, Judge Brown," Mr. Allison said. He turned to me. "Don't you want to say something?" He leaned in. "Remember what we talked about."

I squared my shoulders and swallowed. "No. I have nothing to say." I heard a sob from the back of the courtroom.

Judge Brown paused, then nodded. "Then I'll proceed." She flipped through a file on her desk. "From the evidence presented by the Carson City Police Department, letters received, and the recommendations of Mr. Grimes and Dr. Matthews, I remand Kyle to three years' probation under strict supervision of his parole officer, Mark Grimes, and continued psychological evaluations by Dr. Matthews or any other state-appointed psychiatrist. I also recommend counseling for both families, the Bishops and the Carolls. This was an unfortunate incident." Judge Brown looked at me. "Do you have any questions?"

"But," I said, shaking my head, "but they have to tell

you about me—about what I did."

Judge Brown nodded. "I know what you did, and your sentence is appropriate."

I killed Jason. How could that sentence be appropriate? I turned to the Bishops. "You *saw* what I did. Tell her! *Tell her!*"

Mr. Allison yanked on my shirtsleeve. "Enough!"

"I don't get it. I kill Jase and get a get-out-of-jail-free card? Like nothing? What the fuck is wrong with everyone here? I *did* it. He's dead because of me."

Dad grabbed me by the shoulders. "We're going home, Kyle. We'll deal with this there."

I looked around the courtroom. It didn't make sense. It was an open-and-shut case. I killed him. I confessed. And they send me home because it was an "unfortunate incident"? I felt numb. It was like everything had turned upside down again. Everything was wrong. I squeezed the watch, my heart pounding in my ears.

"Look at me, Kyle. Look me in the eyes." Dad held my jaw in his hand. "We're going home now."

I shook my head. "No. No. No."

Mark came forward and said, "Juvenile Master Brown, clearly Kyle is not himself, and he is reacting to the intense pressure he's been under."

The judge looked at him, then at me. She said almost in a whisper, "You are one step away from being in contempt of this court. You have a second chance because this court believes you deserve it."

Second chance? Tell that to Jason—the dead one.

"This court does not hand out second chances lightly," Judge Brown continued. "You have an opportunity to make something of yourself—to redeem yourself. I never want to see you in my courtroom again. Understood?"

I felt cheated. My life was supposed to have been put on pause, just like Jason's. It wasn't supposed to turn out this way. I wasn't supposed to be allowed to go on. *Freeze frame.*

Every morning since October 8, I'd wished I could wake up to the smell of pancakes and the sounds of Mel's blow-dryer and Jason's snoring. I'd wished that I had a chance to make that day right. It would be so easy if life could be edited. But the movie never changed. And there was no way to erase what I had done or to go back.

"Court adjourned." Judge Brown stood abruptly and left.

The courtroom settled into an uncomfortable silence, something you wouldn't find in a real courtroom drama. I looked back to see Mr. and Mrs. Bishop slip out the door.

Mom muttered, "Thank God. Thank God," all the way to the car.

Mark caught up to us. "Kid, I don't know what the hell that was all about."

Mom stepped forward. "He's upset. His best friend is dead."

"I'm aware that he's upset, but that's the kind of thing that gets a judge doubting a kid. Dr. Matthews is going to have to reevaluate whether or not we should send him to West Hills."

"The mental hospital? Aren't we jumping to some conclusions here, Mark?" Dad opened Mom's door. He was in charge now. "Aren't we expecting a lot of a fifteen-year-old? Under the circumstances, I'd say Kyle is handling things pretty well."

Mark nodded. "It's not an easy time for anyone. But you need to know what I expect of Kyle."

Dad waited, arms crossed. He stood head and shoulders above Mark.

"Kyle's job is to get good grades and stay in line." Mark turned to me. "You still belong to the state. Understand?"

I nodded.

Mark turned to Mom and Dad and softened his tone. "After a while, these kinds of cases tend to take care of themselves. I'll be in contact with Dr. Matthews. I want to see Kyle's progress reports. I'll be talking to you about his behavior and grades, but I hope I don't have to come around too often."

Mom and Dad nodded. Mark shook my hand. "See you later this week, okay?"

"Okay."

We got into the car. Dad's hand shook too hard to put the key into the ignition. "Christ," he whispered.

Mom steadied his hand and guided the key in. Dad rested his head on the steering wheel.

"You okay, Dad?" Mel asked. She leaned forward.

His shoulders shook with silent sobs.

15

The house was quiet. I trudged up to my room and stared at my poster of *Sin City*. Jase had been a Frank Miller fanatic, and it was the only movie poster he ever really wanted. But I didn't give it to him. I never bet him for it, either. Some part of me liked having something Jase wanted.

Did that mean I had pointed the gun at him? On purpose?

I took the poster off the wall, leaving a glaring white spot. One by one, I tore down the rest of my posters, piling them up in the corner. I didn't deserve to have anything anymore. I should've given the fucking poster to Jason.

I looked at the blank walls. Nothingness. That's what I deserved. My mind returned to the scene I thought of at the detention center—my death scene. There was only one way to make things stop now. The ultimate freeze frame. Could I do it?

Shivering, I pulled my knees to my chest and remembered that Jason's duffel bag was pushed into the back corner of my closet from that last night he'd stayed over.

What did he pack? Would I have to return the stuff to his parents?

Jason had used the same duffel for every sleepover since fourth grade. It was blue and white and had a purple stain on the bottom from the time that Jeffrey Mason barfed up his Kool-Aid.

I pushed my shoes out of the way and reached back to drag out Jason's bag. The duffel was heavy. I had forgotten that he had come over right after school. He hadn't even stopped at home. His gym shoes and sweaty clothes were inside. He had brought home his math, science, and history notebooks with every white space filled with drawings and doodles. His doodles were art, not just squiggles.

He had a library book: *The Metamorphosis*. I flipped through the first few pages. Jase read the strangest shit. And the book was way overdue. I bet Scarface Cordoba, the librarian, had already sent out a hit on Jase for not returning it.

Too late, Scarface.

I wiped my nose and wondered if the library had one

of those drop-off slots like they have at Blockbuster so I could drop it off and run. Or maybe if I got to school at five A.M., I could leave it propped against the door.

Leave it to Jase to stick me with facing Scarface with an overdue book. Shit.

Dude, Jase, nice touch. It was overdue before all this happened.

Suck it up, Kyle. Things could be worse.

Yeah, can't argue with a dead guy.

You never could argue with me alive, either, man.

Whatever.

I pulled out his sketchbook and portfolio. They were his latest comics characters: Infinity Detention, Split Infinitive, Formaldehyde, Sketch, Kite Rider, Line Runner, and Freeze Frame. My hands felt clammy; my sweaty fingers smudged the notebook. I put it down, and an application for UC Berkeley's teen summer comic-book art program slipped out. Jason had already filled it in.

So he was going to apply after all.

Jason had big dreams.

Poof! Now they were gone.

I sat with the empty bag on my lap and my hands shook. It smelled like Jason—a combination of peanut butter, damp socks, and chalk. There wasn't a day that went by that Jason didn't eat a peanut-butter sandwich. The guy was obsessed with them—the chunky kind. And the damp socks and chalk smells were everywhere else. I don't know why, especially since damp socks are kind of raunchy, but it was more of a damp-socks-after-going-through-the-wash kind of smell. Damp, clean socks. And the chalk came from all those pastels he used for his art.

I buried my head in Jason's bag and breathed deep. I didn't even hear Mom coming up the stairs.

She opened my door and gasped. "Kyle! What are you doing with your head in a duffel bag?"

I pulled my head out and shoved the duffel and Jason's stuff under the bed. "I'm just thinkin', Mom."

"With a duffel bag on your head?"

"Yeah. I read about it somewhere. You know, to help me think."

"Are you okay?" Mom scanned the bare walls. Dad's frame filled the doorway. He hadn't said anything since we'd left the courthouse.

The smell of Mom's perfume drifted through the room, erasing Jason.

"I guess I kinda want to be alone for a while. If that's okay."

Mom came toward me. Dad pulled her back. He nodded. They backed out of the room. Did they smell Jason too?

"Don't forget we have a family session with Dr. Matthews later today," Mom said.

"Sure. Okay."

Dr. Matthews had a new office. A big one with that same lumpy couch and tiny desk. But she also had beanbags and Legos and stuff like that. Every session with her got worse. It was like she wanted to direct the movie in my head. But she didn't get that the most important scene of the movie had been deleted, and there was no way to recover it.

She wanted us to do family therapy once a month—including Mel. Mel glared at Dr. Matthews the whole visit.

"Now, then. I want to talk about Kyle." Dr. Matthews focused on me and smiled.

She was obsessed with my issues and ticked them off for my family.

I wanted to interrupt and say, *Actually, I killed my best friend. No matter what I do, that's what happened. And I can't go back. And when I close my eyes, all I see is blood and Jason stuffed in a coffin. And his mother made him wear makeup for eternity. That's my real "issue."*

But I didn't say that.

Dr. Matthews leaned back. I wondered if her knotty hair might get caught up in the buttons on the couch cushions. She started talking to my parents, and I played their conversation in fast-forward, listening as the shrill words blended together. Then I stopped and played it backward, so everything sounded like a different language.

".gnilaeh ot pets tsrif eht si gnirebmemeR"

"?rebmemer ot deen elyK seod oS?"

".ti deen ew nehw su stcetorp taht enihcam lufrednow a si dnim ehT .oN"

"?aisenma ekil ti sI"

".emit emos etiuq rof deneppah tahw yltcaxe rebmemer ton thgim elyK"

".sseug I ,gnimlehwrevo neeb lla s'tI"

I looked at the wall. Framed diplomas hung all around the room. I couldn't believe she had actually gone to college for this stuff.

Dad put his arm around my shoulders. Mel rolled her eyes and kept looking at her watch. I let their conversation play in real time.

"We're going to get through this, Kyle." Dad nodded firmly, with confidence.

Dr. Matthews's bright dress blended in with the colorful sofa, and she looked like a blob with frizzy hair. If I squinted, I couldn't tell where the sofa ended and she began.

"Kyle needs to get back to school and start normal activities again. He's been on homebound since the incident and has not progressed. One of the terms of his probation is that he do his homework and get passing grades." She flipped through a folder. "Kyle needs to get moving. Inertia is *deadly*." She leaned over when she said that last part, ruining the sofa-dress-blob effect.

"Okay," Mom agreed. "Kyle will start on Monday."

16

Inertia is deadly.

Life is deadly too. Just ask Jason.

After Mom, Dad, and Mel had gone, Dr. Matthews said, "The disposition was pretty tough."

"It was okay."

"Do you really think you deserve to be sent away for what happened?"

For killing another person? Yes. "The judge didn't."

"But do you?"

"I dunno."

"Can you tell me why, then, you reacted the way you did at the disposition?"

I unclasped the watch, then clasped it again. "I guess I was surprised."

"What surprised you?"

"It's not like I expected to go home, you know."

She pushed a loose strand of hair behind her ear. "Were you disappointed that the judge didn't send you to a juvenile detention center?"

"Yeah," I said, then caught myself. "No. I mean, I dunno."

"Can you explain?"

"I killed Jason." I picked at a hangnail. It started to bleed. I sucked on it, letting the copper taste coat my tongue.

"Did you mean to?"

Since tenth grade started, I had eaten lunch alone in the cafeteria most days; the only time Jason called was to see if I could hang out with him and Chase. So really, it was probably just Chase who wanted to see me. Jason had only hung out with me alone one weekend, and he ended up dead.

Did I mean to?

Is not sharing lunch a motive for murder?

It would make the perfect film noir, like *The Maltese Falcon*. An old black-and-white detective movie with high-contrast photography and over-the-top acting.

Mark, the tough and gritty PO, moonlighting as a private eye, sits behind a desk. Smoke curls up from his unfiltered cigarette while he pours himself another stiff drink from the half-empty bottle of whisky. Sirens wail and a neon sign blinks in the background.

He hears the sound of high heels clacking on the stairway. The door flies open and in walks Dr. Matthews, clad in fishnet stockings and a dress that probably cuts off her oxygen supply. She bats her eyelashes. "Did he mean to? Will you help me, sir?"

Mark looks up at her and tips the brim of his hat.

Dr. Matthews throws herself into a chair, sobbing uncontrollably.

Mark coolly hands her a handkerchief and a piece of paper. "Here are my rates. I'll find out. I'll find out if he meant to. But know this: I won't play the sap for you!"

"Kyle?" Dr. Matthews tapped my shoulder. "Are you listening?"

"Yeah. Sure." The only problem with that movie is that Sam Spade never had a tan. Maybe I could convince Mark to stay away from the tanning beds on Fifth Street before shooting.

"Was there something you wished you could've said to the Bishops?" Dr. Matthews asked.

I'm sorry.

But I didn't say it, and now it's too late—just another scene I screwed up and can't edit. What a fucking mess.

"Okay. Let's try it another way. Are there things you

would've liked to say to Jason but didn't?"

Why did you ditch me for Alex and the guys?

Why didn't you want to hang out with me anymore?

Do you know what happened?

That's what I especially wanted to ask him: *Do you know what happened?*

"Maybe you can write those things down. Write them when you think about them. You don't have to show me," Dr. Matthews said.

I leaned back and stared at the water stain on the ceiling. "Okay."

"Your first day back at school will be tough." She handed me a card. "You can call me if you need to talk."

I hesitated.

"Take the card. You don't have to call. I just want you to know that you can."

The minutes slipped away. I lay in bed and listened to the house, its walls moaning in the wind, the familiar creak of the third step. Every evening the sun dropped behind the mountains, only to come back the following morning, streaming light into my bedroom. Every goddamned morning.

That Sunday, I sat by the front window and watched Chase run up and down the street with one of his kites. There was no wind, but the kid didn't give up. He was out all day long from morning until evening. Nobody helped him at the Bishops' house. Jason would've. Jason was always there for Chase.

My stomach ached, watching Chase drag the tattered kite across the asphalt. His cheeks and nose turned red, flushed from the cold. Once in a while I saw him look toward my driveway.

Help him out, dude. Don't be an asshole and just watch him like that.

Easy for you to say. Your parents don't hate you.

Get over it. His kite's gonna get torn to shreds, and you know Mom and Dad won't get him a new one.

I got out to the porch but then I saw Mrs. Bishop, wrapped in a thick sweater. She called Chase inside. His kite hung limp. He dropped his head and went in just as the sun slipped away.

Don't forget about Chase, man.

I sometimes wished I could shut off the Jason in my head. Especially since he talked to me more often dead than when he was alive this past year.

Mark came by that evening. "Just wanting to check in."

No. He definitely couldn't pull off Sam Spade.

"You're a smart kid. It's time to get back on the bike, Kyle."

I nodded. He loved to talk about bikes. I wondered if he'd ever seen *The Great Escape*, but then figured a PO isn't likely to watch a movie about escaping prisoners, regardless of the cool motorcycle stunts.

"Every action has a reaction," he continued. "Everything we do or say has an effect."

No shit, Sherlock. I bit my tongue.

Mark glared at me, like he knew what I was thinking.

"I'll see you Friday. Time to move on, Kyle." Mark left the house, his motorcycle rumbling all the way down the street. I had to be the only kid with a PO who looked like he belonged on the set of *Easy Rider*.

That night I listened as Mom and Dad argued. The wind rattled the windows, and birch tree branches scratched up against the house.

Time to move on, Kyle. Yeah, right. I thought about stopping time. And I only knew one way to do it. Everybody would be better off. Dying couldn't be so terrible—so hard to do. Besides, maybe then I could be with Jason.

Dawn came when I wanted it least, when I had finally found a quiet moment to escape my thoughts. Mel's alarm clock beeped. Dad had finished showering; his electric razor buzzed across his face. The smell of coffee drifted upstairs and turned my stomach.

I picked Jason's watch up off the nightstand and put it on. It would keep me where I needed to be until I could work up the guts to get there myself.

17

"**K**yle, come down for breakfast." I looked up to see Mom peeking in the door.

Mel thundered down the steps. "I can't do this, Mom. Brooke doesn't even talk to me. Everybody whispers when I walk down the hall. They all stare at me because of—" Mel turned and saw me at the top of the staircase. She looked away.

Mom gave Mel one of those another-word-and-you're-toast looks.

"Well, I'm *not* showing up with him at school today. It's just too weird. It's too—I dunno," she whispered. Like I wouldn't be able to hear her. Cheerleaders definitely don't have volume control. And Mel had freakishly developed vocal cords; she was the only one on the squad who never used a megaphone.

"That's fine—I'm riding my bike." They stared at me.

"Kyle, it's late October. You can't ride your bike." Parents always come up with arbitrary shit like that. What does October have to do with riding bikes?

I didn't hear what else Mom had to say, because I walked into the garage, got on, and rode, taking Elm Street down to Crain to get to Fifth. I didn't want to pass Jason's house.

I checked in at the front office. Mrs. Brawn jumped up and grabbed my shoulders. "Oh, Kyle! How *great* to have you back!" It was weird to have her happy to see me. Mrs. Brawn was about ninety years old, and she had been the school secretary since Charlie Chaplin's silent-movie days.

Supposedly, Mrs. Brawn had once stapled a kid's tardy record to his forehead and made him walk around all day with it. I figured it was a rumor and told Jason it was impossible. "Plus," I said, "it's illegal for adults to staple things to body parts. That's abuse." Though it would make for a wicked scene in some kind of horror flick.

Jason had shrugged and said, "In the old days, teachers and secretaries could beat up kids. Believe what you want, but I'm not gonna piss off Mrs. Brawn."

I always felt a piercing pain in my forehead when I saw her. Jason had told me it was psychological. I supposed I could check with Dr. Matthews about that one.

That morning, walking in through the school doors, I wondered if the knot in my gut was psychological, too.

Mrs. Brawn patted my hand. "You don't want to be late, now. Not on your first day back."

I inhaled the soupy school smells: rusty metal, musty carpets, greasy food, sour sweat. I swallowed and rushed to first period, stalling in the doorway. Almost everybody had settled in. The desk between Catalina and Tim was glaringly empty. I wondered if Mrs. Beacham had erased Jason from her seating chart.

Catalina Sandina   XXXX   Tim Tierney

Was it that easy to do? Just a line through a name and he's gone? I backed up, figuring Mom and Dad could home-school me. Then I wouldn't have to see that empty desk every day. Or maybe I could get out of first period. It was the only class we'd had together.

"Hello, Kyle!" Mrs. Beacham squealed, walking up and squeezing my shoulder. "I'm delighted to see you back in class." Her nicotine-yellowed nails dug into my back as she nudged me into the room.

Everybody stared, then went back to their little gossip circles.

"Uh," I muttered to Mrs. Beacham and shrugged her claws off my shoulder. "Thanks."

I walked past Jason's desk, running my fingers across it, feeling the bumpy etchings other students had carved. Jase liked graffiti. He said it was an art form, rebellion against the establishment. I found my seat between Judd and Marcy. Marcy stared at me, and when I looked up at her, she pretended she was reading.

Judd grunted, "Hey, Kyle." He slumped over his English book and picked his nose.

Jessie Martinez came up to me after third period. "Kyle?" She looked around. "Do you think they're gonna make a movie about this? I, uh, wouldn't want to look bad on the day they film."

"Yeah, Michael Moore's coming this afternoon," I muttered.

"What? Did you say . . ." She flipped her hair and globbed on some sparkly lip stuff that smelled like grapes.

"What's the deal with chicks and fruity-smelling lip stuff?" I'd asked Jason one day.

"It's for hookin' up. Don't be a moron."

"Yeah, like you'd know."

"You've gotta be joking. You've never hooked up? Not even once?"

I hadn't really thought about it much, except for in the bathroom. "Well, yeah, but she didn't have a whole bunch of strawberry shit all over her lips."

Jase grinned. He knew I was lying but didn't call me on it. "It's better with the lip gloss. Try it sometime," he said.

God, I hope Jason had sex. I mean, I hope he didn't die a virgin. I hadn't thought about that before.

I thought about Dr. Matthews's "things to ask Jason" list. *Can people who are dead talk to other people who are dead? That's another one.*

In gym, we played handball. It felt good to throw the ball as hard as I could. Coach Copeland came up after class. "Kenny—no, Karl—no, excuse me, Kyle! You ought to think about indoor-track tryouts."

What a tool. He couldn't even get my name right.

"I don't know, Coach Copeland. I'm kinda busy lately." I went into the locker room to shower and change.

A group of guys, Jason's new friends, hung out by my locker. Jase used to be like me, kind of a loner. But since high school had started, he had friends from all over the school.

"Hey, Shadow." Alex Keller shoved Pinky and Troy out of the way. He came right at me.

The locker room cleared out. I was left alone, trying to get dressed with six assholes staring at me.

Then I thought about Chase. Who made sure nobody messed with him? Who watched out for Chase now that Jason was gone? How could I not have remembered about those kids? The ones who bullied him?

I told you. Don't forget about Chase.

I didn't. I just—

Alex pushed me against the locker. "Kenny—no, Karl—no, excuse me, Kyle, I'm talking to you." Alex and his friends snickered.

"Yeah, what?" I pushed him off.

Alex stood in front of my locker and pushed me back. "You're a freak, dude. We saw you at the funeral. You're a freak. And nice fuckin' shoes."

That was it? That's the best he could do? I'm a freak with bad taste in footwear?

Alex blew a bubble and it popped, *smack*, in my face. He chomped his gum. "You weren't even friends anymore. Why was he over at your place?"

That stung. I felt blood rush to my face, and my lip quivered. I replayed the last two sentences.

"You weren't even friends anymore. Why was he over at your place?"

"You weren't even friends anymore. Why was he over at your place?"

Just because I wasn't a tool and didn't want to ride along in Alex's dumb-ass truck to make Taco Bell runs, that didn't mean Jase and I weren't friends. So they'd shared a couple of taco pizzas. Big fuckin' deal.

I came back to the scene. Alex and Pinky were laughing

about something. I looked down to see a glob of slobbery chewing gum slide down my leg.

"And you just walk around like nothing happened." Alex leaned in closer. "Well, I won't forget what you did to my friend." He shoved me. "Ever."

Yeah, neither will I, I thought. Then I realized that it was a lie, since I couldn't remember to begin with.

I went back to that moment: My pajama pants were wet. I kneeled down to squeeze out the dew. Then Jase was dead. The end.

A crushing pain ripped through my head when Pinky flicked my temple. "See you in math," he said.

Alex sneered. "Like I said, fucking mental." Then they walked out of the locker room like some B-movie bounty hunters.

If I concentrated hard enough, would I disappear? I squeezed my eyes shut.

"Kyle?" Ricky Myers tapped me on the shoulder.

I jumped. Not invisible. "Yeah?"

He looked around. "What's it feel like, you know?"

"What's what feel like?"

"What's it feel like"—he looked around again—"to kill somebody?" Ricky swallowed hard, and his Adam's apple bobbed up and down, bulging out of his neck.

"I don't know," I muttered, and left.

18

The hallways hummed with that prelunch electricity. I walked into the cafeteria. Everybody sat in the places they had staked claim to at the beginning of the year. Plastic trays banged on tabletops. Students ripped into their utensil packs, dropping the plastic bags on the floor beside them. The smell of greasy synthetic cheese permeated the air.

I scanned the tables, looking for a place that looked safe. Kids stopped eating. They whispered. They stared at me until I looked over, then they pretended that I wasn't there. Backpacks filled empty chairs, and guys spread their stuff out, marking territory like dogs pissing on trees.

Alex slammed into me. "Sorry, Shadow. Didn't see you there." Pinky and Troy laughed. "Doesn't look like there's any place for you here." He said it loud.

Everybody looked up and focused on me, the one-man freak show. It was a classic scene, starting with a shot of me holding my lunch bag and a library book. The camera swish-panned the cafeteria, and all I could see was a blur of faces. Then the camera swiveled back to me for a closeup.

Sweat trickled down my temple and back. My face felt flushed.

Fade out. Fade out. Fade out.

That's what I wished I could do. Fade out and go away. Forever. I couldn't handle this anymore.

But the cafeteria stayed the same, with all those faces looking at me. Everyone knew that I wasn't the one who should be standing there. The wrong guy had died.

Rewind, then. Back up. Get out. I reversed into the hallway.

"Hey, kid. Where are you going? Lunch is that way." The hall monitor pointed to the cafeteria doors.

"I, um, I forgot I have to return a library book. And I don't have time after school." I pulled *The Metamorphosis* out of my backpack. "I can't return it late. Mr. Cordoba will have my head."

The monitor laughed like he understood. Nobody returned books late to Mr. Cordoba. "Okay. Go ahead."

I exhaled, not realizing I had been holding my breath, and hurried away. I stood outside the library in the empty hallway, opening the door a crack. Scarface sat hunched over the newspaper. Rumor had it he was in the Witness Protection Program; the Feds wouldn't let the school get rid of the guy.

Some seniors had told Jase that when Scarface was young, he worked with one of the largest cartels down in South America smuggling drugs and shit. That's where he got the nasty scar that ran from his left eye down to his jaw. He was offered a shitload of cash and lifetime protection to testify against the *patrones*.

"Yeah, but why'd he become a librarian? Man, Jase, they'd never give a guy like that a job with teenagers. That's, like, well . . . Couldn't happen."

"I don't know, but that's what I heard," Jason said. "Some seniors said they saw five passports hidden in his office."

No seniors ever talked to me, so I didn't know that kind of stuff.

"Yeah, like the school board would hire him with that past. Don't you figure they at least ask for references— noncriminal ones?"

"Don't be a shithead. The Feds always create these new identities. It's not like his real name is even Cordoba."

Jason had a point. We kept an eye on him freshman year, but in the end, Scarface Cordoba didn't have any of the telltale mob-assassin signs. He didn't even wear nice suits.

"I think he's just a regular old librarian, Jase."

"Maybe."

"Are you in or out, Mr. Caroll?" Mr. Cordoba asked. His left eye sagged a little, pulled taut by the scar. I followed the bumpy, purple skin from the corner of his eye down to his jaw. It zigzagged by his nose, then stopped right below his chin. "Mr. Caroll, are you going to stand there gawking at me all day? In or out?"

"In?" I answered. I couldn't believe he knew my name.

He nodded. A group of students played chess in the far corner of the library. Almost every table had somebody at it. "What can I do for you today, Mr. Caroll?"

I pulled *The Metamorphosis* out of my backpack. "Mr. Cordoba, this is late. Um, a friend of mine had it, and I, uh, just found it."

Scarface took the book from my hands.

"I'm sorry." I figured the late fee would be, like, $245. I'd have to empty my savings to cover Jason's stupid book.

Scarface scanned the book into the system and nodded. "You're set."

"How much do I owe you?"

"For what?"

"The late fee. It's about four weeks late, I think."

"Nothing." Scarface set the book on top of a pile of books. "Find a seat if you'd like. But don't eat and read at the same time. When you're done eating, wash your hands; then you can read. Don't make a mess of my books."

I looked around. Nobody stared at me. Most kids were already reading and doing homework. The only empty table was the one right smack in front of Scarface's desk. I sat down and pulled out my lunch, staring out the window while I ate. The last leaves clung to the spindly branches of the birch trees in front of the school. The grass had already turned yellow from the cold.

When we were in seventh grade, Jason and I went around and raked people's lawns for cash. I was saving up to buy a video camera, and Jase wanted some vintage comic book. But we ended up wasting more time than working, because once we'd raked up the leaves, we couldn't resist jumping in the piles. We came up with some sweet moves: the half pike, the forward flip, the back bend, and the cannonball. I once did a cannonball on a leaf pile in Mr. Bachman's yard and bit through my lip. It bled like hell, and he called my mom, flipped out because he thought we'd sue him. I think he spread the word, because after that, nobody would hire us. My lip swelling to the size of a basketball didn't help with our corporate image. Neither did the fact that I walked all messed up because my ass hurt.

"What's worse, Jase: not being able to eat or not being able to sit?"

Jason laughed. "Well, you've got them both. You tell me."

I would've laughed, too, if my lip hadn't hurt so freaking much.

"Mr. Caroll, are you going to sit there daydreaming all day or actually get something done?"

I jumped. Scarface peered over the top of his newspaper.

"I'm, um, sure. I'll read something." I grabbed the first book I could reach from the shelves.

The Baby-Sitters Club. Shit. I looked over at Scarface. He buried his head in the paper. I sighed, relieved he hadn't noticed.

Scarface cleared his throat. "Mr. Caroll, I didn't know you were a babysitter."

"I, um. I just grabbed something."

"Okay." He went back to his paper.

"Mr. Cordoba?"

"Yes?"

"I don't really know what to read."

"What do you usually read?"

"I don't." I shrugged. "I watch movies."

Scarface raised his eyebrows and peered over the top of the paper. "Well, then, try this." Scarface handed me back

The Metamorphosis. "I assume you haven't read it."

I sat down and started the book. I was still on the first page, where some guy wakes up as a bug, when the bell rang. The library cleared out. I took a deep breath and got ready to go, tucking *The Metamorphosis* into my backpack.

"See you around, Mr. Cordoba."

"I look forward to it, Mr. Caroll."

As I headed out the door, Mr. Cordoba swept through the library, cleaning crumbs off the tables, straightening books, tucking in chairs.

The last two periods dragged. Pinky Deiterstein, the genetic mutant, sat behind me in math. He had enormous thumbs, almost as long as his pointer finger, twice as wide, and really hairy. During the eighth-grade Thumb War Finals, Pinky broke Tim Preston's thumb. We heard the crack when the bone was crushed.

If Pinky hadn't flicked me in the head and whispered, "Murderer . . . murderer," I might've been able to pay attention.

Murderer . . . murderer . . . murderer . . . murderer . . . I replayed the words over in my head. It was the voice-over to my movie—one line, one word: *Murderer . . . murderer . . . murderer . . . murderer.* It echoed against the walls of my mind.

Don't forget about Chase.

Murderer . . .

Don't forget about Chase.

Murderer . . .

I rubbed my temples; my head ached.

While everyone around me was working on some complicated problem with tangents and cosines, I leaned as far forward as I could, out of Pinky's reach, and pulled out one of the notebooks Jase had left at my house.

I thought about *Run, Lola, Run*, the perfect movie. Lola gets this call from her boyfriend, and everything is messed up. So she gets to do the scene over and over again until it turns out the way it's supposed to, always starting with the phone call. I closed my eyes. I remembered my pajama pant legs sticking to my ankles. That's where the scene would have to begin.

Since I couldn't remember that scene in the shed, maybe another director could, like Tarantino, Lynch, or even Hitchcock. Yeah, Hitchcock. That would be sweet, to have him direct a scene in my life. He'd probably get it right.

Don't forget about Chase.

I won't.

You already did.

I was just . . . I didn't . . . I just . . .

I closed the notebook, hoping I could turn off Jason's voice. Announcements crackled over the loudspeaker before the final bell. I gathered my stuff and decided to head over to Chase's school just to make sure he was okay.

It was Monday. I'd see Dr. Matthews the next day and Mark on Friday. All these people had become a huge part of my life because of just one scene. The final bell rang. Pinky brushed by me and pushed my books off the desk. Jason's notebook flipped open to a page where he had drawn Sketch, his latest superhero version of himself. A sinking feeling settled over me.

There was no editing real life.

19

I picked up all my papers and stuffed them into my backpack. I left without stopping at my locker for homework.

Orange doors opened and slammed. The halls filled with students, but I pushed my way through. Buses lined up and I darted between them, ignoring the teachers' shouts, "Hey, you, get back over here! Hey! Stop!"

I got onto my bike and rode as hard as I could. My lungs burned from the cold air. I looked at my watch: 10:46. *Shit!*

I knew I only had about ten minutes, so I pumped hard until I got to Chase's school. The buses were already lined up, idling, belching out puffs of black smoke. I hid my bike behind a bush and walked between the buses until I found bus 12. It was the first in line. There were some Dumpsters right at the corner—perfect for hiding.

The bell rang and kids spilled out of the school, running around with macaroni art projects in their hands and winter hats with pom-poms on their heads.

Then I saw a familiar green hat with multicolored stripes. Chase was walking and reading a book at the same time, probably science fiction or something about kites.

Every year he picked a new thing. Last year it was dinosaurs. Two years ago it was space travel. He was a walking encyclopedia. The kid would be great for *Jeopardy!* someday.

The same bullies who had been giving Chase shit since kindergarten walked behind him, stepping on the heels of his shoes, shoving him along. Jesus, those kids were only eight, but they were already total jerks. Didn't their parents know? Do parents know when their kids are shitheads?

Julian, the leader of the pack, was a short, freckly punk with greasy red hair. He had buckteeth and warty hands. It was kinda sad, really. I didn't remember the others' names. One looked like he had flunked a few grades. He was shaped like a bowling pin. And the other kid looked pretty normal except for this really irritating eye twitch. I listened for the trill of the whistle from that old Clint Eastwood western. This one would be called *The Warty, the Fatty, and the Twitchy.*

Bowling Pin pulled off Chase's hat. "Thanks for the hat, Chase-Basket-Case. I needed a new one. Tomorrow I'll need a scarf."

Chase didn't do anything. He didn't turn around. He didn't stop them from taking his stuff. He just dropped his head and walked on.

Keep your head up, Chase. Keep it up.

Tears stung my eyes. I hated those kids for making Chase feel so small. I scanned the area. None of the bus-duty teachers were looking my way, so I stepped from behind the Dumpster, cutting the three off.

"Hey, cool! It's a high-school guy! What are you doing here?" Julian wiped his hand across his face. A glistening trail of snot stuck to his jacket arm.

Why are the snottiest kids the bullies?

I didn't say anything. I looked over at Chase getting on the bus and looked back at the three kids. "Leave Chase alone. Got it?"

Bowling Pin stepped forward, then looked like he changed his mind mid stride and stared at the ground. "Okay." His voice cracked at the end.

Poor kid.

Twitchy stood behind. I noticed his lip quivering.

Jesus, they were just kids. I felt like such a tool messing with eight-year-olds. But they were mean little shits. And Chase didn't have anyone else.

"Leave him alone."

They nodded, turned, and ran to their buses. Julian dropped the hat.

The buses chugged out of the lot. I picked up Chase's hat and waited for all the teachers to go back to the building.

I looked across the empty field, remembering how big I used to think the playground was. I walked over to the swings and sat down for a second, the chains pinching my fingers. They were the same swings we'd played on; the same ones Jase had fallen off and gotten a concussion.

I had about two hours until Mom and Dad would be home. I hated counting hours and minutes. I needed someone to talk to. I wanted to see a friend. So I got on my bike and rode until I got to the cemetery.

20

Nobody was around. I guess not many people take time to visit the dead. It's hard enough to get people to visit their great-aunts and grandmas when they're alive. Plus grave-yards are creepy.

I opened the gate and wheeled my bike in. The gate *chink*ed closed behind me. I jumped.

"A little nervous, boy?"

Some old guy holding a rake stepped out of a small office.

"Uh." I looked around. If he hadn't talked, I would've probably thought he was a zombie. This guy was straight out of *Night of the Living Dead*. He had to be a thousand years old.

"Looking for something?"

"Yeah." I nodded. "A friend."

"Here's the map." He pointed out a map that had the names of people and their grave numbers. There were hundreds.

"Thanks."

I skimmed over the names. I'd never known a dead person before, except for Jason's grandma Peters. But she was old dead. That's different. I found him. Jason G. Bishop—R—317.

"Find it?"

The *Living Dead* guy was still there. It was like he didn't breathe or anything, he was so quiet. Maybe he didn't want to wake them all up. Couldn't really blame him. It didn't look like it'd be too long before he'd be joining the ranks.

"Yeah, thanks."

I walked along the winding paths. Tufts of dying grass grew around cracked tombstones. The farther I walked, the fewer tombstones there were. Most graves had stone plaques marking the ground, covered by dirt and dried leaves.

An old oak tree stood in the middle of a bunch of graves, and I pictured its roots webbing around coffins like gargoyle claws. I shivered.

Then I saw it. Jason. The earth was fresh, a rusty color, loosely piled. Flowers surrounded the grave. They were pretty wilty, but they still looked okay. There was a wooden box with water-stained, muddy pictures inside, CDs, a bag of marbles, a Jack Sack—all sorts of things. Tattered satin ribbons were tied around the box with popped balloons on their ends.

I hadn't brought anything.

I dug around my pockets and pulled out a quarter and a wad of chewed gum that had stuck to my pocket lining. I had nothing for him, not even a comic book.

"Fuck," I muttered. My voice sounded like an invader in the heavy graveyard silence. Plus I didn't think *fuck* was the most appropriate thing to say. "Excuse me," I whispered, looking around.

Jesus, who was I talking to?

I stared at Jason's grave.

Jason's grave. My stomach lurched. I could feel the acid work its way up. I swallowed hard and breathed. My legs felt heavy, but I forced myself forward.

Jason G. Bishop
Son, Brother, Friend
He walks with God

I ran my fingers across the black granite set flush with the earth. I think I would've put ARTIST on the stone, too. Some people think that you have to actually be famous and stuff to call yourself something. But Jason really was an artist, even if he hadn't sold anything yet. Yeah: Jason G. Bishop, ARTIST, SON, BROTHER, FRIEND. He would've liked that. I wasn't so sure about the *He walks with God* stuff though.

The slate gray sky darkened with heavy clouds. My fingers burned from the cold. I crouched down.

"Hey."

Leaves rustled.

"So this is it." I rubbed my arms and sat by the stone, pulling my knees to my chest. "Thought you might like a little company."

It was actually a peaceful place. Maybe that's what bugged people so much about graveyards. They were silent. Nobody hollered or shouted in a graveyard. The traffic was miles away. And dead people were a quiet bunch.

Silence is pretty shitty when you don't want to hear your own thoughts.

BROTHER: I traced the word with my finger. "I haven't forgotten about Chase. I'm gonna take care of him. Somehow I'm gonna make things okay for Chase. I promise."

The wind whined in the trees. I opened my backpack and pulled out a crumpled paper. "I, uh, I have a few things I've been wondering about. And things I guess I've wanted to say to you. I don't know if it's anything you can help with, but, well, I've just been writing this shit down as it comes to me."

I waited. The wind picked up a little, and one of the ribbons came loose and skipped across Jason's grave. I was never big into signs, but I figured that anything was better than nothing. Maybe Jason was around.

"Okay. Well, first of all, it's been a hundred and eighty-five days. You know. The orange shoes and all. I betcha you didn't think I'd go through with it, huh?"

I cleared my throat and straightened out the paper. "I'm also just kinda wondering if you're lonely. Is it the same kind of lonely we have down here?"

I paused. I had been lonely way before Jason died, but it wasn't like this.

"This is the thing. If I wait for a sign every time, this might take all year. So I'm just gonna read through the list, okay? Just thoughts and stuff. No big deal. All right. Here goes: Are there angels? Like with wings? Are there ghosts? Are you a ghost? Can you pick to be a ghost or angel or is it kind of assigned?" I paused. "Can you, um, talk to Grandma Peters? Can you hang out with other dead people? Like if I died, could we hang out?"

I looked around. It had to be the loneliest damned place on Earth. I shivered and zipped up my jacket. I held Chase's hat in my hand and shoved the questions into my pocket.

"Do Alex and the guys come?" I wiped my nose. "Were they really good friends? That good?" Well, they didn't fucking kill him. That's gotta top the shitty-things-to-do-to-your-friend list. I breathed in deep.

"Dude, I messed up. Big-time. I just don't know what to do. These questions and stuff, they're just dumb. Dumb shit I think about so I don't have to think about this. About you. Here, you know? I just don't know how—how that could've happened. Anyway, I fucked up. I know I did." I closed my eyes and slumped against the pile of dirt. I thought maybe I could just never get up. Simple. Just sit and sit until I became one of the dead.

When I opened my eyes, the sky had turned purple-black. The first stars had popped out. My teeth were chattering.

I stood up and my feet tingled from the cold. I blew on my stiff fingers. "I've got Chase covered. I guess that's the most important thing, right? That's the one thing I can do right."

I looked at the headstone again. *Jason G. Bishop.* At least they hadn't spelled out Gabriel. He hated his middle name.

I turned back. "Hey, Jase? What's worse: killing your best friend or being killed by your best friend?"

No answer.

I kinda think the first one is worse. But that's because I don't know what the second one is like. Jase probably had his own ideas about that.

21

Riding home, I felt a little bit of relief. I had one thing under control: I could keep Chase safe. Maybe if I did that, kept my promise to Jase, I'd have a reason to stick around. I coasted into the driveway and saw Mark's motorcycle.

"Shit."

I threw open the front door.

"He's home now. He's here." Dad was talking to someone on the phone. Mom and Mark rushed toward me.

"Where have you been? We've been worried sick!" Mom shook my shoulders. Dad came over and pried her fingers off. "Do you have any idea what time it is?"

I looked at my watch: 10:46.

"Kyle, are you listening? Do you have *any* idea what time it is?"

God, I hated questions like that. If I knew the time, I was screwed. If I didn't know the time, I was screwed. Parents always get pissed because we don't have the right answers. They never figure that they have the wrong questions.

What if I didn't give a shit about the time?

I shrugged. This was definitely a scene I wanted to skip. Fast-forward.

They paced up and down the hall in jittery movements, their words coming out in high-pitched screeches. It was like watching one of those old quarter-machine westerns in Virginia City where you get to crank the action, and it goes as fast as you want.

I returned to the scene when Mark was getting ready to go.

He glowered. "Kyle, you messed up."

"I was just riding around."

"You don't get it, do you? You can't be anywhere without telling us where you are. *Anywhere.* If you pull another stunt like this . . ." Mark didn't finish the sentence. It was one of those if–then statements, without the *then*. Those were the worst, because you knew the *then* had to be pretty awful. "I'll call tomorrow." He looked from Mom to Dad. "And get him a damned cell phone." He left; his Harley rumbled down the street.

"Where were you?" Dad asked, steering me into the kitchen. "We were worried."

"I was just riding my bike around. That's all." I suppose they figured I had nowhere to go but school and home now that I'd killed my only friend.

"In the dark? Riding your bike?" Dad rubbed his eyes and leaned on the counter. "Things are—" he started to say. "Kyle, we don't—" He couldn't finish a thought. "We're really worried about you. We're just . . . is Dr. Matthews helping? Do you need to talk to someone else?"

The only person I needed to talk to was Jason. I couldn't shake the cold and stomped my feet on the kitchen floor, shivering.

"You're freezing. Go upstairs and get a sweatshirt. We can talk about this after homework and you eat your dinner. It's in the microwave."

Dad went to his office and closed the door. I walked upstairs. Mom was slumped against Melanie's door. I could hear Melanie's sobs. "They all hate me, Mom. They do," she bawled. "Brooke decided to quit cheerleading. She can't stand to be around me. And then you and Dad . . ." Her words were muffled by a new wave of sobs.

"Honey, I'm so sorry. You have to expect that things will be different for a while." Mom's voice sounded raw.

Different? Painting a room is *different*. Killing Jason could hardly be called *different*.

Mom turned and tried to smile at me. It was one of those forced it's-not-your-fault-you-ruined-our-lives smiles.

Through her door I heard Melanie say, "I hate Kyle. He ruined everything."

I went into my room and closed the door. At least she said what everybody else thought.

Somebody knocked.

"Come in." I flopped on my bed.

Mel walked in with puffy, red eyes. "I didn't mean that."

Yes you did.

"I just never want to go back to school again. I'd rather die." Melanie buried her face in her hands.

I knew how she felt.

"Things are that bad?" I asked.

She wiped her sleeve across her eyes. "I guess they aren't much better for you."

I shrugged. "I'm not a cheerleader. I'm pretty low profile, you know."

She sighed and sat next to me on the bed. "I didn't mean that. Really."

"It's okay." It felt good to sit next to Mel. Almost like things were before she got boobs.

"Maybe we can change our identities and move away," she said.

"Don't think I haven't thought about it."

"And I can't believe you're getting a cell phone." She punched me in the arm. "God, life is so unfair."

Mel had wanted one for about a year. I elbowed her. "Yeah, unlimited minutes with my PO."

She shook her head. "God, everything sucks. Life sucks."

I wanted to ask Mel if she thought it was always going to be this awful, but before I could, she got up and left.

I thought about Clock Westergard. Everybody at school laughed at him. He had stringy black hair and was too skinny. One arm was longer than the other, so when he raised his hand in class, it looked like either six o'clock or twelve thirty. He smelled like photo chemicals because he spent most of his time in the school's lab. He always walked around with this beat-up camera.

The "cool" kids messed with him. They hit his books out of his hands, shoved him into lockers, and gave him cans of soda shaken up. In ninth grade Troy Beckett slipped snow through the vents in Clock's locker. Kids laughed, like getting schoolbooks wet was the most hilarious thing ever. We knew that Clock's grandma didn't have money for new books and shit. All Clock did, though, was take out his books and dab them dry with a dirty gym shirt. Then he stood up and looked Troy in the eyes. We thought they'd fight, but all he did was hold his books and stare Troy down. Troy backed up and left. Then Clock looked each one of us in the eyes. It was like he was saying, *Fuck you*. I avoided him after that.

I wondered if I should talk to him, ask him how he got up to go to school each day. Christ, I didn't even know his real name. I think even the teachers called him Clock.

I stared at the words in my history book: *The Egyptians were among the greatest architects in the history of the world.*

I read that sentence seven times before I closed the book and looked out the window. A porch light flickered on at Jason's house. It was funny how from the outside everything could look the same.

Tuesday morning was more brutal than Monday, like the day was being played in slow motion.

At lunchtime, I headed straight to the library, but the door didn't open. I jiggled on the knob, thinking maybe it was jammed or something. Locked. Kids streamed by.

I zoomed in on the sign on the door: LIBRARY CLOSED FOR LUNCH ON TUESDAYS.

Fuck.

I held my lunch and *The Metamorphosis* in my hands and looked down the hall toward the cafeteria. I definitely didn't want to repeat the scene from the day before. The hall monitor had gone, so I snuck back by the science classrooms. Nobody ever hung out in the science hallway, because it smelled like chemicals and dead animals.

I leaned against some lockers and started to read.

"Mr. Caroll?" Scarface towered over me, holding a pile of science books.

I jumped. "Oh, um. I, um, was just on my way to the cafeteria." *The Metamorphosis* slipped from my hands and thunked on the floor.

Scarface nodded. "That's unfortunate. I could use some help in the library today." He turned to go down the hallway.

"Oh. I've got time." I cleared my throat.

He nodded.

I carried Scarface's books and followed him into the warmth of the library.

"Eat lunch—then you can help me with the books. You should have time for a little reading before the bell rings."

I sat at the table in front of Scarface's desk. He pulled out a Tupperware container of salad and some pita bread.

I chewed on my ham sandwich. I like it when the bread gets smooshed with the ham, cheese, and mayo and sticks to the roof of my mouth. Then I try to peel it off with my tongue without breaking apart the bread-ham-cheese mass. Jason used to do the same with peanut butter and jelly.

"What do you think about the book?"

I was in mid peel when Scarface spoke. I choked down the bite. "What?"

"The book. *The Metamorphosis.*"

"Oh. It's pretty weird, you know." Who would direct *that* movie? Maybe David Cronenberg. He was real into disease and weird transformations. Maybe he'd film it in a seedy downtown motel off Fourth Street in Reno. It would make a wicked flick.

Mr. Cordoba watched me. He didn't say anything but waited. Shit, he probably wanted a report or something. "I don't really remember where they are, um, which city." I opened the book, looking frantically for something about the setting, themes, main conflicts, and all the other crap Mrs. Beacham harped on.

"Mr. Caroll, I'm not asking for a presentation. Just tell me what you think about the book—about what you've read so far."

"Um, well, I'm not far or anything, but I kind of think it's . . . not too believable."

"How so?"

"Like who's gonna wake up a bug?"

"Don't you think somebody's life can change drastically from one day to the next?" Scarface asked. "One moment to the next?"

I paused. "I never thought about it like that."

"Sometimes you have to look beyond the words." He took a sip of water and said, "If you woke up one morning with your reality horribly altered, what would you do?"

151

I thought for a long time. "If I turned into a bug, I'd do anything to feel normal, I guess."

Scarface nodded and turned back to his work.

"Mr. Cordoba?"

He looked up.

"Do you think they ever made a movie out of this book?"

"Most likely. But I don't really know." He pulled some books out of a box. "We need to code these for shelving."

I helped him organize books, then read until the bell rang. "Mr. Cordoba?"

"Yes?" He looked up from his computer.

"Is the library open at lunch tomorrow? You know. It's kind of hard to read in the cafeteria. Lots of noise and all."

"Yes."

"Okay." I picked up *The Metamorphosis* and put it in my backpack. "It's a pretty cool book after all, huh?"

"That it is. See you tomorrow, Mr. Caroll."

"See you." I walked down the hall, thinking about all the ways *The Metamorphosis* could be filmed.

23

"**H**ey, Shadow!" Pinky came up to me and threw me into the wall. He kneed me in the stomach, over and over. I gasped and could feel my air shutting off like a valve.

Alex and Troy stood behind him, laughing.

"Dude, Pinky. We don't wanna kill the guy. Jesus Christ." I wondered if it could end like this; then it would all be okay. It would be over.

But what about my promise? What about Chase?

I fought to hold on as his knee kept jabbing me. Major fade-out. Just as everything started to go black, he stopped. I slumped to the floor, choking.

"Yeah, real tough, punk," Troy said. They walked off laughing, and the hallway cleared out.

Crash! Bang! Pow! Back to reality, comic book–style.

Nice friends you've got there, Jase.

They're not bad, once you get to know them.

Not bad? Pinky just tried to de-entrail me.

They're just . . . They're probably bummed too.

Oh yeah. I forget you were Mr. Popular. You know, you didn't need them.

Dude, I wanted to do other stuff.

What's that supposed to mean?

I just didn't want to watch old cult movies with you every Friday night for the rest of my life. What's the big deal?

Sorry to have cramped your style.

Whatever.

"Murderer . . . murderer . . ." The sound track kept playing, like one of Dad's scratched records.

The days passed. It didn't take long for teachers to start giving me notes to take home. "Dear Mr. and Mrs. Caroll: I'm concerned that Kyle has not turned in homework since his return to school."

I shoved the notes into my backpack. I didn't figure my teachers would cut me any slack if I told them I was too busy rewriting that scene. Dr. Matthews was still on a big memory kick, wanting me to remember everything about Jason, but black thoughts crept through my brain, staining everything.

"Why don't you try thinking of it as a movie," Dr.

Matthews had said. "Write the whole movie and see what happens when you get to that scene."

But I didn't want to write the whole movie. I wanted *Run, Lola, Run,* a chance to redo that scene until I got it right.

```
SCENE THREE: Take One—Tarantino style
"Comanche," by the Revels, is blasting in the
shed and fades out completely before fading
in again when the action begins.
```

```
FADE IN: Kyle's pajama pants are wet,
sticking to his ankles. He crouches down
to squeeze out the dew. He breathes in deep.
Jason holds the gun out for Kyle to get a
closer look.
```

```
CLOSE-UP of Jason twirling the gun in his
hand.
```

JASON

> Check it out, Kyle. It's pretty
> tight, huh?

KYLE

> Sweet, Jase. That's sweet.

CUT TO: Kyle's mom framed in the doorway, silhouetted by the October light.

FADE IN: Jason lying in a pool of blood, then the camera cuts to the gun in Kyle's, alias Shadow's, hand. The camera pans the shelves of the shed and focuses on an old suitcase and a samurai sword.

WIDE-ANGLE SHOT: The Mexican standoff between Kyle, Jason, and Kyle's mom. Kyle holds the gun. Mom holds a pancake spatula.

CUT TO: CLOSE-UP of the gun in Kyle's hand.

WIDE-ANGLE SHOT: The entire shed is coated in blood. Blood sprays from Jason's bullet wounds like in a Manga comic strip.

FADE OUT: Jason lying in a pool of blood.

I reread the scene.

Wrong.

It was like failing a test about the memories of my own life. How pathetic could I get? Maybe I had early-onset Alzheimer's.

Dude, you're really calling it Scene Three?

Yeah. So?

So that last scene of my life is called Scene Three?

I can't think of anything else right now.

You've gotta do better than that.

Give me time and I'll come up with a name for the whole thing.

Jesus, Kyle. Scene Three.

My teachers' notes padded the bottom of my backpack. I looked at the blanks of missing homework. Egyptian pyramids just didn't seem all that important. When I woke up, the only thing that got me through the day was Chase. Lady Macbeth and her damned spot seemed pointless. All she needed was a little bleach. It had worked in the shed.

I had to be totally mental. Maybe I *did* need Dr. Matthews after all. Even if she didn't seem to help.

I saw Clock one day on my way back from the nurse's office. I was in a hurry to get to Chase's school.

"Dude, you okay?" Clock asked. He pulled his hair back into a ponytail and leaned against the wall, his arm outstretched.

Six fifteen, three thirty, six fifteen, three thirty.

Clock stared at the bag of ice I was holding to the back of my head. "What happened?"

My head throbbed. The nurse had said ice would stop the swelling, but the ice was melting, dripping all over me.

Clock shrugged and left. I didn't get how anybody could be like Clock. Carson High was a school of sheep, but Clock didn't give a shit.

"Clock!" I shouted, and ran after him. "Man, I'm sorry."

"About what?"

"Dude, I don't know. Just stuff, just life."

He turned to go.

"Clock, uh, what's your name, anyway?"

He grinned. "Clock."

I had to get to Chase's school, but I needed to know who Clock was. "Your real name, I mean. What's your real name?"

"What's it to you?"

"I dunno. It's just . . ." My voice trailed off. What *did* it matter? "I guess I'd just like to know."

He leaned against some lockers and didn't say anything for a long time. He just stared at me, like the time he had stared at Troy, with his black eyes. Icy eyes.

But I didn't look away.

Then he smiled. "It's Kohana."

"That's different."

"It means 'fast' in Lakota." Clock zipped up his coat and walked away. "I'm gonna be late."

I looked at my watch: 10:46.

"Shit, what time is it, uh, Kohana?" I called after him.

He looked back at me. "Time to get a new watch."

"Yeah, yeah. What time is it?"

Clock pulled out one of those old-fashioned pocket watches on a rusty chain. He flipped open the lid.

"That thing works?"

"Better than yours. It's two fifty-five."

"Shit! I've gotta go."

I rode as fast as I could and got to Chase's school just as the lines of kids were piling into the buses. Chase got on and found his favorite seat, three rows from the back on the right-hand side next to the window. He sat with his head leaned up against the pane, his breath fogging the glass.

He was okay.

24

I shade my eyes, trying to block the glare of the fluorescent light.

All I can hear is the spinning of a gun cartridge and a click when it's shoved back into place. "One bullet; one chance." Jase holds the gun out to me, twirling it in his fingers. "Take it, you fucking pansy. Do it."

Canned laughter from an audience. My eyes adjust and I see Alex, Pinky, Troy, and Jase sitting in a circle. Each holds a gun to his neighbor's head. The entire school is watching us.

"Sit the fuck down, Shadow," Alex sneers.

Sweat beads on my forehead and I take the last empty chair. Jase shoves the gun into my hand. "What're you gonna do?"

The lights dim and it's just Jase and me, facing each other

in the shed. "Whaddya wanna do?" he asks.

"Whaddya wanna do?"

"Whaddya wanna do?"

I jerked awake and stumbled to the bathroom. The porcelain felt cool on my face. Everything was blurry. I tried to stand, but my knees buckled. Clutching the toilet, I retched, squeezing my eyes shut, trying to erase that day. What did we do in the shed? How did it happen?

My nightmares were getting worse. It was easier not to sleep.

I listened to the darkness and watched Jason's house through the window. Mrs. Bishop had put a candle lamp in the window. She never turned off the light. I read that's what people used to do for sailors or soldiers, waiting for them to come home.

Didn't she know he was never coming back?

I walked out to the shed, locked with a padlock now. I touched its cold metal doors and leaned my face into it. Did it smell burned inside, like ashes and fire?

I imagined Jason and me switching places, him having shot me. Things made more sense when I thought about it that way. People loved Jason and would understand. People would forgive. Dying wouldn't be so hard.

Then I thought about Jason gasping for breath, his eyes glazed over, the blood seeping through his T-shirt and

161

pooling on the shed floor.

It took him ninety minutes to die. Less time than a movie. Ninety minutes from the bang to time of death.

How long did they work to revive him? Did he hurt the whole time?

I sat in the shadows, writing in the dim light of the streetlamp, trying to remember, returning to the same place, the same moment, the same scene. I needed to remember.

SCENE THREE: Take Two—Lynch style
The theme song of Scene Three by Angelo Badalamenti plays softly in the background, leading Jason and Kyle to the shed. The light sputters on and buzzes, never giving the viewer a full view of the scene. The shed is bathed in green by the flickering fluorescent light that hangs from the shed's rafters. The hum is barely audible above the haunting score.

CUT TO: Man in a cowboy hat behind the shed, peering in through the window.

POINT OF VIEW: Viewers see the shed through Kyle's point of view. The camera pans the

shelves of the shed. They are blurry because
Kyle is trembling. The music fades out and
changes to "Dance of the Dream Man."

FADE IN: Kyle's pajama pants are wet, sticking
to his ankles. He crouches down to squeeze
out the dew. He breathes in deep. Jason holds
the gun out for Kyle to get a closer look.

                    JASON
         (Holding the gun out to Kyle)
         Check this baby out. It's pretty
         tight, huh?

                    KYLE
    Sweet, Jase. That's sweet.

                    JASON
    What do you wanna do?

                    KYLE
    I dunno. What are we s'posed to do
    with it?
                    JASON
         (Pulling his collar up to look like
         a minister)

                     163

> Well, Kyle, let's see what our
> options are. We could put the gun
> away and continue to freeze—

FADE OUT: The shed doors wail, and Kyle's mom
comes in, blue box in her hand. Behind her,
Jason's mom is holding a ring. Their dresses
are identical.

> MAN IN THE COWBOY HAT
> Just say, "He's the one."

> KYLE'S MOM
> He's the one.

CUT TO: CLOSE-UP of the gun in Kyle's hand.

FADE OUT: Jason lying in a grotesque position.
He is deformed, so a sheet covers his face.
There is no blood.

I read the scene. At least I got a little more dialogue this
time. "What are we s'posed to do with it?"

Did Jase want to put the gun away?

Or did I just take the gun and squeeze the trigger?

Any way I wrote it, Jason ended up dying.

164

At school, everybody was pumped after a crazy Halloween weekend. Somehow dressing up like a ghost didn't seem that fun anymore. I biked over to the cemetery.

"I'm on a pretty tight schedule now, with Dr. Matthews and Mark. It's hard to get away."

I rubbed my eyes and crouched down to pick up the red M&M's that were scattered everywhere. Chase had been there. He only ate the red M&M's. I put them back in the small jar and gathered a few rocks to keep it steady.

"Anyway, I read *The Metamorphosis*." I waited. "I liked it."

A family walked by and gathered at a fresh grave. They piled flowers on the black soil. "And Chase is doing good. I mean, I haven't talked to him or anything. But I can tell he's doing good. Those kids stopped messing with him. He leaves you these M&M's." I jiggled the jar. "Have you ever wondered what he does with the other colors?"

I wiped the mud off Jason's marker.

"I'm still wearing the orange shoes. It's been a hundred and ninety-five days, counting today."

I scuffed my shoe on the patchy grass. "I still feel bad all the time, Jase. And I have these dreams. *Nightmare on Elm Street*. It's awful." I wiped the tear that dripped down my nose. "Is it better there? Where you are?"

The wind cut through my jacket. The family huddled over the other grave, humming, praying. I kneeled down and leaned my forehead on Jason's marker, waiting for an answer.

Then I heard soft footsteps padding down the walk. I turned to see the Bishop family—all of them. Mrs. Bishop held a bouquet of bright flowers in her arms.

I jumped up and knocked the M&M's all over the grave. "Shit!" I looked for a place to hide. Leave it to the Bishops to bury Jason on the only treeless hill. The only way out was across the graves.

I ran, hopping from grave to grave. "Sorry, sorry, sorry, excuse me, sorry, sorry." The last thing I needed was to piss off half of Carson City's dead. "Excuse me, sorry. Sorry." I didn't stop running until I got to my bike. It took me a while to steady my hands to unlock the chain. As I pulled my bike out, I noticed that somebody had put a small jar of red M&M's in the drink holder. I looked back. The Bishops had disappeared behind a short hill. I put the jar in my pocket and rode home.

25

Lunchtime in the library was like a frame still. I could always count on the chess club taking over the back table; the skinny girl with glasses sitting at the table kitty-corner from me; Brady, the junior class president, coming in to read the newspaper; and Joaquín Sánchez, the center for the varsity basketball team, coming in twice a week to tutor his little brother in math. It would've made a great publicity shot.

At the end of the period on a Friday, I handed Cordoba *The Metamorphosis*.

"Mr. Caroll, do you need another book?"

"Yeah. Maybe."

He pulled down books from the shelves. "What would you like to read?"

I picked up *The Time Machine*. "Maybe this one." I looked at the names of those who had checked it out but didn't see Jason's. I wished I had asked him about more of the books he'd read. Maybe Mr. Cordoba knew.

"That's a classic, Mr. Caroll." Mr. Cordoba stamped the book. "See you Monday."

"Sure. Thanks." I sighed, glad to have something to read over the weekend.

Mel met me out on the porch that day with her you're-in-deep-shit look. "Kyle, you messed up. They got your progress report today, and Mom freaked out. Big-time. She won't even talk."

"What shade of red is she?"

"God, Kyle. This is huge. It's about as bad as it can get."

"Man, I didn't think progress reports came until mid-November. That's weird."

"Kyle, it *is* mid-November."

I imagined a scene where the camera cuts to pages of a calendar flipping through the days, stopping on November 11. Somebody tears out the date; the camera zooms in on the piece of paper drifting into the wastebasket. I go back and change the scene. It would be better to stop and tear out October 8.

"Thanksgiving is in two weeks." Mel snapped her gum and grabbed my arm. "Jesus, I sometimes wonder what planet you live on. What have you been doing all these weeks in your room after school?"

Nothing, I thought. Absolutely nothing. Could Mel understand how much energy *nothing* took?

I heard Dr. Matthews's voice saying, "Inertia is deadly." It echoed down the streets.

At least it was a better voice-over than *murderer . . . murderer . . . murderer.*

"C'mon, Kyle." Mel pushed me through the door. Mom held on to Dad's hand so tight, you could see the white in her knuckles, just like at the disposition. Freeze frame: Mom and Dad on the couch.

I wondered if they were trying the whole stay-still-so-the-Earth-swallows-me-up thing. I could've told them that it doesn't work. Mark had his arms crossed in front of his chest. I concentrated on the bulging Chinese tattoo. Jesus, the guy even had muscular wrists. I hadn't even noticed his Harley at first. It was as if all my life scenes were blurry.

"Kyle, we need to talk."

Nothing good ever follows *We need to talk.*

"We received your progress report today." Mom rubbed her temples.

"We didn't realize things were this bad." Dad leaned on the coffee table.

Mel shoved me into the easy chair and sat down on the arm next to me.

"You haven't turned in one homework assignment for over a month, since October." Mark's temple vein pulsated. His tattoo twitched. What if the tattoo guy had written *Dog shit* in Chinese instead of *Control, Determination, Peace,* or whatever the hell it said? How would anybody know? Anybody not Chinese, I mean. I pictured Mark visiting Carson City's Golden Chopsticks Chinese Palace and having all the waiters laughing at his *Dog shit* wrist. "You're failing every class." Mark looked back at the progress report. "Every class but PE."

Mom clenched her jaw and glared at Mark.

I looked from Mom to Dad. How could I explain to them how pointless homework seemed?

Dad said, "Remember what Dr. Matthews said? Remember how important it is to get back into life?"

Back into life? As if I ever got out of it. That was Jason. Out of breath. Out of time. Out of life.

It was like somebody had shouted, "Cut! That's a wrap!" as soon as that ER doctor walked into the waiting room at 10:46.

That's a wrap, Jase.

Yeah. Scene Three.

I don't have time for this shit right now, okay?

Whatever. Scene Three.

"What work did you bring home this weekend?" Mom asked, and reached for my backpack. She opened it and pulled out *The Time Machine*, my notebook filled with Scene Three, sixteen tardy notes, seven notes from my teachers, and a detention warning. "What the— Jesus, Kyle.

Why didn't you give me these notes?"

I shrugged.

"Why didn't your teachers call? What the hell is going on with the school? What happened to open communication?" Mom paced back and forth, reading through the notes.

"It's not a big deal," I muttered.

"Being sent to a juvenile detention center? Not a big deal? Is that what you want?" she cried.

To go away forever and never have to face anyone again? Never have to look at the shed again? Never have to look at the Bishops' house again?

But then again, I had Chase. And a promise to keep.

Plus, I had seen some raunchy movies about prisons. Maybe I'd end up being some fat guy's bitch. That would suck. Alex and "the guys" were better than that.

Mark leaned in and skimmed through some of the notes. "You've been given a second chance here, and look what you're doing." He pulled a faded piece of paper out of his pants pocket. "This is a grade contract. Sign here. If you blow your grades again, we'll have to come up with some alternative plans."

"What's that supposed to mean? Alternative plans?" Mom clutched my backpack.

Alternative plans probably mean a place in the Willow Springs or West Hills psych wards. White walls. White tiles. White jackets. White noise. Stanley Kubrick.

171

He turned to Mom and Dad. "Kyle needs to learn that he is responsible for his own actions and poor choices."

Did I choose to point and aim and shoot?

Dude, I still can't believe you're calling it Scene Three.

Ah, fuck you, man.

Mark glowered at Mom and Dad. "Probation is about monitoring, listening, keeping track of what's going on. And that's obviously not happening here."

"So we're supposed to know everything about a fifteen-year-old boy who hardly speaks? He walks into his room and sits there all afternoon until the next morning. What am I supposed to do about that?" Mom turned a deeper shade of red.

I could've made a sweet documentary about what happens to parents after their only son fucks up their lives.

Mom's eyes darted between Mark and me. "Kyle, we want to help you. I'm afraid—" She gripped the notes in her fist. When she realized that they had formed a sweaty ball, she let them drop to the table, then tried to straighten them out. "You're just so disconnected," Mom said. She kept her head down. Mom didn't like to cry in front of anybody.

Dad cleared his throat. He sat on the end table next to my chair. "It's not just the grades."

Then the room fell silent. No comic relief for this scene. Finally Mark stood to go. "I'll set up a meeting with Kyle's teachers and Dr. Matthews for next week." He shook

Dad's hand. "We'll get things worked out." Mark thumped my shoulder. "Last chance, kid." He motioned to the grade contract.

Mom finally looked up from the crumpled notes on the table. She nodded. A solution had been placed on the table. A meeting. With adults. Talking about how to fix me—the one who broke everything else.

Mark left and Mom returned to my backpack. She picked up the copy of *The Time Machine* and ran her fingers along its crooked spine. Her voice trembled. "Are you reading this book for a report?"

"No."

"Okay. Then what are you studying in your classes?"

"I don't know."

She sighed. "Okay. Okay. This is my fault."

Why did they always want to take the blame for the things I did wrong?

"We need to get this homework in order," Dad said.

We, we, we, we, we . . . I wondered if Hannibal Lecter's parents said shit like that. "Hanni, honey, we need to try to stop killing people, then doing nasty things like broiling them for supper. . . ."

"Can't you call a classmate to ask for some assignment—any assignment?" Dad asked. He rubbed Mom's shoulders.

I shook my head. "I don't have anyone to call."

26

Tuesday morning, Dad took me to school. "Kyle, you need to stay after school for a while today. We arranged for you to go to the library. Mom and I are having a big meeting with your teachers. You need to get back on track."

Back on track.

Back on the bike.

Back from the dead.

The day sucked. I thought about all of them—my teachers, my parents, Mark, and Dr. Matthews—sitting in Principal Velásquez's stuffy office. I hoped *all* my teachers didn't have to be there.

After the last bell, I rushed to Chase's school and came back as fast as I could. It took longer running, since I didn't have my bike that day. I looked at the clock in the hallway outside the library. I was forty minutes late. Maybe Mr. Cordoba didn't know what time I was supposed to get there.

I stood outside the library in the empty hallway. Lunchtime was one thing, but almost nobody went to the library after school. Nobody who didn't have to, anyway.

"You're late."

I jumped. It was like the guy could see through his newspaper and the door. I cleared my throat. "Sorry."

"Get in, then."

I handed *The Time Machine* to Mr. Cordoba.

"Well?" he said.

"Well?" I echoed.

"Tell me about the book."

I paused. "Really, I guess I was kind of disappointed. I expected to get answers, you know?"

"Disappointed? Answers?"

"It didn't help me much, Mr. Cordoba." I cleared my throat and stared down at my shoes. The orange had faded, so they looked more like a dirty peach. I had to find a way to glue the peeling rubber back on.

"What do you want help with, Mr. Caroll?" he asked.

"Um, I dunno. It's just that I guess I wanted something else. Something about being stuck in time."

Mr. Cordoba put his paper down. "Stuck?"

"Have you ever wanted something so bad, you thought there had to be a way for it to happen?"

That's one of the last things Jason had said to me. We ran into each other Thursday after school. He was hanging out by the flagpole, waiting for Alex to pick him up.

"Where're you guys heading today?"

Jase shoved his books into his backpack. "Nowhere." He looked real down.

I sat next to him. "What's up?"

"Have you ever wanted something so bad, you thought there had to be a way for it to happen?"

I shook my head. "Whaddya mean?"

Jase pulled out a letter from UC Berkeley. He handed it to me. I skimmed it over.

"Oh, shit, Jase. I'm sorry."

"I thought I could get into the winter comic-book art program for teens, you know? I've even been working on this new portfolio." He pulled out a sketchbook of school superheroes and villains. "But I'm just not good enough."

"Dude, there had to be major competition. Plus you submitted your old stuff. It's not as good as this." I pointed to Infinity Detention, who shaped his body into the infinity sign, zapping his enemies to the detention room forever. Split Infinitive was awesome. Her body would divide in two, and she'd crush her enemy's brain if he messed up on grammar.

Jason smiled. "Check out Formaldehyde. He's the master villain. He doesn't even kill his enemies, but preserves them in these massive jars and leaves them in the science hall on exhibit."

"And you?"

Jason flipped the page. "I'm Sketch. I can draw anything the superheroes need. So if Kite Rider needs a kite that spouts fire and shit like that, I draw it and it comes to life. Or if Freeze Frame needs a stopwatch, I draw it up."

"Freeze Frame?"

He turned the page. "Check him out. Look familiar?"

I grinned. "Freeze Frame rocks."

He nodded. "I was debating between Freeze Frame and Director's Cut. I went for Freeze Frame so you could stop time. You're the only force that can stop the *zap* of Infinity Detention."

I flexed. "Freeze Frame. This is sweet." I skimmed through the notebook and saw Line Runner. Some lame-ass basketball guy who looked like Alex. I cleared my throat. "You should try again for next year."

Jase shrugged. "I was thinking about the summer program, but that one's even harder to get into than the winter one. I'm not even gonna try."

"Don't quit. You'll get in. I'm sure of it. Especially with this new stuff."

Jason bit his lip. "Nah. You just like being a superhero."

"Who wouldn't?" Alex probably did, too. "You'll get in."

"Probably not."

"For sure. What's worse: never trying and never knowing, or trying and getting your ass kicked once in a while?"

Alex drove up. He rolled down the window. "You tagging along, Shadow?"

I didn't get why Jase would even bother being friends with those ass wipes. I shook my head. "Nope. Busy today." I got on my bike.

"Hey, Kyle?"

"Yeah?"

"You still thinking about trying out for basketball?" Jason asked.

"Yeah, maybe." Basketball was my latest lame-ass effort to keep up with Jase and his new friends. My friendship with Jase had become a pathetic game of follow-the-leader with him sitting in the director's chair.

Alex snickered.

Jason lowered his voice, like he didn't want Alex and those guys to hear. "Wanna shoot hoops after the homecoming game, then?"

"Cool." Then it slipped out. "You can stay over tomorrow night if you want. I just got the uncut version of *A Clockwork Orange*." Fuck, why did I invite him? He probably had a few parties to go to with Alex.

"Yeah. Sounds good. See you tomorrow."

"See you."

∞∞∞∞∞∞

I hadn't really known what Jase had meant when he said he'd wished for something so bad, but now I did. I wish I'd never seen Jason after school that day or that the dialogue was different. It would've been an easy scene to fix. All I had to do was leave it at playing basketball after the home-coming game. Easy.

Mr. Cordoba tapped a pencil on his desk, waiting.

Maybe he would understand. "Have you ever wanted to go back and edit something in your life?" I asked, staring at the carpet.

"Yes, I have."

I looked up. "Really?"

Mr. Cordoba was nodding. "Really."

I waited for a while, hoping he'd tell me. But he sat quietly behind his desk, watching me.

"So what did you do?"

"To what?"

"To change the past? Or"—I paused—"to delete it."

Mr. Cordoba frowned. "Delete it?"

"I guess. I mean, I dunno. It's confusing."

"The past will never go away, Mr. Caroll. But you can make peace with it."

"How?"

"By facing it."

I sighed and sat down. As if it were that easy. I pulled out the notebook and wrote:

SCENE THREE: Take Three—Hitchcock style
A carnival organ pipes "It's a Most Unusual
Day" in the background. FADE IN: Kyle's
pajama pants stick to his ankles. He crouches
down to squeeze out the dew, then sits next
to Jason on the workbench. The contents of
the shelves blur behind them.

DOLLY ZOOM/HITCHCOCK ZOOM: the shelves. The
shelves overwhelm the foreground. The viewer's
attention is taken away from Kyle and Jason
and directed to the contents of the shelves.
The viewer sees a newspaper clipping, with a
picture of Hitchcock advertising a weight-loss
product, lying on top of an old dollhouse.

CLOSE-UP of the dollhouse staircase.

WIDE ANGLE: Jason is facing the camera. The
viewer sees the back of the murderer. He has
shaggy brown hair. He is short and thin. He
looks like Kyle from behind, but the viewer
does not see his face. He breathes in deep.
Jason holds the gun out.

CLOSE-UP of gun in Jason's hands.

CUT TO: Kyle wiping his hands on his pajama pants, trying to keep his hands from trembling.

                    JASON
          (Jason holds the gun out to Kyle.)
          Check this baby out. It's pretty
          tight, huh?

                    KYLE
          Sweet, Jase. That's sweet.

                    JASON
          What do you wanna do?

                    KYLE
          I dunno. What are we s'posed to do
          with it?

                    JASON
          (Pulls up T-shirt collar around
          his neck, making him look like a
          pastor. He scowls.) Well, Kyle,
          let's see what our options are.
          We could A: put the gun away and
          continue to freeze, or B: put the
          gun to good use.

                    181

CUT TO: the gun passing from Jason's hand to Kyle's.

HITCHCOCK ZOOM: to a mirror behind Jason. The viewer's attention is directed to the mirror, where he sees, reflected, the face of the killer. The killer is holding a glass of brandy and the gun.

I was just up to the part of the scene where I was going to drink the brandy when Mr. Cordoba interrupted me. "Mr. Caroll, you have a lot of catching up to do, from what I understand." He eyed the notebook.

I put it away. The master of suspense would have to wait. Nobody argued with Cordoba. Ever. I opened my history book and started on the day's assignment. It wasn't as boring as I thought it would be. The only noise for the next hour was the sound of Mr. Cordoba working on the computer and the scratch of my pencil on paper.

"Mr. Caroll, it's time to find your parents."

I looked at the clock: 4:45. It was the fastest hour I'd had after school since— Well, for a long time. As I was packing up my stuff, my parents appeared at the library door. For a second they looked like strangers. Mom looked skinnier. Dad's shoulders slouched. He opened the door.

"How did it go?" He was looking at Cordoba.

"Give us a few more minutes." Cordoba nodded his head in my direction. Dad closed the door. "So, Mr. Caroll, I think our trial period went well. I'll expect you here every day after school as well as at lunch. On time."

Our trial period? Every day? On time? What about Chase?

"Uh, Mr. Cordoba. I can't."

"You can't what, Mr. Caroll?"

"I, um, I can't be on time."

Mr. Cordoba arched his eyebrows and cracked his knuckles. "Because?"

Because I stand behind a Dumpster to watch out for my dead best friend's brother. Too weird. I didn't want to sound like a stalker. "I just need a half hour."

He waited for me to get my arms through my backpack straps. "So it looks like you'll be getting up a half hour earlier, then, to get here before school."

I groaned. I didn't mean to, but it escaped out of my throat. I didn't care about lunchtime and after school. Getting up to spend even more hours at school—that kind of sucked.

Mr. Cordoba lowered his voice. "You need your half hour after school? I need your half hour before school." He cracked his knuckles again. "Do you need another book?"

I nodded. "Yeah. Thanks."

Mr. Cordoba nodded and handed me *A Separate Peace*.

"Don't we have to read this in eleventh-grade English or something?"

"Probably."

I raised my eyebrows.

"Read it twice."

I didn't argue. I looked at the signatures of kids who had checked it out. Jason hadn't.

"Mr. Caroll, your parents are waiting." He opened the library door. "I'll see you tomorrow morning."

"Okay, Mr. Cordoba." For a moment, just a moment, I felt almost normal.

27

After Mom and Dad's conference with all the Carson City school district's employees, I became every teacher's project. I couldn't go anywhere without being mobbed by somebody who wanted me to be *involved*.

At home, things weren't much better. Uncle Ray came down from Reno at least once a week so he and my dad could have breakfast. They invited me once, but I couldn't stand the breakfast smells: syrup, pancakes, fried sausage. I felt nauseous and had to go sit outside. The only things I could stomach for breakfast anymore were cereal and Pop-Tarts.

I went to Dr. Matthews's office every Tuesday, the only day I had left to visit Jase because I got out of library duty for the shrink.

At Dr. Matthews's I hardly ever spoke. Every week she asked me to tell her about October 8. Over and again. Once I asked, "Tarantino or Hitchcock style?"

It threw her for a loop. That afternoon, neither of us said much.

The days dragged. At school, I couldn't understand how Karen Jacobs and Maria Ramirez were excited about Sadie Hawkins. I couldn't understand why nominating the winter homecoming court was so important. The only things that made sense were watching Chase, going to the graveyard, and the library.

Then I saw the flyers.

Memorial Assembly for Jason Bishop: 5th Period

How long had the flyers been up? Why hadn't I seen them before? They were pasted everywhere with a picture of Jason from freshman year, when he didn't have long hair. He hated that picture.

The sophomore class officers handed out flyers and balloons that read: JASON, YOU'RE IN OUR HEARTS FOREVER. They all wore black, and Sarah McGraw, class president, dabbed her eyes with Kleenex. I'd never even seen her talk to Jason. They swept through the hallway like storm-troopers.

186

Jesus, they were probably going to read some bad poetry, the kind you find on greeting cards and bumper stickers. I bet I was the only one who knew that Jason's favorite poet was e. e. cummings.

All of last year, Jason had refused to capitalize his name in English class. The student teacher, Miss Torrence, marked Jase down for bad capitalization one day. He brought in e. e. cummings's poems and said, "If he doesn't have to, why do I?"

A few months ago, I saw Miss Torrence working at Costco. I think she decided not to be a teacher after all.

The flyer felt like lead in my hand. The first bell rang for fifth period. "Shit," I muttered. I crouched down between some lockers, behind a trash can, waiting for the tardy bell to ring. The halls emptied as kids rushed to the gym. I had to get out of school before the assembly began.

When I stood up, prickles of light ripped through my skull. For just a second everything went grayish black. Steadying myself on the lockers, I walked down a side hallway nobody used except for the smokers. They had rigged the door of the emergency exit so the fire alarm wouldn't go off. The hall smelled like potpourri spray and old cigarettes. I saw Clock walking across the field and thought I could catch up to him. I almost made it through the door when I felt a hand on my shoulder.

"Going somewhere, Mr. Caroll?"

Cordoba.

"Mr. Caroll, are you lost, perhaps?"

There was no escape. My eyes darted around the hallway.

Cordoba leaned over and picked up the flyer. "I need some help reshelving books in the library. I think you just got the job."

He didn't smile. He didn't give me one of those bummer-you-killed-your-friend looks. He didn't give me a Mrs. Beacham–style sympathetic shoulder squeeze. He just pointed toward the library. Relieved, I followed Cordoba down the hall. I took out *A Separate Peace* and handed it to him.

"You finished quickly."

"Yeah."

Cordoba raised his eyebrows. I knew the drill; it was book confession time.

"It was so-so."

"Why so-so?"

I sighed. "I dunno. I didn't get it. How could Finny be so okay with everything after what Gene did to him?"

"So Finny shouldn't have forgiven Gene?"

"I think there are some things . . ." I cleared my throat. "Some things aren't forgivable."

"Even between best friends?"

I thought for a bit. "Especially between best friends."

"How so? What isn't forgivable?"

188

Living. Being alive. Breathing, eating, sleeping, jacking off.

I heard "The Star-Spangled Banner" blaring out the gym speakers. Mel slumped into the library and sat next to me. "Didn't feel much like an assembly today." Her mascara was smeared underneath her eyes. I was relieved to see her. I didn't want to talk about Cordoba's books anymore.

"Me neither," I whispered.

"They're all assholes, Kyle. You know that."

I didn't know who "they" were, but I figured it had to do with her cheerleader friends. It sucked to see Mel so sad all the time.

Sorry, I wanted to say. But it just seemed like such a copout.

"The Bishops are coming. They're planting a tree with a plaque or something."

The knot in my stomach moved up to my throat. My eyes burned. It was like everybody wanted to relive it over and again. But they weren't there. They didn't know how awful Jason had sounded—gurgling, gasping, dying. It wasn't like it was in the movies. It was final. It was over. What good was a fucking tree? Trees died too. And it was November. You can't plant a tree in November.

They should've made some kind of cockroach memorial. Those prehistoric fuckers never die. They'll live way longer than the whole human race. It could be the cockroach memorial to Jason Bishop. It would've been perfect

189

because of *The Metamorphosis*. Jase would've liked that.

Mr. Cordoba watched Mel and me whispering. He cleared his throat. "Mr. Caroll, why don't you help me reshelve these books? Miss Caroll, I assume you've got a note."

Mel handed it to him.

"Are you ready to work too?"

Mel nodded.

I liked the smell of the library. I liked the feel of the book pages between my fingers, and the crinkly sound of the plastic covers. We spent the afternoon sorting and shelving books.

"It's time to go now." Mr. Cordoba pointed toward the clock: 5:00.

It was weird how the library was the only place where time meant nothing to me. There were no ticks or pings. I felt like I could sit there forever without wanting to go backward or forward.

"Let's go home, Kyle." Mel grabbed her keys and put on her coat.

"Yeah. Wait a sec. Um, Mr. Cordoba. Do you have a book by that poetry guy, e. e. cummings?"

"Poetry guy," he mumbled, shaking his head. "Interesting choice." He pulled a book down and handed it to me. I should've taken the time to read e. e. cummings while Jason was still alive.

All evening, something didn't feel right. As I listened to

the sounds of nighttime, I saw the jar of red M&M's on the nightstand and realized what it was. Chase. I'd forgotten about Chase. I couldn't even keep the simplest promise.

"I'm so sorry," I whispered. "I'm so sorry."

28

I stood behind the Dumpsters. The bell rang and kids came running out with construction-paper turkeys in their hands. Some class had made stick mobiles with glittery winter scenes dangling from the tips. A little girl tripped and crushed her mobile. Poor kid. She couldn't stop crying.

I saw the circus act. They looked over at me. Julian looked especially pale and ran to his bus, leaving Bowling Pin and Twitchy behind.

No Chase.

Kids piled into the buses. The crusty snow looked dirty and tired after being trampled by little feet. The buses pulled out.

No Chase.

My heart raced.

Maybe he's sick. Yeah, he's probably sick.

An icy tightness gripped my stomach. I had missed yesterday and now there was no Chase. I stood up to leave when I felt somebody tugging on my coat sleeves.

"Chase, what are you doing here?"

"I didn't see your orange shoes yesterday." Chase had a huge bruise on his left cheek. His eye was a little swollen.

"What happened? Who did this to you?"

Chase shrugged. The kid could talk a thousand miles a minute, but only when he wanted to. "What happened to your neck, Kyle?"

I had gotten so bruised and beaten lately, I had lost track. A few days earlier Alex had elbowed me in the neck and left a huge black-and-blue mark that was fading to a yellowish green. I'd been wearing turtlenecks so my parents wouldn't see. They didn't need anything else to worry about. But there was no fooling Chase. Looking up at me, the way he was, he saw the bruise where it poked above my shirt.

"So? What happened to your neck?"

"It doesn't matter. Are you okay? What are you doing here? Why aren't you on the bus?"

"Where were you?"

"I blew it. I didn't come."

"Yeah, they didn't see you and kicked my butt. Plus it was a GCP day. Not good."

"GCP?"

193

Chase nodded solemnly. "Green corduroy pants day. Whenever Julian wears his green corduroys, somebody gets beaten up. Usually me." Chase pulled out a piece of paper. "This charts the days Julian beats me up. Here, you see what he wears. Sixty-two percent of the time he beats me up, it's a GCP day. You can't refute the facts."

I studied the chart. "Maybe it's a coincidence."

"Kyle, in life there are no coincidences."

"Maybe he doesn't have a lot of pants."

Chase took the chart back and tucked it into his note-book. "So where were you?"

Chase looked so small. I crouched down. "I'm so sorry," I said, trying to control my voice. "It won't happen again. I'll always be here."

"Even if you're sick?"

"Even if I'm sick."

"Even if you have to have an emergency appendectomy?"

"Oh. In that case, maybe not."

"So you won't always be here."

"I'll always . . ." I sighed. "I don't know. Chase, buddy, you can't let them do this to you. You've got to stand up for yourself."

"Do you?"

"Do I what?"

"Do you stand up for yourself?" Chase pointed at my turtleneck.

194

"That doesn't matter."

"Do as I say, not as I do?"

I tried to smile, but only one side of my mouth curved up. Chase was one of a kind. "Do you know how to throw a punch at least?"

Chase shook his head. Another boy came around from the Dumpster. Chase nodded at him. "This is Mike. He's my best friend. He has a GCP chart, too. His is forty-one percent."

Mike shrugged. "They just kick my butt a lot." He gawked at me. "Geez, you're big."

I stifled a laugh. I was 5'8" and weighed 120 pounds. Real big. "Nice to meet you, Mike."

"How much do you charge?"

"For what?"

"To be Chase's bodyguard?"

Chase looked at Mike as if he'd asked the dumbest damned thing. "He does my work pro bono."

Chase killed me. Where'd he come up with this stuff?

"Okay, this is the thing, guys. These kids—that freckled guy, Julian, and his friends—they'll never leave you alone if you don't stand up for yourselves."

"Maybe they'll grow out of it." Chase shrugged. "Maybe he won't buy any more GCPs after this year."

"No, Chase. They won't grow out of it. Never. You have to stand up for yourself. I'll be here. But what if I'm not here forever?"

"Will you go away like Jason?"

Tears stung my eyes. "No, not like that. But maybe I'll have to get a job or something."

"Oh. This isn't your job?" Mike asked. He was even smaller than Chase. "Is that why you come late sometimes?"

Chase nudged him. Then he pulled a red Spiderman watch out of his pocket and handed it to me. "This is for you. I bought it with my allowance."

I held the watch in my hands. "For what?"

"To tell the time, Kyle."

"I've got a watch."

"Oh." He inspected my wrist. "That's Jason's old watch—the one you traded. It's broken. I knew the watch was the problem—why you come late."

"It's not—," I said.

"Did you really think it was ten forty-six?" Chase asked.

10:46.

"Anyway, I had to decide between Spiderman and the Hulk and decided Spiderman fit your profile better. The Hulk is entirely too conspicuous. This should help you get here on time, every day." Chase took off my old watch and fastened Spiderman around my wrist. "It's already set and has a new battery. Do you want me to throw this one away?"

"No!" I snatched the watch from his hands. "I, uh, maybe I can fix it." I stared at the two watches. One stopped at 10:46. The other ticking away, like nothing had ever happened.

"Okay." Chase looked at Mike, and they both shrugged.

The Bishops' minivan was idling in the school driveway. "There's Mom. She wanted to come pick me up today because of yesterday. I don't think you're supposed to be here."

I bit my lip and ducked back down behind the Dumpsters. "I know. I know." I swallowed hard. "Go on. I'll see you tomorrow."

Chase's eyes got really big.

"I promise, Chase," I said.

A large shadow blocked the sunlight. Mr. Bishop towered above me.

"Dad!" Chase said. "Kyle was just—"

"Chase, Mike, get in the car."

"Dad, but—" Chase said. He reached out for my hand.

Mr. Bishop pointed to the minivan. "I said *'Get in the car!'* Now."

Chase nodded. He and Mike looked back at me.

"What the hell are you doing here? At Chase's school?"

I couldn't even begin to explain. "I, um. I . . ."

Mr. Bishop clenched his fists. "You are to stay away from my family. Understood?"

I tried to stand, but my legs wouldn't hold me. I swallowed. *I'm so sorry,* I wanted to say. *I'm sorry.*

My hands burned with the icy snow. Mr. Bishop kept talking, but I couldn't hear him. I only heard a buzzing in my ears, like when I shot the gun. His mouth moved, but no sound came out. Someone had muted the movie.

I finally got the strength to stand and get to my bike. Mr. Bishop stood behind the Dumpsters staring at me, fists by his sides.

I rode to the library as hard and fast as I could, the cold air piercing my lungs. My hands trembled, and I could barely open the library door. I sat in the first chair I found with my head between my knees, trying to control my breathing.

Mr. Cordoba peered over his newspaper. "Everything okay?"

"Sure. Yeah." My voice wavered.

"Do you need anything?"

"I just want to sit right now, okay? Just sit," I whispered. Vertigo. The floor spun, the colors of the carpet blending. I squeezed my eyes shut, hoping that life could stop, but all I could see was Jason's dead body crumpled up in Dad's shed.

I hugged my knees, listening to my heart thud against my hollow chest.

Mr. Cordoba set his newspaper down on his desk and

half read, half watched me.

The minutes ticked by. Fiery orange light streamed through the windows, and pink clouds streaked from behind the mountains. Everything became blanketed in purple. I got up and started to pull down book after book, searching for Jason's name. Which books did he take out? What did he use to read?

Cordoba watched as the tables piled with books.

"Are you looking for something?"

"I just need to find," I said, choking out the words, "I just need to find a book. That's all. I don't need your help. I don't need anybody's help. I'm just looking for a . . ." The titles blurred before me. My voice cracked.

"Why don't we call your folks?"

"No." I shook my head. "I just need a book."

Mr. Cordoba approached me. "Can I help you pick one out?"

"I don't want *your* books. Don't you get it?"

He put his hand on my shoulder. "Mr. Caroll, it's time to go home."

"No." I pushed him away.

"Why don't you get your things out of your locker and come back here? We'll find whatever book you want."

"We will?" I whispered.

Mr. Cordoba nodded. "We can look all night if we have to."

"Okay," I breathed. "Okay."

The hallways were empty. Most teachers had gone home. Sometimes after the library I could hear a vacuum in the distance. Sometimes, if varsity basketball practice was running late, I could hear the pounding of rubber balls on the court and the squeak of basketball shoes.

Something felt wrong. It was later than usual, too dark. Too quiet.

I was walking down the hallway when I heard glass shatter; then I felt thunderous pain in my head.

"Fucking pansy. Hiding out in the library behind that freak, Cordoba. Didn't even have the balls to show up at the assembly."

I staggered back and felt blood trickle down behind my ear, matting my hair. Dripping. Clumping.

"What's the matter, Kyle? Not so tough without your gun?" Troy asked.

"You're the one who shoulda died," said Alex. "You're the fucking loser who followed Jason around. You're the fucking shadow."

A quiet rage surged through me. Troy, Pinky, and Alex turned crimson, erasing the gray of the hallway and the purple of the evening light. I reached for Alex's neck and shoved him against the locker.

He trembled, his breath rank with fear.

29

"**H**ow could you do this, Kyle? This isn't you." Mom paced back and forth. "This is— Jesus, I need some air."

Who am I, then?

I held an ice pack to my head.

I didn't remember the explosion. I didn't remember anything but Cordoba holding on to me. Holding me back. Bringing back the gray. And Alex. Whimpering, crying, begging, pissing.

That would be some mess for Janitor Parker to clean up.

Principal Velásquez tapped her fingernails on the desk. *Tackity-tackity-tackity* . . . pause . . . *tackity-tackity-tackity.*

Mark stormed in through the door. "What happened?"

My head throbbed. Alex's mom held him in her arms. He sobbed in the corner of the room, far away from the rest of us.

We waited for Troy's and Pinky's parents to come. When they arrived, we all sat around an oval table in the meeting room, Alex included. Mom and Dad stood behind me.

"Kyle, why don't you begin?" *Tackity-tackity-tackity . . .* pause.

"I, um—"

"He was gonna kill me!" Alex shouted. "That's what was gonna happen. He had me in a choke hold. He wouldn't let go. He's a freak. A killer. He probably killed Jason on purpose too." Alex wiped his nose.

The hair bristled on the back of my neck and my breathing became shallower. Maybe he was right.

Mrs. Keller hugged Alex and stroked his hair. "My baby, my baby," she whispered. She was one of those hair-spray casino moms. Lots of makeup, glittery jewelry, and high heels.

"Kyle," Dad said, moving forward. "Can you tell us anything at all?"

Indiana Jones was named after George Lucas's dog. Fuck or derivatives of the word are used 272 times in Reservoir Dogs. The Blair Witch Project *was filmed in eight days.*

"Kyle, I'm talking to you." Dad pulled up a chair beside me and put his hand over mine.

I jerked my hand back, then felt embarrassed for Dad. His only son couldn't stand to be touched.

Jesus, I'm a freak. They're right. They're all right.

Dad crossed his arms and sighed. "Kyle, can you tell us anything?"

I thought of the soft library light, the quiet dark hallway, and the thundering pain. "I don't know."

The other parents started to talk at once about my mental instability; my obvious psychopathic tendencies; my explosive temper. "I demand that he be expelled today, right now. I will *not* have my son go to school with such a violent boy." Pinky looked really small next to his parents. Even his thumbs. So much for genetic engineering. They were a family of mutants.

What's worse, Jase: being a freak or a mutant?

What's the diff?

Good point.

"He didn't do anything wrong," Mr. Cordoba said. "As I said before, he was protecting himself. Do I have to point out that Kyle is the only one here bleeding?"

Nobody said anything. The meatheads' parents glared and stayed quiet for a while.

"Who, then, hit you with the bottle today?" *Tackity-tackity-tackity . . .* pause.

"I don't know." That was the truth. It was too dark. "One of them, I guess, since they were there and all. But I don't know who."

"Principal Velásquez, every student has a right to defend him- or herself from harm. Kyle was, in my opinion, doing just that." Mr. Cordoba crossed his arms. He looked even bigger than Mark.

Mr. Cordoba's defense propelled Dad and Mom into action. They were exempt from guilt—from having to live with the possibility that their only son was a serial killer, stalking popular kids throughout high schools everywhere, ruthlessly murdering them. "Kyle, have they attacked you before? Do they bully you?" Mom asked.

I wasn't gonna rat. Rats sucked more than the fucking jock squad. "Um, in PE things get a little rough sometimes. Normal stuff, though. No big deal."

"Bullying?" Pinky's mom pushed her chair out and stood tall. Everybody else followed suit, leaving me alone at the table. It was like a scene from *12 Angry Men*. I could've renamed it *12 Angry Parents, Parole Officers, and School District Employees*. Pinky's mom towered over everyone except for Mr. Cordoba. "There's no proof that my son has ever laid a finger on your son." She glared at me. "And only one boy in this room has a parole officer." She flashed Mark a look.

I kept my mouth shut.

"Well, if there's bullying going on at this school, I think we need to address it, Principal Velásquez. Here and now." Mom was on fire. She didn't even reach Pinky's mom's shoulder. I hoped she'd be able to run fast in case we needed to bolt. I looked at Pinky's mom's thumbs. Huge. And she had the arm span of an ape.

"Bullying? In this school? It has never been brought to my attention." *Tackity-tackity-tackity, tacka-tacka-tackity.*

The only thing separating these guys from gangsters was their letterman jackets.

"Are these boys the perpetrators, Kyle?" Mom asked.

Perpetrators? "It's just PE class. No big deal."

"But he tried to choke me," Alex whined.

I didn't remember that part. I just remembered the red—the anger.

"All of you get in-house suspension. All four of you." *Tackity-tackity-tackity.*

"What about basketball? We haven't lost a game all season." Alex jumped from his chair. Snot bubbles formed and popped.

Principal Velásquez crossed her arms in front of her. "Well, I guess you'll enjoy watching it from the stands. You're all off the team until after your suspension."

"Oh, you'll be hearing from us, Principal Velásquez." Pinky's mom stomped toward the door. Principal Velásquez's diplomas rattled against the walls. "We're not through here."

"Oh, Ms. Deiterstein, I do believe we are finished." Principal Velásquez didn't take shit from anybody—especially parents. "And all of you will complete these anger-management and conflict-resolution packets. Due after winter break in January."

Nobody said anything.

"Tomorrow you gentlemen will begin your in-house suspension. I've got a couple of phone calls to make tonight—including one to Coach Copeland. Thanks for coming, everybody." She grabbed each parent's hand. I wondered if her nails dug into them when she squeezed.

Mark nodded triumphantly and shook Mr. Cordoba's hand. "Thanks." Then he clapped me on the back . . . again. "Never again, Kyle. This can never happen again. Got it?"

"Sure, Mark. It won't."

"You've got to let it go. Let it go when these kids go after you like that."

"Yeah, okay."

"Okay, Kyle. Good. We're good now." Mark put on his jacket.

Pinky, Troy, and Alex followed their parents out the door.

"I can't believe she thinks she can kick me off the basketball team," Alex muttered.

Mr. Cordoba cleared his throat. "I don't think it would be prudent for the four of them to be together. Kyle had better do his suspension in the library."

Tackity-tackity-tackity . . . pause . . . *tackity-tackity-tackity.* "Sounds reasonable."

Mom, Dad, and I walked to the parking lot. It was like the reels of our lives had been taken and filmed over—just blurry images were left on the film. I wondered if Jason's death would eat us away, bit by bit, until we crumbled into nothing.

Mark rumbled off on his Harley. Mom and Dad got into the car.

Mr. Cordoba walked next to me. I half waved and said, "Thank you."

He stopped and looked me in the eyes. "A book must be an ice axe to break the seas frozen inside our soul."

I sighed. "What?"

"Kafka," he said, and handed me a book.

My head hurt too much to even think about some nutty novel. I looked down. *The Catcher in the Rye.* I flipped it open and saw Jason's crooked signature—no caps. Tears burned my eyes. "Thanks," I whispered.

Mr. Cordoba put his hand on my shoulder and nodded.

30

They wanted to take me to the ER to make sure I wasn't brain damaged or something. But they calmed down once my head stopped bleeding.

We dropped Dad off at the Hub. He had to relieve some worker who'd called in sick. Everybody called in "sick" around the holidays, especially Thanksgiving.

When we got to Richmond Avenue, I looked in the Bishops' front window. Mrs. Bishop still had that candle lamp lit, waiting for Jason to come back. Mom didn't talk until we walked in the door. "Sit. Now." She pulled out a kitchen chair. "We need to talk."

Not that again.

"Look at me." Mom crossed her arms.

I rolled my eyes. "It's not a big deal." I went to the

fridge for some peanut butter and jelly.

"Kyle Michael Caroll, I want to know what's going on with you. You're distant, withdrawn, and now this? I'm worried about you."

"So, what? I can't defend myself?"

"You know that's not what I'm talking about," she said. "It's . . . it's everything." She paused. "That boy was terrified, Kyle."

My jaw muscles tightened. I clenched my fists around the jar of jelly, feeling an electric surge shoot through my body. It was like I was at the edge of a cliff and any minute, any second, I could jump and crash to the ground.

"We just—" She sighed. "We want things to be normal for you again."

"Why? Why do you want things normal for me? So life can be easier for you?" The burning started up in my stomach again.

"Kyle . . ." Mom's voice trailed off.

"Why doesn't anybody have the balls to say that things will *never* be the same again? How come that's so hard to say?" I felt the sting of tears in my eyes. I swallowed and bit my lower lip.

"You keep pushing us away. You won't let us help. You won't move on. We don't know what to think, Kyle."

Move on? Move on? I have no right to move on.

I felt the heat creep up my body and fill everything with

crimson red. The edge of the cliff was a step away. I jumped into the void. "I'm sick of all the bullshit." I clutched the jelly jar. "You have no idea how I have felt every single day since then. You have no idea," I whispered. Sweat beaded on my forehead. "And you want me to move on? Tell that to Jason. Tell that to Chase. Tell that to the Bishops!" I squeezed the jar. It shattered and fell to the floor. I looked down. Drops of blood mixed with globs of raspberry jelly.

Everything went into slow motion. Mom and I looked from the blood to my hand to outside the front window. We watched Mel drive up and run into the house. She came into the kitchen and looked from me to Mom. "Oh, wow, Kyle. Are you okay?"

I nodded.

"Can I help?" She came forward.

I shook my head. "I'm fine."

"Okay." Mel stepped out of the kitchen.

Mom grabbed a towel. "Put your hand over the sink. I need to pull out the glass."

I wanted to close my fist and grind the pieces into my palm. But Mom looked horrified, so I held my throbbing hand over the sink, watching the blood trickle out of the cuts.

"Kyle?" Mom said. "What can we do? What can we do to help you?" Mom held my hands in hers.

I looked down at where my orange sneaker tips poked out from under my pants. I didn't know if I'd make it another 144 days. I didn't know if I could even make it one more day. "Nothing."

Mom ran her fingers through her hair. "Okay. I, um, maybe we should call Dr. Matthews?"

I sighed. They hadn't realized that my visits with Dr. Matthews were a waste of time.

On the way to my room, I turned around at the top of the staircase. Mom looked so far away, like I was seeing her through a camera lens.

In my room, I flicked off the lights, threw myself onto the bed, and stared up at the ceiling. Somehow, I finally fell asleep.

The rope burns, scraping across my neck. "Nah, you do it."

"Fuck, why do I always have to do things first?"

"You're taller." I loop it around his neck.

"See, that's not so hard. Watch this." He jumps, swinging back and forth, back and forth, a happy grin on his face.

Then his body jerks.

Hiccups.

Spasms.

He smiles.

I watch the smile fade—first the lips disappear, then nose, eyes. A blank face. Nothingness.

I jerked awake and gasped for air. I grabbed a blanket and crept into the hall. Lying outside Mel's door, I waited until the first light of morning.

When light from Mom and Dad's room spilled into the hallway, I tiptoed back to my bed.

"Kyle? It's time for school." Mom called through my door.

I faked a horrible cough and lay under the covers, working up a sweat.

Mom knocked on the door. "Can I come in?"

"Yes," I said in my most gravelly voice.

Mom came in and placed her hand on my forehead. "You have a fever."

I nodded. It wasn't too hard to look sick, since I'd lost about fifteen pounds over the past eight weeks and had hardly slept in days. My face had taken on a kind of skull-and-crossbones look.

Dad came in. "He'd better stay home today."

Mom looked worried. "I can't miss another day of work. Are you covered at the Hub?"

Dad shook his head.

"I'll be fine," I whispered. "I just need sleep."

Mom bit her lower lip and scowled. She looked at her watch.

"It's just a few hours. I'll come home after the lunch rush," Dad said. "And he can call me if he needs anything. You'll call, right, Kyle?"

I closed my eyes and pretended to drift back to sleep.

"I'll tell the school." Mom's heels clacked down the stairs.

The familiar sounds of breakfast drifted to my room. Mom burned Dad's eggs again. I heard Mel laughing at something Dad said. They actually sounded happy. Free. Free from Kyle.

Before leaving for work, Mom slipped into my room and kissed my cheek, her eyes filled with concern. "Will you be okay for a few hours?"

I grunted. "Yeah. Don't worry."

She put my cell phone on the bedside table. "You call Dad if you need anything, and he'll be home before you know it." She bit her lip. "You know how much we love you, right?"

I listened as they left the house, the front lock clicking

and car doors slamming. Then I got up and grabbed my notebook. Maybe if I remembered, it would be okay.

SCENE THREE: Take Eleven—Chinese fantasy (Zhang Yimou) style
Dissonant violins play in the background. The sound of bullets ricocheting off objects overtakes the score. FADE OUT score.

WIDE-ANGLE SHOT of the scene. The shed is at the left-hand corner of the shot. It's a high-contrast color shot; the white of the shed stands out against the green grass and bamboo in the background.

CUT TO: Kyle crouching down to squeeze out the dew from his pajama pants. He pauses, catches his breath, then stands again.

CUT TO: Jason, holding the gun, twirling it, and shooting at various targets in the shed.

The camera ZOOMS OUT, and we see light streaming into the shed like crisscrossing strings, surrounding Jason. Kyle is in the background, hardly visible in the shadows.

ZOOM OUT: Jason shoots, the bullet piercing
the roof of the shed.

CLOSE-UP of Kyle. He pauses, then does a
martial-arts triple flip and pokes his finger
through the bullet hole in the ceiling,
landing safely on the ground.

                    JASON
          (Holds the gun out to Kyle.)
          Check this baby out. It's pretty
          tight, huh?

                    KYLE
          Sweet, Jase. That's sweet.

                    JASON
          What do you wanna do?

                    KYLE
          I dunno. What are we s'posed to do
          with it?

                    JASON
          (Pulls up T-shirt collar around his
          neck, like a pastor. He scowls.)

Well, Kyle, let's see what our
options are. We could A: put the gun
away and continue to freeze, B: put
the gun to good use, or C (and my
personal favorite): rob the local
convenience store, frame Mel and
Brooke, move to the Cayman Islands,
and never, ever have to work again.

                    KYLE
(Relaxes his shoulders and laughs.)
We don't work now, you moron.

CLOSE-UP shot of our hero—Jason.
Blindfolded.

                   JASON:
Do it! Just do it!

Silence. The ricocheting bullets have stopped.
We hear a sickening sound as the bullet
pierces Jason.

ZOOM OUT. The shed is in the left-hand corner
of the shot. Fall turns to winter to spring,
then summer, then fall.

ZOOM IN. Jason lying in a puddle of blood.

CUT TO Kyle, staring at Jason.

CUT TO the gun in Kyle's hand.

The dissonant sound of violins begins again, accompanied by the sound of the wind through the trees. FADE OUT.

I reread the entry. More dialogue, but still incomplete. I closed my eyes. *Remember,* I thought. *Just remember.* But nothing came. Just the shrill sound of the bullet as it left the gun's barrel, and Jason buckling over. I put my notebook away and got dressed. I walked out to the shed and held my hands against the door. The cold seeped from the metal surface through my gloves. Snowflakes tumbled from the sky. Gusts of wind whipped them into a whirling frenzy. I clasped my hands in front of me and closed my eyes.

What are you doing out here?

The whine of the wind grew. My teeth chattered.

I blew it, you know. With Chase.

The snow fell faster, like it was in some kind of hurry to get where it needed to go. A film of snow covered my body. My teeth knocked hard against each other. Jason didn't say anything,

Do you believe in signs? Like dreams that tell you what to do?

I waited.

What am I supposed to do?

Silence.

It doesn't matter anymore, anyway, does it? Nothing matters anymore.

Silence.

Asshole.

God, I'm such a freak show. I'm pissed off at a dead guy. I brushed the snow off my coat and pants. "See you soon," I whispered.

Chilled, I walked back inside, changing out of my snowy clothes into dry ones before Dad got home to check up on me. *You'll catch your death,* he would say.

That's the point. But that's the kind of stuff a kid really shouldn't say to his parents.

32

I woke up to Mom and Mel arguing in the hallway.

"But Mom, you guys promised you'd go."

"We can't leave him here alone. One of us has to stay."

"He's just sleeping anyway. And you promised," Mel cried.

My door opened a crack. "Kyle?"

I didn't answer.

"Don't wake him," I heard Dad say. "How long is the program, Mel?"

"It's just a couple of hours. And we've been practicing since September."

I had forgotten it was Mel's regional cheerleading competition. Carson High had made it to the finals.

"We need to go, Maggie," Dad urged Mom.

"But you didn't see him." Mom's voice sounded strained. "You didn't see the look in his eyes yesterday."

"We were all tired. It was a long day, and he was coming down with something. I've been here all afternoon, and he hasn't moved. He just needs sleep."

"Please," Mel begged. "Please, Mom."

Mom came in and touched her cool hand to my forehead. I lay still. She walked back into the hallway.

"Well?" Mel's voice had a whiny pitch to it.

"He was fine alone this morning," Dad said.

"How about if I stay just through your performance, Mel?"

"That's perfect."

I listened as they put on their heavy jackets and winter boots. Downstairs, Mom, Dad, and Mel shuffled out the door and got into the car. I took out my notebook and read through each scene. The words ran together. Tears smudged the writing.

I can't do this anymore.

Then don't.

You always have the answers, huh?

Depends on the questions.

Fuck you.

I threw the notebook across the room. The lamp teetered on the edge of my nightstand and shattered on the floor. I crawled to the corner and squeezed my head between my knees. The pounding had to stop. The hurt had to stop.

"Go away," I said. I rocked back and forth.

Every time I closed my eyes, the walls closed in.

"Breathe. Just breathe," I whispered.

I looked around the room, desperate, and pulled out the phone book. "Cordoba, Cordoba, Cordoba."

Fuck, what's his first name?

I dialed the first number I saw under Cordoba. Maybe we could talk about books. I just needed to talk—to hear somebody besides Jason.

Three rings. Four rings.

"Hello?" Out of breath, low humming voice.

Deep breaths, slow deep breaths. Count to ten.

"Hello?" she repeated.

"I—" I cleared my throat. Inhale, exhale, inhale, exhale, inhale, exhale . . .

"You kids have nothing better to do than this?" She hollered to somebody, "It's another one of those prank callers. We need to get caller ID."

"Please," I whispered.

Click.

I went to sit at the top of the stairs. Mrs. Schneibel had already strung up her Christmas lights. The glow of the colorful lights reflected off our living room windows.

'Tis the season. Fucking holidays.

Mom had left the radio on in the kitchen. It was a crackly old radio—you had to turn the dial and mess around with a duct-taped antenna to hear anything. And if you moved it, even the tiniest bit, you lost the station and had to start again.

I walked into the kitchen and cranked up the staticky Christmas carols the radio stations had been playing since October. I stared out at the Bishops' house. The candle was lit. A warm light glowed between the slats of the blinds. They were home. Shadows moved behind the Bishops' curtains. Maybe they were watching TV.

"'Tis the season to be thankful. 'Tis the season for forgiveness and love. It's time to reach out." The DJ was really caking on the love and forgiveness stuff. He was taking calls and listening to everybody's sappy reconciliation stories.

I bit my lip and looked at the calendar.

November 23.

Last year at this time, Jason and I were probably eating the crust off Mrs. Bishop's homemade apple pie. Last year Jason and I had a Coen brothers movie marathon. Last year, as soon as Jason got back from church, we spent the rest of Thanksgiving weekend sledding up on C-Hill.

I laid my head on the cold countertop. Tears pooled on the tiles.

The DJ ho-ho-hoed in some hokey Santa voice. "Come on, everybody! What are you waiting for? I challenge each and every one of you to—" I bumped into the radio and it went fuzzy.

I pulled on my winter hat and coat and walked down the street. I fought to steady my breathing. My stomach burned when I saw that Mrs. Bishop had hung up her old wooden turkey. It was the same one she hung up every year.

My hand trembled when I rang the bell.

I heard shouts inside and Brooke opened the door.

Freeze frame.

I opened my mouth. The words got trapped in my throat. I struggled to breathe, fighting to push the words out.

I'm sorry. I'm sorry. I'm sorry. I'm sorry.

But nothing came out. As soon as I tried to say them, I knew the words wouldn't change anything. They wouldn't bring him back. Sorry was the cheap way out.

Brooke narrowed her eyes. "Who the hell do you think you are, coming here? At Thanksgiving?"

"Who's there, honey?" Mrs. Bishop hollered from the kitchen. The house smelled like pumpkin pie and apple cider.

I tried to say something, but nothing came. Not even tears.

Mrs. Bishop came out from the kitchen with a plate of cookies. "Kyle!" she said. She dropped the plate and it shattered on the hardwood floor. Her mouth quivered and her eyes closed. She covered her face with her hands and muffled a sob.

The next thing I knew, I was standing in front of the shed again. I had no clue how I'd gotten there.

33

I stared at the shed. It had been there since before I was born. The hinges never worked on the right-hand door, and the white paint had flaked off over the years, giving it a splotchy look, like it had psoriasis or something.

I looked for the key above on the ledge, but it wasn't there.

Maybe that was one of Mark's suggestions. "Hide the fucking key, man. Don't let your kid in there."

Not a bad suggestion, really.

I stepped back and punched the doors. My knuckles cracked on the cold metal. The padlock rattled and clanged. I kicked and punched the doors again and again until my hands were bloody and numb. The metal dented and crumpled under the weight of my fists and boots.

Fucking piece of shit cheap shed.

I went around to the back, where a small window faced the neighbors' yard.

Crash!

The rock ripped through the flimsy glass, leaving jagged edges. I punched the glass and heaved myself inside.

It smelled the same. It smelled like damp wood and fertilizer. It smelled like grease and dry grass.

It smelled like death.

I pulled the cord hanging from the fluorescent light. The light sputtered on, and the whole shed glowed an eerie green.

The floor was filthy except for one really white spot.

I kneeled down and touched where his blood had pooled.

I tried to replay it all. But I still didn't know how it happened. How could something like that happen? It was just one second. Not even a second, really. Then the burn, the powder, the ashes.

Ashes, ashes, we all fall down.

What had I done?

I circled the shed and moved toward a box of rope. Frayed ends and knots, lots of rope. Lots to tie. Lots to hang.

You're the one who shoulda died.

You're a nobody.

226

You did this.

You have no right.

You're a freak.

I hate Kyle. He ruined everything.

Stay away from my family.

Everything seemed clearer. My breathing evened out. I held the yellow rope in my bloody hands. They'd all be better off.

I just wanted to stop thinking about whether I had done it on purpose. How I had ruined everybody's lives that day. I wanted to get away from that scene—that moment.

I grabbed a pencil and scrap of paper and wrote: *The End.*

My heartbeat steadied. I made a loop. The perfect size.

The rafters were too high to reach from the bench. God, I was so fucking short!

Jumping up, I tried to loop the rope around. Wood splintered and creaked, and the bench collapsed.

I crashed to the floor and felt the rope, raw in my fingers. I clenched the rope between my teeth and curled into a ball. Hot tears spilled down my cheeks and into my ears, my sobs trapped in my throat.

I couldn't even kill myself. I couldn't even do that right.

My body trembled.

What would Jason do?

What would Jason say?

Dude, Kyle, don't be a shithead. Don't do it.

But what else is there? What if I meant to kill you?

Shit happens, Kyle.

Shit happens?

Yeah. So what?

You come to me with the great philosophy of "shit happens"?

Man, you'll figure it out.

Cold seeped through my clothes. My teeth chattered; I shivered. My hands throbbed and bled.

Suppose, I thought. *Suppose I lived.*

The light in the shed wavered, dimmed, then died. Everything was bathed in night, and objects became formless shadows, lumps on drooping shelves. I don't know how long I stayed in the shed, replaying my death scene in my head. After a while, I slipped out the broken window and walked into the house, welcoming its familiar smells of toast, vacuum dust, and Mel's perfume.

My hands ached and shook when I cleaned off the blood, wrapping them in bandages. I stared at myself in the bathroom mirror, pushing my hair behind my ears. He said I'd figure it out. Maybe—just maybe—I would.

I walked up to my room and opened my shades. At night, snow made the world seem like day. The bright white filled the room with reflected moonlight.

I put my notebook back into my drawer and hid it under some CDs. I buried my head in Jason's duffel bag and breathed deep. It was losing its smell.

I didn't even hear the car pull into the drive.

Mom opened my door. "What are you doing?"

I looked up at her. Her cheeks were flushed from the cold. "Are you feeling better?" She came in and put her hand on my forehead. Her breath smelled like peppermint. I shoved the duffel under the bed and hid my hands under the covers.

Dad came in with a steaming cup of peppermint chocolate. Mel bounded up the stairs. "We won, Kyle! Look!" She barreled into the room.

I smiled. "That's great, Mel. It really is."

She plopped next to me. "You look like shit."

"Thanks."

"Are you feeling okay?" Dad asked.

I think so. Maybe. I nodded.

"Why don't we let Kyle rest?" Dad motioned Mel and Mom to leave the room. He put his hand on my shoulder. "Do you need anything?"

I shook my head, still hiding my hands.

"Sleep. Maybe you should get more sleep." Dad looked into my eyes.

I looked away. "Yeah."

He paused. "Can I sit here for a while?"

I concentrated on the streaks of peeling paint on my bedroom wall. "Sure."

He sat on the edge of the bed. I felt him watching me, like he was looking for a sign that I was okay.

I turned and smiled. "I'll drink this when it cools down. Thanks."

"You're welcome." He got up. "I'm right down the hall if you need anything."

"Sure."

He left me alone. I flicked off the lights and stared at the glow-in-the-dark planets that Jason and I had pasted on my bedroom ceiling. We each got a set for Christmas when we were in fifth grade. When we were sticking mine up, Jason slipped on the ladder and pasted Pluto overlapping Saturn. My solar system was totally lame. We tried to scrape it off, but it stuck. So Saturn looked like it had an extra moon and Pluto didn't exist.

I was pissed at the time, but now I actually liked my Pluto all wrong. It was better. It made me remember something other than the shed. I let the memory wash over me and I held on to it as long as I could, hoping it wouldn't disappear into blackness. I was just about to remember what Jase sounded like when he laughed when I fell into a dreamless sleep.

35

I woke up to the sound of pebbles hitting my window. Chase stood below with his hands cupped over his mouth, hooting like an owl.

"What are you doing here?"

He held up an orange card, then hid it under a rock in the yard. He waved and ran away. I slipped out the front door and opened up the card.

Dear Bodyguard,

Your presence behind the Dumpsters has been missed. Luckily, we haven't had any GCP days, and we're learning tactics to get through the school day unscathed.

We look forward to your rapid recovery.

Our best, Chase and Mike

I smiled. Getting through the day "unscathed" took a lot of energy. They had included a drawing of me with my orange shoes, a hole in the left one.

My stomach growled, and I went inside to get breakfast. Mom dropped the raw turkey on the kitchen floor when she saw my hands.

We spent the rest of Thanksgiving morning in the emergency room getting X-rays and a cast for my broken left hand.

"Sorry about Thanksgiving, Mom."

"It doesn't matter. We'll order Chinese."

When we left the ER, Dad and Mom walked ahead of me, whispering to each other. They looked like an old 1920s silent movie, their black jackets a stark contrast to the fresh-fallen snow. Dad wrapped his arm around Mom's hunched shoulders. The snow muted the sound of our footsteps.

He opened the car's back door for me and helped me tuck my head in so I wouldn't whack it on the doorframe. I clicked my seat belt and turned to look out the back window. Everything looked the same as that day. The outside of the emergency room had the same concrete walls, painted white and stained with exhaust fumes and who knows what else.

We walked into the house. Melanie was watching the Macy's parade. She flicked off the TV. "What happened?"

I covered the cast with my jacket. "I'm fine."

Dad shook his head. "I just don't know what to say."

"I think we might need to see Dr. Matthews. Maybe today? Should I call her?" Mom tipped my chin up so she was looking into my eyes.

"Dr. Matthews. Sure, Mom. That sounds good." Not like she helped any.

Dad pulled the note out of his pocket. "What does this mean, Kyle? 'The End.' I found it in the shed beside the broken bench."

"I just had a bad night, Dad. No big deal." I turned my face away from Mom and took the note. I crumpled it up and tossed it in the garbage. "It didn't mean anything."

Yesterday I'd wanted to die.

Today I didn't.

How can you explain that to your dad?

"I'm just gonna hang out in my room until we go."

"Okay, honey. Sure." Mom stepped forward like she was going to hug me, but I moved back. I felt like I was directing a part in a movie where the camera goes from close-up to wide angle, pulling away from the actors. I saw Mom, Dad, and Mel at the end of a long tunnel, far, far away. I went up to my room.

Mel knocked on my door. "Can I come in?"

"Yeah."

She hesitated, then came and sat on the bed. "What do you think Dr. Matthews and Mark will say?"

I shrugged.

She puffed out her cheeks. "Kyle, how do you feel about what happened? Would you like to talk about it?" She actually did a pretty good impersonation of Dr. Matthews.

I tried to smile.

Mel grabbed my hand—not the broken one. "Do you want talk about it? For real?"

"Not really."

"Those guys roughed you up pretty bad."

"Nah. I'm okay."

"What happened last night?"

I pulled my hand away. She scooted closer to me.

"Just a bad night, I guess."

Mel looked into my eyes. "Don't do that, Kyle. Ever. Okay?" She laid her head on my shoulder. "Promise me," she whispered, her voice cracking.

I squeezed her hand. "I promise." Somehow I knew this was a promise I'd keep.

She looked up and moved my bangs out of my eyes. "Growing your hair long?"

"Maybe."

She wiped her nose. "Looks cool."

"Thanks."

"Talk to her, Kyle."

"Who?"

"Dr. Matthews. Or Mr. Cordoba. Anyone, really. Just talk, okay?"

Dr. Matthews leaned back and laced her fingers around a steaming cup of tea. I sat across from her in a retro chair shaped like an egg. The orange plastic was pretty hard on my ass, and she kept asking me questions I didn't want to answer. "How would Jason like to see you today?"

"Whaddya mean?"

She pointed to the notebook I always carried around: the one with Scene Three. "What would Jason like to see you doing? Maybe you can write about it."

"Writing doesn't help."

"What do you write about?"

"That day. I need to figure out if I—" I stopped.

"If you what?"

"Nothing."

"Maybe you could write about other things."

I chewed on my lip. The edges of the notebook curled in. I had filled every page but one with that scene.

"Just think about it, Kyle. What would Jason wish for you?"

"Does it really matter?"

"I think it does."

I glared. "Why? Why would that matter?"

"Because you were friends. I think you forget that sometimes."

I shook my head. "I never forget that Jason was my best friend."

"No. But you do forget that you were *his*."

36

It was weird to be alive. Everything was under my control that night in the shed. I was even relieved. It made sense to me. I wanted to die.

Then I didn't.

I had Chase. I had books and Mr. Cordoba. And I didn't want to leave them. But I was stuck. I didn't want to be Freeze Frame anymore. I didn't want to live my life in Scene Three. But I didn't know how to move forward, either. Jase had said, *Shit happens*. Maybe that was his way of telling me I hadn't killed him on purpose. Jase would be the first to hold that against me if I had. He'd have probably found a way to haunt me, like in *The Amityville Horror*, or possess me like in *The Exorcist*, if that were true. And so far I hadn't projectile-vomited green baby food.

Over the weekend, most of the snow melted, leaving patchy spots of dirt and ice all over the graveyard. If I squinted, it almost looked like a winter quilt. I brushed a pile of slush from Jase's marker.

"Chase left me this great drawing." I sat on the least snowy spot near Jason's grave. "He might be an artist like you someday." I pulled out the drawing. "See? He even drew the orange shoes."

I tucked the drawing into my pocket. "I guess I just wanted to tell you I'm still here. That's pretty dumb, I know. If I weren't, you'd probably be the first to know." I tapped my fingers on his grave. "And, um, thanks, you know, for the message. I think I get it."

When I got up to go, I left a piece of apple pie on his grave, without the top crust. "I miss you, Jase," I said.

I returned to the library early Monday morning to start my in-house suspension.

"Mr. Cordoba?" I peeked in the door.

Cordoba sat reading the *The Nevada Appeal*, sipping his morning cup of coffee. "Nice to have you back, Mr. Caroll."

Relief flooded my body.

"Well, get in and close the door." He handed me a pile of worksheets and instructions from my teachers. "It looks like you'll be busy."

"Yes, sir." I picked up my assignments and took them to the table.

"What happened to your hands?"

"Just an accident."

Mr. Cordoba looked at my cast and bandaged hand, then back into my eyes. "Are you okay?"

"Yeah, I think I am." I sat down and stared out the window. The buses pulled into the parking lot, spewing students out into the winter grayness. My notebook lay in front of me. One page left to fill—one director left to use. And then I'd need a title. I'd written fourteen different versions, from Tarantino to Iñárritu. None of them, though, had turned out quite right. I flipped through the pages, scene after scene, until I got to the last page. Blank.

"You returned the book of poems," Cordoba said.

I nodded.

"What did you think?"

I shrugged. "I've never really read poetry before." I looked around the library. This was definitely not something any self-respecting fifteen-year-old guy would want people to know about him.

"Most people don't."

"Don't what?"

"Read poetry."

I nodded. "I can see why."

"Why is that, Mr. Caroll?"

"Well, um. It's kinda weird. Words missing. A little confusing. No connectors. Mrs. Beacham is big into connectors."

"Connectors?"

"*And. But. However. Whereas.* You know."

"Were there any poems you liked?"

I thought for a while. "I liked the one called 'Suppose.' I really liked the title."

"Why?"

I leaned close to the radiator, warming up. "Because *suppose* means, I dunno, I guess it means there're other possibilities." I remembered the shed. *Suppose I lived.*

Mr. Cordoba nodded.

I got up and tossed my notebook into the garbage. *Suppose. Suppose I forgot about it. All of it. Suppose it didn't matter if I remembered.*

That afternoon, I crouched behind the Dumpsters and peeked around the corner, watching the kids trudge to the buses.

"Hey Kyle. *Pssst!*" Chase stood in front of the Dumpster.

"Chase! What're you doing here?"

"What happened to your hands? How come you're wearing a cast?"

"Nothing."

"Did they do that to you?"

"Who?"

"The ones who hurt you before?"

"No, Chase. I don't think I have to worry about them anymore."

"Oh." He let out a slow whistle. "Then what happened to your hands?"

Unless I told him, he'd never quit asking, and we'd be out there all afternoon. Chase could go on for hours, and I had to get back to the library. "I punched the shed the other night. No big deal."

"Oh. That's not a smart thing to do."

"Yeah, I know."

"Is it scratchy?"

"What?"

"Your arm."

I knocked on the cast. "No. Not really."

"That's good, then." Chase looked relieved.

"Anyway, thank you. For the card and the drawing." The buses started to pull out of the lot. "You're going to miss the bus, Chase."

Chase shook his head. "I'm going to Mike's today. He's over there keeping watch." I peered around the corner. Mike was on his hands and knees staring at something in the grass with a magnifying glass. Great lookout.

Chase opened his backpack and pulled out some duct tape. "We noticed you could use this."

"For what?"

Chase pointed to my shoes. "The sole is coming off. And neither of us are cobblers. But we saw on the FX Channel that duct tape is great for everything."

"You're allowed to watch FX?"

"Mike's family has DISH, and his big brother let us watch it the other day. We watched *The Man Show*. It was quite informative."

"Yeah, I bet."

Chase pulled out some scissors, and the two of us taped the sole of my left shoe back together. He stood back and admired the patch job. "That stuff is really great." He eyed the tape I held in my hands.

"Why don't you keep it? If I need more, I'll borrow it."

He grinned. "Good idea. I think I'm more organized than you, anyway." He looked down at my shoes. "I've been thinking you need a bodyguard name," he said. "Like . . . Orange Dragon."

"Orange Dragon, huh?" It sounded like a superhero Jase would've drawn. "I like it."

"Me, too," said Chase. "Very scary."

A car pulled into the parking lot. Mike whistled three times, then hooted like an owl. Chase hooted back. "That's our signal."

"Yeah. I remember."

"Listen closely. Mills Park. Saturday. Noon. Fly kites."

"On the sly?"

He nodded. "It's BYOK."

"BYOK?"

"Bring your own kite."

"Oh. Yeah."

Mike hooted again and Chase left.

One morning, Mr. Cordoba was busy in his office. I wandered around the library, browsing the shelves, looking for other books Jason had checked out. I'd already read *The Catcher in the Rye* twice but didn't want to let it go just yet.

The back windows of the library faced the track. The cheerleaders were practicing some pyramid thing. Mel's cheeks were flushed in the chilly December wind, her hair pulled back in a ponytail. I didn't see Brooke anywhere.

Kohana walked by with his camera hanging around his neck, his black hair sticking out of the bottom of a stocking cap, green jacket flapping in the wind. He had his hands shoved into the pockets of his baggy jeans. He'd stop and stare at something for a while, fidget with his camera, then snap a picture. After a while, he made his way to the flagpole and sat at its base.

The radiator clicked on, its heat fogging the windows. I leaned against the pane, icy glass cool against my forehead. I returned to the tables and started on the day's assignments.

"It looks like you need a new notebook, Mr. Caroll." Cordoba held my notebook in his hands. "I found this in the garbage."

It was like the damned scene was chasing me. "Did you read it?" I grabbed it from him.

"No."

I sighed, relieved.

"I noticed that you write a lot."

"This? It's just, um, director's notes." How lame did that sound?

"Director's notes?"

"Yeah. It's a dumb thing I started to do. Writing out a scene from my life, but trying to figure out how some of my favorite directors would direct the same scene."

"So that entire notebook is just one scene from your life?"

I flipped through the pages. "Yeah."

"That's impressive."

"Not really."

"How many directors did you use?"

"Fourteen."

"Is it finished?"

"No. I still have room for one more director."

"And?"

"Couldn't think of one." I moved to throw the notebook back in the garbage and hesitated. "Besides, no director can edit the past. These directors can't even remember it."

Mr. Cordoba took a sip of coffee. "Why don't you just set it aside?"

I walked to the garbage can. "That's what I tried to do until you took it out of the garbage."

"I see. You're throwing away the past."

"I'm trying."

Mr. Cordoba went back to his desk and opened up a book to read.

"What?"

He looked up from the book. "What, what, Mr. Caroll?"

"Aren't you going to come at me with one of your philosophies? About making peace with the past?"

"What would you like me to say?"

"I don't know."

Mr. Cordoba closed his book. "Will the past make sense if you throw it away?"

I shook my head. "I don't know. Maybe." I chucked the notebook in the garbage.

Mr. Cordoba's fingers slid over the bumpy scar. He went back to his office and returned with a notebook.

He handed it to me.

"I can't write that scene anymore, Mr. Cordoba."

"Then don't. New notebook. New scenes." He returned to his book.

What scenes? I was already a master of forgetting, not even counting the shed. It was like in *Eternal Sunshine of the Spotless Mind*, when a guy gets his memories erased. One by one, and no matter how hard he tries to hold on to them, his memories disappear.

That had started to happen to me. I was forgetting what Jason looked like. His face got blurry in my mind, like in those old family photos. You knew who the people are, but they aren't in focus. Same with his voice. I tried to remember how he sounded when he laughed. I didn't think I'd ever get his voice back.

It made me so sad to see that Jase was fading away. Fade out. Jason.

Mr. Cordoba had put his book on the desk. He watched me and motioned to the notebook in the garbage. "Can I hold it for you? If by the end of the year you don't want it, you can throw it away."

"Whatever." Cordoba could be really weird some-times, fishing old notebooks out of the garbage. I flipped through the blank pages of the new notebook. "So which director should I use for the new scenes?" I asked aloud, kind of to myself.

"Why not you? You could direct your own memories." Cordoba looked at the clock. "It's time to get to work, Mr. Caroll."

I worked through my day's assignments. The new notebook lay on the desk, hundreds of blank pages before me. I had a lot of scenes to write.

My pajama pants stuck to my ankles. I crouched down to squeeze out the dew. I did that only to catch my breath. I'd never seen a gun before.

"New notebook," I whispered, crossing out what I wrote. "New scenes." Now I just had to remember.

38

In-house suspension were some of the best weeks I'd had. I finished my work early, then read. Sometimes I'd practice remembering. Something—anything—about Jase that didn't have to do with the shed. But all the memories got mixed up, out of order—just like that guy in *Memento*. He had to write notes all over his body to remember, and he still got it wrong in the end.

Leaving the library one afternoon, I ran into Kohana sitting at the base of the flagpole. "Miss the bus?"

He nodded, cleaning the lens of his camera.

"How long do you have to wait?"

He pulled out his watch. "Just a few more minutes. Then my grandma will be here."

We sat for a minute in silence. I messed with my bike gears.

"You still stuck at the library with Scarface? I heard what happened with Alex and those guys."

I leaned my head against the flagpole. "I'm not suspended anymore, but I go to the library a lot."

"Does Scarface ever talk to you?" Kohana asked.

"Cordoba? Sometimes. I don't think he likes to talk, though."

Kohana wasn't big on talking, either. He looked at my cast. "What happened to your hand?"

"I, um, punched our shed."

"Shitty day?" He put his camera away.

"Yeah. I guess you could say that."

"So how do you ride your bike?"

I smirked and showed him how I managed to balance and steer with my cast while using my bandaged hand for brakes.

"Impressive." He nodded. "Very Cirque du Soleil."

"So"—I motioned to his camera—"what do you take pictures of?"

He arched his eyebrows. "Everything. Some might say nothing."

"What do you mean?"

"I take pictures of things—things most people don't pay attention to. Objects tell stories, you know." He shrugged. "You probably don't get it."

"Yeah, I do." I touched the Dimex in my pocket.

"Maybe your shed has stories," he said.

The metal from the flag clinked against the pole. "Too many."

He zipped up his backpack. "You get it."

"So, um, who started calling you Clock?" I asked, just to get away from the shed's stories.

He smirked. "I did."

I must've looked pretty shocked, because he laughed aloud. "Irony, man. Irony. You're the only one at school who calls me by my name."

"Really?"

"You're the only one who knows it."

"Why?"

"No one else ever asked." Kohana shivered and leaned against the flagpole. I sat next to him and picked at the tape on my shoe.

His grandma pulled up in an old two-tone Dodge Dart. She had long black hair clipped behind her ears, and black eyes. She wore tight jeans and a tighter sweater. Kohana's grandma was hot.

"Dude, that's your grandma?"

Kohana nodded. "It kinda sucks to have a grandma better-looking than me. Like, she's way out of my league."

I cracked up. "And I thought a cheerleader for a sister was bad."

"Yeah, Melanie's pretty sweet-lookin'."

I cringed.

"Well, you're the one checking out my gram."

Then we both laughed.

Kohana's grandma leaned her head out of the car. "Kohana, are you ready?" she asked.

He turned to me. "Gotta go. Thanks for the company."

I was biking off when Kohana shouted, "Wait! Just a sec." I pedaled over to him. He pulled out his camera, lay on the asphalt, and snapped a picture.

"What'd you take the picture of?" I asked, looking on the ground.

"Another story," he said, getting in the car. "Maybe someday you'll tell it to me."

I looked under the bike and all around.

"See you tomorrow, Kyle." He waved.

"See you."

39

I held Jason's Dimex in my hand, just one of the many things he had left behind—one of the many stories. I liked how Kohana thought about objects.

The planet set on the ceiling told a story—like the *Attack of the Killer Tomatoes!* and Frank Miller posters, my orange shoes, a ton of things I hadn't thought about. I scanned my bedroom and saw the pieces of paper sticking out from the pages of the R volume in the encyclopedia set my parents were so excited to get me for my thirteenth birthday—now with one volume missing. All I wanted was the original poster from Mel Brooks's *Silent Movie* that Jase and I saw on eBay. That or a dog. Hell, even a T-shirt would've been okay. But Mom and Dad had gone on a

better-my-mind-and-purge-it-of-popular-culture kick.
Probably because I had gotten four Cs the first semester.
I pulled the pieces of paper from the encyclopedia and
smiled.

Only Jase could turn a disastrous thirteenth birthday
into something cool.

I brought out the notebook and wrote.

UNTITLED: SCENE ONE—PTBP Syndrome (Post-
Traumatic Birthday Present Syndrome)
A blazing cake glows through the window. A
family gathers around the table singing "Happy
Birthday."

CLOSE-UP: Kyle has his eyes closed.

CUT TO: scene in Kyle's head: He's hanging up
Silent Movie next to his *Blazing Saddles* poster
to complete the Mel Brooks movie poster collection.

WIDE ANGLE: Camera pans the faces of everybody
at the table, brimming with expectation. The
gifts are passed down the table and Kyle rips
open a comics-wrapped DVD of *Plan 9 from Outer
Space*.

KYLE

Thanks, Jase!

FADE OUT: "Happy Birthday" music, then, like Ravel's "Bolero," background starts softly with John Williams's theme to *Jaws*. The music gets louder and louder.

CUT TO: Scene where Kyle's parents unveil the encyclopedia set.

KYLE

[Milk-curdling scream.]

A later scene, not filmed at this time, shows Kyle's mom throwing all dairy products out of the refrigerator.

MOM

So you really like it. That much?

DAD

We just *knew* you would.

He lovingly takes Mom in his arms and they stare at the new encyclopedias in the bookshelf.

Background music fades out. Silence. No music.

CUT TO: Kyle's bedroom. Kyle and Jason sit on the bed, staring at the books. Camera pans the encyclopedias in the new bookshelf and returns to Jason and Kyle.

> JASON
>
> That sucks.

Kyle nods his head. Eyes glaze over, looking at the shiny bindings. Jason waves his hand in front of Kyle, but Kyle doesn't flinch.

> JASON
>
> Dude, it's your thirteenth. And you're going through PTBP Syndrome—Post-Traumatic Birthday Present Syndrome. Unreal.

Kyle's eyes dilate, then do that swirly, bulls-eye cartoon thing. In the background we hear the *boing!* cartoon sound.

> JASON
>
> It's supposed to be a cool birthday.

We gotta do something about this.

Dazed, Kyle walks over and pulls out the R volume of the set. He flips the book open, and there's a deafening crack from the new binding being opened. Jason claps his hands over his ears. Kyle winces. Then he begins to read aloud.

KYLE

>R. "Rickets. Rickets is a softening of children's bones potentially leading to fractures and deformity. Rickets is among the most frequent childhood diseases in many developing countries. The main cause is a vitamin D deficiency, but an inadequate supply of calcium in the diet may also lead to rickets." (He looks at Jason.) I don't figure we have rickets.

JASON

>C'mon. I've got an idea.

Jason pulls out two sheets of paper from a notebook. He hands one to Kyle with a pen and takes one.

257

KYLE

Great. Homework already.

JASON

Rip the paper in half. We're gonna
write about where we'll be in ten
years. The same thing on each half.
Then we'll each keep one of each.
But we can't read them until your
twenty-third birthday. Deal?

Kyle raises his eyebrows.

JASON

For real. None of that Mr. December
shit, either. Where are we gonna be
in ten years? Ten years from today.

ZOOM OUT: Kyle and Jason are writing on their
slips of paper. They fold them up and
exchange papers.

JASON

Now put your two pieces in here. R.
Rickets.

KYLE

Where'll you put yours?

JASON

Give me a letter.

KYLE

(Sweeps his hand over the encyclopedias
like Vanna White) Well, Mr. Bishop,
pick a letter. There are twenty-six.

JASON

(Jumps up and down and squeals like
a game-show contestant) GIMME AN X!

KYLE

OOOH! Risky. (He hands him the
volume that includes X words.) I
still don't get how these (he shakes
his papers in the air) makes *this*
(he motions to the encyclopedias)
less uncool.

JASON

Ahhh, young Luke. (Perfect Yoda
impersonation.) This is not merely
an encyclopedia set. It's the crypt

that holds the secrets of our
future.

KYLE

Yoda, Yoda, how could I ever have
doubted your wisdom? (He bows down
and hands over the WXYZ volume.) But
first please read us something from
those ever-so-informative pages.

JASON

(Clears his throat) X. "Xerophagy.
Xerophagy means 'dry eating.' In
some cases, this means bread and
water, especially if being used as a
form of discipline or hunger
strike." (Jason looks up.) I guess
like that Gandhi guy.

KYLE

Forget the commentaries, O wise one,
and just read it.

JASON

Look who's loving his new
encyclopedia set. (He laughs, then

returns to the encyclopedia to read.) "Involuntary xerophagy" (Jason looks up), aka starvation, "is imposed as punishment to heretics, infidels, and evil-doers, adding to the misery of their imprisonment."

KYLE

I thought for sure you'd go for xylophone.

JASON

Dude, xylophone would've been so obvious.

KYLE

(Laughs and places "R" back in the bookshelf) X. Xerophagy. Good word. Want more cake?

JASON

Now we're talking.

I held the pieces of paper in my hand. I couldn't bring myself to read Jason's page and slipped our futures back into R. Someday. Not today. I hoped Mrs. Bishop hadn't thrown out that XYZ encyclopedia. Maybe I'd ask Chase.

I read over the scene and smiled. It felt good to remember—to have a piece of Jason back. Maybe my mind could get him back, more than just Scene Three.

40

Everybody was psyched for Christmas break and the Winter Ball. The school looked like it had been transformed into some kind of *Hallmark Hall of Fame* movie set. But those movies always had happy endings. It had never occurred to me before that the holidays could suck for some people.

Later that week Mark came over and said, "Your grades are better. You're up to date on your homework. Your teachers say you've never been a better student. What's up?"

I couldn't win with this guy. "Nothing. Just studying."

"Spending lots of time in the library, they say." Mark flexed his biceps. I wondered if he did it subconsciously. "What about sports? What about extracurricular activities?" Mark rubbed his head.

"I dunno, Mark. I don't think I'll be elected class president anytime soon."

"You know what I mean."

"I like the library."

Mark leaned against the doorframe. "Dr. Matthews says you still don't talk about any of it."

"Isn't there a law against doctors talking about their patients?"

"Not when they belong to the state of Nevada. So what's up? Why don't you talk?"

I'd seen a show called *Taxicab Confessions*. The cabdriver just drove around like normal, but people told him everything. It's not like he even asked them anything. They started blabbing and blabbing about all their problems and stuff. It was funny, but weird.

"Maybe I should take a ride in a taxi." I shrugged.

Mark rubbed the back of his neck. "It's Christmastime. It's a tough time for everyone, I know."

Shit happens. That's what Jase said. But just because it happens doesn't mean it's okay.

I looked down the street at the Bishops' house. "Maybe I'll make some popcorn strings to wrap around the tree."

People on Richmond Avenue strung up their holiday lights as if nothing had happened—all except for the Bishops. Mrs. Bishop hadn't even put out her nativity scene.

I held the poinsettia in my hands. I had bought it the week before but couldn't bring myself to face them, especially after what happened when I went over at Thanksgiving. The leaves had gotten pretty wilty, even though I'd watered it every day.

Sorry about Jason.

No.

I thought you might want a poinsettia. And, well, sorry.

No.

Every time I tried to cross the street to go to their house, I'd feel a dizzying wave of nausea and would have to lie down on the ground until my world stopped spinning. It took me an hour, but I finally worked up the courage to go. I stepped off the porch and faced their house, clutching the poinsettia.

But the movie got all messed up again. I had almost made it to their house when I saw Mr. Bishop walking out, carrying a suitcase in each hand. His shouts echoed down the street. "There's no way to get him back! He's dead!" The last word hung in the air like one of those cartoon bubbles. *Dead!*

I pictured Mrs. Bishop holding on to fifteen years of birthdays, Christmases, family holidays—fifteen years of memories and photos. They'd all fade away, though. And maybe a day would come when we wouldn't think about him. Not once.

Then he'd really be gone—dead.

The camera panned down the street. Chase sat on the corner, rocking back and forth, his hands covering his ears. Brooke hugged him, begging him to go back inside.

It was a slow-motion shot of all of them turning to look at me—Jason's killer—holding a half-dead plant. Pause. Nobody moved. Nobody said anything. Mr. Bishop looked like he was suspended in time.

Play. Brooke ran at me. She screamed, "A poinsettia! You come to us with a fucking poinsettia!" She ripped the poinsettia from my hands and threw it at me. The pot shattered on the street, the plant's roots curling in the dirt.

Mr. Bishop pulled out of the driveway. Mrs. Bishop looked at me, her eyes filled with tears. I couldn't let Jason be gone forever. I had to find a way to bring him back to them—to Chase. And Mrs. Bishop.

I'd be the one to remember.

I tried to find Chase at school, but Mike told me he was home sick. "Do you maybe wanna come around anyway?" Mike scuffed his boots in the snow. His ears turned red. "Just, you know. So you don't lose practice at being a bodyguard."

I smiled. "I'll be here, Mike."

"Really?"

"Sure."

"Wait a sec." He pulled a sweaty dollar bill out of his pocket. "This is all I've got." He looked worried. "Will that cover it?"

"Keep it, okay? I'll be here."

Mike wrapped his arms around my waist and squeezed. "Thank you, Orange Dragon."

"Don't miss your bus."

"I won't!" He skipped to his bus and waved at me from the window. Real discreet.

Every time I saw Kohana taking pictures, I thought of the stories that went with each one. He showed me a picture he had taken of my backpack, my notebook poking out the top. "I want this story," he said, pointing to the notebook.

I laughed it off. Nobody could have those stories.

Jase had a bunch of stories because he had a shitload of stuff: his art supplies and favorite jeans. And his secrets—the leftovers that Mrs. Bishop would've found.

The secret stash.

You forgot about it, huh?

Yeah. You still got everything?

Yeah. Mom'll probably flip out when she finds the stuff.

Maybe she'll get them to change your headstone. Turn WALKS WITH GOD into ROAD TO PERDITION.

Ha ha. Quite the comedian.

I do what I can. And the book?

Yep. The book.

You're so screwed when Brooke finds out it was you.

A little late now, huh?

I guess.

268

UNTITLED: SCENE TWO—The List
FADE IN: Kyle and Jason are whistling tuneless songs while rollerblading up and down Elm Street. They skate, pause in front of Jason's driveway, and continue to skate.

CLOSE-UP: Jason's front door. Brooke and Mel leave the house. Off camera we hear laughter and car doors slamming. Camera remains focused on the front door.

CUT TO: Jason motioning to his eyes, military style, and back at the house.

CUT TO: Kyle nodding.

FADE IN: Larry Mullen Jr. and Adam Clayton's score from *Mission: Impossible*. Jason and Kyle slip ski masks over their faces, and their Rollerblades turn into climbing shoes. Jason and Kyle elbow-crawl up to the house. Jason opens the door and the hinge creaks. The *Mission: Impossible* music ends with the sound of a needle scratching across a record.

                    MRS. BISHOP

     (Off camera.) Boys? Is that you,
     Jason? Do you need a snack?

                       KYLE
     Real incognito, Jase. Smooth.

                      JASON
     Should we call off the mission?

                       KYLE
     No way. Not now.

                      JASON
     You won't really do it.

                       KYLE
     Watch me.

FADE IN: *Mission: Impossible* sound track. Kyle
sneaks past the den, where Mrs. Bishop is
watching TV, and slips up the Bishop staircase. He stands in front of a door.

ZOOM IN: to sign on the door. "KEEP OUT. That
means you!" Kyle slips his library card into

                       270

the doorjamb and clicks it open. Soundless.
(Homage to classic *Mission: Impossible* scene
where Ethan Hunt/Tom Cruise dangles from a
cord while retrieving information from the
computer.) Kyle dangles from a bungee above a
dresser. Sweat drips from his brow as he
plunges his hand into the top drawer.

                    JASON
          (Speaking through the door) What's
          taking you so long?

                    KYLE
          You didn't tell me I had to look
          through her underwear drawer to
          get it.

                    JASON
          Dude, you'd better not be checking
          out my sister's underwear.

                    KYLE
          (Has a pair on his head and rips
          them off). No way, man.

CAMERA PANS THE ROOM—from Kyle's

point of view—and stops on a
glittery pink book tucked behind
a tattered purple teddy bear.

                    KYLE
Got it.

CUT TO: Jason and Kyle in Jason's room. The
door is bolted with seven locks, and a chair
rests under the doorknob.

ZOOM IN: The book and the first page, written
in curvy letters. "HOT LIPS LIST." Shot from
view of Jason holding the book.

ZOOM OUT: Kyle is looking over Jason's shoulder
at the book.

                    KYLE
     That's it? That's what all this was
     for? A hot lips list?

                    JASON
     Ahh, my friend. This is much more
     than a book. This is blackmail.

                    KYLE
        (Nodding, then grinning) Hey, Jase.
        (He clears his throat and rubs his
        palms together.) Am I on the list?

                    JASON
        (Rolling his eyes) You're not serious,
        are you?

ZOOM OUT: Jason and Kyle laughing.

I laughed. Brooke and Mel tried to torture us into telling them about where we hid that dumb book. But we never gave it up. Honestly, it wasn't even that interesting. They had rated the "kissable" guys from their class with lipstick kisses: one being "good enough for practice"; five being "steamy tongue-twisting." And the highlighted entries were the ones they'd actually hooked up with—with the corrected lipstick kisses to the side. Big deal.

I wondered if Mrs. Bishop had found the book and sent Brooke to do extra church time. Maybe she found all of Jase's stuff. What did she do with it? What happened to Jason's locker? What does the school do with a dead kid's locker?

It was the last day before Christmas break. The day before any school vacation is a waste. In most classes, we just hung out and ate candy. Mrs. Beacham decided to have a Shakespearian insult competition. I won a box of caramel chocolates with "Swim with leeches, thou gorbellied, codpiece-sniffing maggot pie!"

After the bell rang, I walked down the empty hallways. Carson High had become a ghost school. Everybody—students, teachers, custodians, secretaries—had run for home as fast as possible. Mr. Cordoba sat alone, working at his desk, like it was another regular day at the library. I opened the door a crack.

"Mr. Caroll, it's nice to see you here. What with all the holiday festivities."

"Yeah. I wanted to return *The Catcher in the Rye* before the break." I'd re-checked it out twice, just to hold on to it.

He scanned the book. "What did you think?"

"I liked it. A lot." I wondered if Jase had liked it as much as I did.

"You sound surprised."

"Well, you wouldn't think a story about some kid's weekend in New York would be so good, but it was."

"Why?"

I fidgeted with my backpack. "I really liked Holden, you know?"

"What did you like about him?"

"Well, he's funny. And real."

"Real?"

274

"Yeah. Honest. He definitely isn't the type to have to hang out with the popular kids just to be cool."

Mr. Cordoba tapped his fingers on the desk. "Do you know anybody like that?"

I thought about Kohana. "Yeah. I do. But he doesn't have a lot of friends. Funny, huh?"

Mr. Cordoba shut down his computer and looked at me. "Does Holden have a lot of friends?"

I shook my head. "No. It seems like he could use one."

Mr. Cordoba waited and leaned on the desk. He hadn't scratched his temple yet, so that meant I wasn't done talking about the book. He always scratched his temple when he didn't want to talk anymore. He probably wasn't a very good poker player.

"Why?"

"I dunno. He seems kind of lonely."

"That must be hard."

"It is . . . I guess." I blushed.

Mr. Cordoba scratched his temple. "I agree."

"You think Holden would be a good friend?"

"I think *you* would be a good friend to Holden."

I stood there stunned until Mr. Cordoba said, "So— what book are you taking home for the holidays?"

"Um, I dunno. Could you maybe pick out a book you like—really like, though? One you read not because you *had* to read it? Maybe I'll like it, too." I scuffed my shoe against the carpet. I'd already had to change the duct tape twice. I'd used Dad's because I didn't want to bug Chase about it.

He pulled a book from the shelves and handed it to me. "This is one of my favorites. Let's see if we have the same taste."

I flipped to the front. No Jason.

He took it back and registered it in the system while I fished for my library card at the bottom of my pack.

"Mr. Cordoba?"

"Yes?"

"Did you know Jason? Jason Bishop?"

He nodded.

I turned away from Mr. Cordoba's steady gaze. "Did you know him well? I mean, did you talk about books a lot?"

"No. I didn't know him well."

"That's too bad." I sighed. "Did he check out a lot of books?"

"Some."

I looked around the library. "What other books did he like to read? Do you remember?"

"He spent a lot of time looking at the art books," Mr. Cordoba said, pointing to the reference section. "And he used to check out graphic novels every now and again."

I stared at the flecks of brown in the worn library carpet.

I didn't want Mr. Cordoba to think I was stalking a dead guy. "Okay. Just wondering, you know."

"I understand."

"You do?"

"What people read says a lot about them."

"Yeah. I guess it does." I looked at the book in my hands. "So what does this book say about me: kid who doesn't know what to read?" I laughed.

"Or what does it say about me?"

"Oh. Oh yeah." I looked at the title: *Chronicle of a Death Foretold.*

"Merry Christmas, Mr. Caroll."

"You, too. And thanks." When I walked down the hall, I felt like I carried the secret to who Mr. Cordoba was in my backpack. But I wasn't sure if I wanted to know what that secret was.

42

Since the day with the poinsettia, I hadn't seen Mr. Bishop's car. Snow piled on the Bishops' walk and driveway. I started to get up early to shovel it. Then I shoveled both their next-door neighbors' walks and driveways, too, so Mrs. Bishop would think it was one of them. It was hard to do with a broken hand and in the dark. At least my cast hand had healed quick. Sometimes it took me a couple of hours.

I cradled a hot chocolate against my fingers after one morning of shoveling, inhaling the smell of sticky-sweet marshmallows. I opened *Chronicle of a Death Foretold,* and an envelope dropped out. *Mr. Caroll* was scribbled on the front.

I hadn't gotten a Christmas card from anyone. My Secret Santa in math class never even gave me a present. I took out the card. It was simple, with a small tree on the front, encircled by the words PEACE ON EARTH. I opened it.

> Dear Mr. Caroll,
>   I wish you peace. Happy
> Christmas.
>   —Mr. Cordoba

I held the card in my hand, unable to believe that we had ever thought Mr. Cordoba was a heartless assassin. The guy handed out PEACE ON EARTH Christmas cards. No mafia guy ever sends cards. What would Capone have written on his cards?

> Merry Christmas. Hope I don't
> have to off you this year.
>   —Al

I turned the card over. It smelled like books. Do people always smell like their jobs? If so, it would totally suck to be a proctologist.

Good one, Kyle.

Thanks, Jase.

I smiled and put the card back in the novel.

Christmas Eve loomed over us like some kind of black cloud—like that 1978 horror flick *The Swarm*, where a mass of African bees invades and kills thousands in Houston. Mel and I were anxious. Mom had baked three kinds of desserts to calm her nerves. And it was all Dad's fault. He had invited Uncle Ray and Aunt Phyllis. Having to spend any amount of time with Aunt Phyllis topped Jason's and my "what's worse" list.

"I want everybody to be on their best behavior tonight," Dad said. He looked at Mom when he talked. "I mean everybody!"

When we heard Uncle Ray and Aunt Phyllis's car in the drive, Mel and I bolted upstairs. Mom met us at the top of the stairwell and growled, "Don't you *dare* think of escaping tonight. Now get downstairs and *be nice.*"

After dinner, Aunt Phyllis sat down at the piano and started pounding out Christmas carols. At first it was totally embarrassing and lame, but after a while, all of us were singing—even Mom.

"I think she's drinking something a lot stronger than eggnog," Mel whispered.

Mom's cheeks were pink and her eyes looked droopy. "Maybe," I agreed.

Aunt Phyllis and Uncle Ray took Mel's room. Mel took my bed, and I slept on the floor. I slipped into my sleeping bag. Sleeping bags are always the same—same feel, same smell. There's something nice about things that don't change.

I peed in my bag once at summer camp in fourth grade. The next morning, everybody knew who had wet their bags because the sleeping bags were hung up on the camp clothesline.

Jeffrey Mason razzed me, but Jason stepped up. "Listen, purple puke face, I wouldn't mess with Kyle if I were you."

That was a great line: purple puke face. I started to write out the next scene in my head.

UNTITLED: ~~Scene Three~~Scene Four—The sleeping bag Campers sing "Kumbaya" in the background.

FADE IN: Camera pans a typical summer camp in the mountains. There's a bonfire, and one kid's marshmallow goes up in flames.

ARC SHOT of boy and burning marshmallow. A dizzying look at the hazards of summer camp.

CUT TO: A group stands around the sleeping bags hanging on the line.

CLOSE-UP: The blue sleeping bag with green lining. Kyle is written in huge letters across it.

```
The camera swish-pans the faces of the
campers using a fish-eye lens. Their faces
are blurry and distorted as they laugh and
point at the sleeping bag.


                    JASON
         (Standing tall) Listen, purple puke
         face, I wouldn't mess with Kyle if I
         were you.
```

"Kyle?" Melanie interrupted the memory while I was thinking about the color of Jason's bag. Was it red or orange? It bugged me that I couldn't remember.

"Are you asleep?" she asked.

"No." I looked up at Pluto and sighed.

"Can we talk for a sec?"

I propped myself up on my elbow. "Huh?" I hoped Mel wasn't going to start talking to me about Jake Sanders, her latest boyfriend. Everybody called the guy Hoover. Since Mel had started hooking up with him, she wore turtlenecks a lot.

"It's just— Well, you're different. That's all." Melanie moved to the end of the bed and peered over at me.

Pluto was starting to blur into Saturn. Everything seemed too heavy to hold inside. I couldn't move. I couldn't breathe.

Mel leaned over and grabbed my hand. "I wish we hadn't fought that morning, you know? I mean, it was stupid."

I wished we hadn't fought, too. I nodded.

"I think about it a lot. Sometimes I wonder if things could've been different if only—" Mel wiped her nose. "It's stupid, I guess."

"It's not your fault, Mel."

"I sometimes think it is."

"Why?"

"I was mad at Jason, you know? And I just hated seeing him there that morning."

I sat up. "What for?"

"He'd totally ditched you for those losers. Then he came over and sat at our table, eating Mom's pancakes like everything was the same. Dad even went out to get syrup for him. Like when would that have ever happened in a normal world? King Jason. I wished he'd go away."

And he did.

She wiped away some tears. "Now I feel like shit all the time, because . . ."

I squeezed her hand.

"God, it sucks."

"Mel, it's not like what you thought made a difference. If you had that power, I would've spontaneously combusted about five years ago."

She laughed through her tears.

"Do you ever talk to Brooke?" I asked. Melanie had lost a best friend, too. I never told her how bad I felt about that. I just never knew what to say anymore.

She shook her head.

"That sucks."

"No big deal. She dropped out of cheer— It doesn't matter. Anyway, we were just friends because of habit, you know. It's not like we had a lot in common anymore."

I knew what she meant. Kind of.

"Hold on a sec." Mel ran out of the room and came back in. "Here. It's your Christmas present."

I opened up a gift certificate to Sundance Books. "Sweet, Mel. That's cool."

"Yeah, you've been reading a lot. Maybe if you have any left over, you can invite me for a coffee there."

"Like a ten-dollar latte? That's half the certificate!"

"Cheap ass."

I laughed. Mel brought her hand down on my head and ruffled my hair. She slipped off the bed and sat next to me. "You know, I'm glad you're here. I wouldn't trade you for anything."

Maybe she was worth that ten-dollar latte after all. I leaned into her. "All right. But make it a small latte without all those foo-foo add-ons. And it'd better not be fat-free decaf shit, okay?"

"Deal," she said, and kissed me on the forehead. She

climbed back into bed and whispered, "Merry Christmas, Kyle."

"You, too, Mel." I listened as her breathing steadied. "Thank you," I whispered.

When Mel finally fell asleep, I went to sit at the top of the staircase. The house smelled like pine. The glow of the Christmas tree was the only light left. Last year Jase and I would've been stuffed with Mrs. Bishop's caramel cookies and hot chocolate.

What would Jason wish for you now? Dr. Matthews's question popped into my head and wouldn't leave. I wished I knew the answer.

I went back to bed and listened to the quiet house until the blackness of night lifted.

Merry Christmas, Jase, I thought.

43

At dawn I snuck out. The moon still hung low in the sky. I walked to the Bishops' and tapped on Chase's window.

He popped his head up and peered out. He smooshed his nose against the pane and started to laugh, so that the whole window fogged up.

I put my finger to my lips. "Shhhh." I stomped my feet, trying to keep warm.

"What?" he mouthed.

I motioned him to go to the back door and jumped the side fence to meet him.

"I'm sorry about your dad, Chase." He covered his ears and turned his back to me. I walked around and faced him. "We don't have to talk about that. Okay?"

He uncovered his ears. "Whatcha doin' up so early?" he asked. "Do you need help shoveling today?"

"You know?" I asked.

"I figured it was you."

I lowered my voice. "Does your mom know?"

Chase shook his head. "She doesn't get up that early anymore. She sleeps a lot." He faced the rising sun, squinting in the early-morning light. "Did you know that the sun has been called Helios and sol? Nuclear fusion produces a really cool energy output of three hundred eighty-six billion billion megawatts. And there are over one billion stars in our galaxy. The sun's just one of them. Funny, huh? One in a billion."

"Did you get a new book?"

Chase grinned. "You do know the difference between a solar system and a galaxy, don't you?"

I rubbed my arms to warm up, still stuck on Helios and his 386 billion billion megawatts.

"Anyway, the sun has eight satellites. We like to call them planets. You know Jason had the sun's satellites all messed up on his ceiling. He mixed up Saturn and Jupiter. And Pluto isn't even considered a planet anymore, scientifically speaking. Maybe historically we can talk about Pluto as a planet, but it's not really. I mean, how could Jason *not* know that?"

Since when was Pluto not a planet? "Hey, are the

planets still there? On Jase's ceiling?"

Chase nodded. "Yep."

"Don't take them down. I mean, if you don't have to."

"Mom doesn't touch anything in Jason's room. It's like a museum."

"Chase, I can't stay long. Here, I got you something."

"Wait a sec." Chase ran back into the house.

God, I hope he isn't getting his mom.

He came out and handed me a card. "It's a winter solstice card. I meant to give it to you on December twenty-first, but Dad picked me up that day."

I smiled. "Wow, Chase." I held the construction-paper card in my hand. It had a picture of the sun and some stars. And on the inside he had written, *I like your orange shoes. Keep your head up, Orange Dragon.*

"Mike helped me with it. He's still really into hiring you."

I took a deep breath and tried to control my voice. "Maybe after your gig is over."

Chase's eyes got real big. I cracked a smile.

"Nah, you wouldn't ditch me," he said.

"Never."

"Never."

"Thanks," I said. "It's the best winter solstice card I've ever gotten—the best card, really."

"So how many days has it been?"

"Has what been?"

"The orange shoes? The bet? I told Mom that Jason owed you his 1948 Captain Marvel Adventures number eighty-one if you wore them for a year straight."

"Oh yeah? What'd she say?"

"She didn't say anything. She just cried. She always cries."

I kicked some snow off the back porch. "Yeah, well, the comic books don't really matter."

"So why do you wear 'em?"

I shrugged. "Just because."

"Honoring your bet?"

"I guess so."

"Good enough. Well, I knew you'd like the card." Chase eyed the present I had in my hands.

"Oh, so you want this?"

I handed it over, and he tore open the wrapping paper. "No way! It's a dragon! It's a red dragon!"

"I couldn't find orange."

"That doesn't matter. Orange is a by-product of red and yellow. This is the best!"

"Just don't drag it on the street or anything. Maybe we can fly it at Mills. Saturday. Noon."

"On the sly?" Chase grinned.

"Sure. On the sly." I laughed. "Now go hide it. Don't tell anybody."

Chase crossed his heart. "Boy Scout's honor."

"Chase, you're not a Boy Scout."

"But I have honor."

"Yeah. Happy Christmas, okay?"

"Happy late winter solstice to you." Chase left the wrapping paper soaking in the snow and went inside. I scooped it up and walked by his window. He pressed his whole face against it this time. Then he pulled back and mouthed, "Thank you."

"**A**ny New Year's resolutions, Mr. Caroll?" Mr. Cordoba asked, placing *Chronicle of a Death Foretold* on a pile of books.

"No. I, uh, don't make resolutions—not anymore, anyway."

Mr. Cordoba tapped his finger on the book. He flipped through the pages. "What did you think?"

"I really liked it. Maybe I can read more by that author."

He nodded. "He's Colombian."

"Really?"

"From my hometown."

"Oh, yeah?" No wonder everybody thought he was some kind of mafia guy. Carson City was so lame. Had

Cordoba been from Cuba, everybody probably would've thought he was a commie spy.

"Aracataca. He won the Nobel prize."

"For what?"

"For literature."

"Oh. That's a pretty big deal."

Mr. Cordoba looked at me over his glasses. "Pretty big. So why did you like it?"

"I dunno. I guess I liked how this guy wanted to go back and find out what happened, but it turned out everybody had a different story."

"Memory is tricky, isn't it?"

"It is." I wondered what Chase remembered about Jason. If it was different from what I remembered. I pulled out my notebook. "I wrote this line down: 'The broken mirror of memory.'"

Mr. Cordoba nodded. "That's a great way to describe memories. It's like your director's notebook."

"How?"

"Fourteen versions of the same scene."

"Yeah. I hadn't thought about that. It's just that none of them turned out right."

"You haven't found the right director."

I shook my head. "Not yet."

"You will." Mr. Cordoba watched me intently. Waiting. "Are you going to do homework today?"

"I don't really feel like it."

Mr. Cordoba raised his eyebrows. "Come help me out, then." He handed me a pile of envelopes to lick.

"What are these for?" I passed my tongue across the sticky sweet glue.

"I'm trying to raise money to open a boxing gym in Aracataca."

"So you're a boxer?"

"I was."

Cordoba was actually telling me stuff about himself—not his books. Maybe I'd tell Kohana. I paused. "Do you still box?"

"Just for exercise and training."

"You train boxers?"

"A little—down at the community center gym."

"Were you a good boxer?"

"Some say so."

"Were you pro?"

"Almost."

"What happened?"

"I came here and became a librarian."

Intense! "Why a librarian? I mean, you could've been a boxer. You could've been superfamous or something." Mr. Cordoba looked up from the letters he was folding. "Well, not that a librarian can't be famous. I'm sure there are famous ones out there." I felt my face get hot.

Mr. Cordoba pointed out the books on the shelves. "Because here, every day, I can be anything I want to be. There is no limit to what I can do here"—he tapped his temple—"and here." He pointed to the books.

I shrugged. Weird. After that, we didn't talk for a long time. I just licked and sealed envelopes. The silences with Mr. Cordoba were cool, too.

"Do you need another book, Mr. Caroll?" Mr. Cordoba asked while I gathered my things.

"Sure. That'd be good."

He handed me *The Outsiders*.

"Hey! This is a great Coppola movie."

Cordoba smiled. "I've never seen it."

"You don't like movies?"

"I never know what to watch."

"Oh, c'mon, Mr. Cordoba. I can give you a list a mile long of movies to watch."

"Okay, then, pick one, and I'll watch it this week."

"Narrow it down to one? Let me think." I zipped up my pack and grinned. "*Black Mask.*"

"*Black Mask*?" Mr. Cordoba wrote it down.

"If you have trouble finding it, I can download it for you."

"Thank you, Mr. Caroll. I look forward to watching it."

When I turned to go, I asked, "Mr. Cordoba, um, can I ask you one more thing?"

He nodded.

"Is that how you got the scar? Boxing?"

"No."

My ears prickled. They were probably about the color of Mark's head after his trip to Cancun over the holidays. "Uh, sorry. I just thought . . ."

"See you tomorrow morning. Don't be late."

The sun was about to drop behind the mountains. I rode home as fast as I could, pumping my legs, feeling the burn in my thighs and sweat trickle down my back. My heart pounded, and I think I was smiling.

Mr. Cordoba was a boxer.

45

Everything started going back to normal all around me. Almost like October 8 had never really happened. I worried that I was the only one remembering Jase, keeping him from disappearing forever. After school one day I went to look for Jase's locker. I just wanted to see it. Instead, I found Alex and his friends surrounding Kohana in one of the back hallways. Pinky and Troy held Kohana down while Alex ripped his photography portfolio out of his hands. "Nice pictures, man." Ever since they had taken the heat off me, I'd noticed them hanging around Kohana more. They never did things other than say lame-ass stuff and try to look cool. Kohana didn't put up with their shit, anyway. The day before, when Alex tried to trip Kohana after school, Kohana slammed him into the flagpole. Alex had been alone. It looked like Alex got his henchmen to take care of things for him again.

Alex showed Kohana's photo to Pinky and Troy. He tore it down the middle. The vein on Kohana's temple pulsated as he tried to break free. I felt the red rage again and raced down the hall. No teachers were around. These guys thought they ruled the fucking world.

I threw myself into Alex, and the portfolio went flying. Pinky and Troy pounced on me. "Get your photos, Kohana! Get 'em!" Kohana ran to his portfolio as Troy kicked me in the stomach. Not this again.

"Oh, look who we have here, guys. A true hero, huh?" Alex stood up, brushing off his pants. His voice quavered.

Fucking pansy.

Pinky and Troy pulled me up and shoved me into the lockers. My hand throbbed. I'd only had the cast off for a week, and it still hurt—useless for a fight.

Kohana was a step from his portfolio when he turned around. "Leave him alone, assholes."

"How sweet, Clock. You found yourself a little friend." Alex laughed.

Friend. I had never thought that I was Kohana's friend. I just kinda figured he put up with me after school since he didn't have a lot of company.

Alex kept laughing. But nobody else did. Not even Pinky and Troy. Pinky looked at Troy and shrugged, still holding me against the locker doors.

I felt like I was in a spaghetti western with a really bad script. I looked down the hall for a tumbleweed and listened for Ennio Morricone's theme music.

I tried to push Pinky and Troy off, but they were too strong.

Alex sneered at me. "Yeah, and we know what happens to Kyle's friends."

"I said, 'Leave him alone,'" Kohana said, and shoved Alex against the lockers across the hall. "Back off," he whispered. "Leave us alone. Just back off." Kohana looked from Alex to me. He cocked his head to the side. "What, Alex, you gonna piss yourself again?"

Pinky snorted. "C'mon, guys. They aren't worth it," he said. Kohana let Alex go. "Maybe they'll go off and watch one of Kyle's weird-ass movies together."

How did they know about the movies?

"It was Jase's own fault he died, hanging out with a freak like Kyle," Alex said.

That sent me reeling. I yanked myself free of Troy and Pinky and raced at Alex. The hallways turned red. The rage overtook me, and I don't know what I would've done if I hadn't felt Kohana's hand on my shoulder. "He's not worth it, man. Let it go." Kohana brought me back to the hallway. Alex whimpered. Troy and Pinky didn't move.

Then I saw Alex, really saw him. A pathetic shit of a

friend. And scared. It was like I could see his movie projected ten years into the future. He'd be that guy at the class reunion who still talked about being homecoming king; that guy who'd buy beer for the keggers at the creek, hanging out with the high school kids when his friends were long gone; that guy who wore his letterman jacket after graduation and never let go of the past.

I didn't want to be like him—stuck on a day, stuck in an era.

I watched the three of them walk away. Troy and Pinky walked ahead—the first sign of the end of Alex's golden years.

I sat against the lockers to catch my breath.

Kohana grabbed his portfolio and sat next to me. "You okay?"

"Yeah. You?"

"Yeah. Thanks."

"You, too, man." I rubbed my temples.

"What they say about Jason and stuff. That's not cool. They're losers."

I leaned my head against the lockers. "Fuck, it's complicated." Kohana flipped through his portfolio. "Are your pictures okay?"

"Thanks to you."

"I know they mean a lot to you." I sighed. "Your stories."

Kohana took out his camera and took a picture of the hallway. "This was a good story, too."

"What's the story? Getting picked on by the school tools?"

Kohana shook his head. "No. Friendship." He cleared his throat and smiled.

I wondered if that was okay. Would it be okay with Chase and Jason that I had a friend? Plus I still wasn't completely sure I hadn't shot my last one on purpose. Maybe I ought to come with a "friendship warning label." I closed my eyes and sighed.

"How can you be so okay with things, Kohana? Doesn't it just piss you off?"

He laughed. "Seriously, nobody's worth that."

"Worth what?"

"There's this old Native American thing Gram said to me one time. It sucked at first, growing up here. My mom died. Dad left. He didn't want to be the dad of a deformed kid. I had no friends." Kohana wiped his camera lens. "I didn't see the point of anything, you know. One day Gram said, 'Kohana, I want to know what sustains you from the inside when all else falls away.'"

"Huh?"

Kohana sighed. "That's what I said. I was only eight. But I got it after a while. Everything fell away, you know. And I was alone. So I had to figure it out."

"Figure what out?"

"What sustains me."

We sat in silence for a while.

"Gram gave me this camera, the first one she ever used. She was a professional photographer before I came along."

"Is that what sustains you?"

"No." He shook his head. "It can never be a thing. This is just a tool. But it helps. So that's what you've got to figure out."

What sustains me? I'd have to think on that. "Hey, thanks." I said.

"For what?"

"For your story."

"Yeah, and what about yours?"

"Another time?"

Kohana nodded. "Another time."

"I think you should take a picture of your camera."

Kohana smirked. "Kinda hard to do."

I stood. "Maybe you want to hang out at the library?" I'd never wanted to share that space with anybody before.

Kohana pushed his hair out of his face. "I dunno. I'm not really a group person."

"Three people are a group?"

"Hey, man. I'm used to hanging solo."

"True. It's a good place, though. I'll introduce you to Mr. Cordoba. He seems mean, but he's not. He's a"—I mumbled the words—"a friend."

"Then he must be pretty okay," Kohana said.

We walked down the hall. "You know, Gram has a friend with a cabin up in Squaw Valley. Sometimes we go for the weekend to hike and mountain bike and stuff."

"Yeah? Sounds cool."

"Maybe you can come next time."

"I'd like that." Then I paused. "Squaw Valley's in California, right?"

"Yeah."

"Shit, man, I'm not sure if I'm allowed to leave the state."

"Oh." He looked disappointed.

"I can ask my PO."

"PO?"

"Parole officer."

Kohana turned to me. I shrugged; then we buckled over, laughing.

46

I started to sleep better at night, but I'd always wake up really early in the morning. The mornings were the hardest. The house was so damned quiet and the neighborhood looked dead, like an empty movie set. Nobody'd show up until seven A.M. to bring it to life. I wished Mr. Cordoba would open the library at five A.M. or something. That would've helped. At least sometimes there was shoveling to do.

One morning, I couldn't take the quiet anymore, so I got dressed and stood outside Chase's window. "Chase," I whispered and tapped on the window.

Nothing.

"Chase!" I flicked a couple of stones at the window.

His head popped up and he rubbed his eyes. "What?"

I motioned to the backyard and jumped the side fence.

The back door creaked open. Chase peeked his head out. "I don't pay overtime, you know."

I shook my head. "You don't pay me at all. Remember? Pro bono."

"It's dark. It's cold."

I nodded. "I know. Get your slippers and robe on."

It took a thousand years, but he finally came out all bundled up.

"What took you so long?"

"Had to brush my teeth."

"No you didn't."

"I always brush my teeth first thing when I wake up. Don't you?"

"Okay. Yeah."

"Breathe on me. I betcha you don't."

"I do, too, Chase."

"Breathe on me."

I breathed.

"You have smelly breath. You didn't brush."

"Okay, so I forgot. It's early. I usually wait until after breakfast."

"How many cavities do you have?"

"Not many."

"How many?"

"I don't know."

"*Hmmph.*"

We sat on the back porch and looked up at the stars. "Can you show me dandelion?"

"You mean *Taraxacum officinale*?"

"Yeah. I never remember the name."

Chase looked around and pointed up to a cluster of stars. "That's it." He turned to me. "That all you need?"

"Are you doing okay? About your dad and all?"

Chase turned away. He got up and said, "I'm going now."

"Wait, Chase." I patted the step beside me. "I read this book a little while ago. It was really weird. It was about this guy who woke up one morning as a bug."

"What kind of bug?"

"Um, an insect."

"More than one million species of insects have been identified. And in all, there are over ten quintillion insects in the world. So you might want to narrow it down."

"Oh. Well, um, the book doesn't really say. But he goes to sleep as a man and wakes up a bug. An insect. But it's not science fiction or anything."

Chase chewed his bottom lip and sat down. "Tell me more."

So I told him about *The Metamorphosis*. We spent about an hour on the porch. The black night turned to the purple dawn. Porch lights flickered off. "I'd better go, Chase."

"See ya this afternoon, Kyle. Don't be late." Chase pointed to my watch.

"Never."

"Never?"

"Well, almost never."

"Close enough. Don't forget to brush your teeth."

"I won't."

"And Kyle?"

"Yeah?" I had to get back before the Bishops came out, before Mom and Dad were up.

"You can come and tell me about your books whenever you want. You read good books."

"Cool. I'll be back then." I waved from the sidewalk. Chase looked a little like an old man in his tattered robe and slippers. I hoped he wouldn't be too tired at school.

47

Dr. Matthews strummed her fingers on her desk. She'd been losing weight and had gotten thin enough to stop wearing curtain-dresses. She was wearing pants and a sweater. She looked kinda nice. Chubby nice. "New journal?" Dr. Matthews pointed to my notebook.

I nodded.

"And?"

"I'm, um, trying to write the whole movie now. Like you said." I cleared my throat and pretended to be really interested in the books she had on her shelves.

She smiled at me—a real smile. And I told her about the time Jase and I got grounded for taking his grandma's car down the street when we were twelve. How were we supposed to know it wasn't like driving bumper cars?

At first the memories came back one scene at a time. I'd find something, like my old Rollerblades, and that would remind me of the time Jase didn't brake right and he ended up with eight stitches in his forehead. After a while, though, the stories flowed. It was easy to go back in time and find a piece of Jason in practically every object I had in my room.

With my director's notes, I felt like I could edit the bullshit. I didn't care about the times Jase blew off my Friday-night movie marathons. The new notebook let me write about the important stuff.

It was like Kohana and his camera. He could choose which stories he wanted to photograph. It could be anything—from a spray-painted locker to the bottom of somebody's desk. He didn't have to take pictures of the bad stuff. Neither did I.

Kohana sometimes came to the library when he missed the bus. He never bugged me about where I went for a half hour after school, and I never asked him why he liked to sit outside so much. Sometimes I'd wait with Kohana at the flag-pole after library time until his grandma came around. He'd show me his pictures. We'd talk about the best angle to take a shot, to film a scene. Or we wouldn't say anything at all.

I almost told him about the notebook a million times, but I didn't want to ruin the magic. It was almost like Jason was coming back to life in the notebook Mr. Cordoba had given me. I wished, though, that I could take all those memories and bring him back to the Bishops—to Chase.

At the library I spent more time writing than doing homework. Homework was easy, so I usually got it done fast so I could do the other stuff. I had always been a "solid C" student until that last fall. Then I crashed to Fs and rose to Bs. My teachers almost glowed when they handed out semester grades.

"You're really reaching your potential."

"Oh, Kyle, I am so pleased with your effort and academic success this term."

And Mark was right there behind them—proud of *his* success story—his grade contract. Even Mel took me out one night with her new boyfriend, Hoover, after progress reports came. We went out for buffalo wings, then to a movie. Hoover paid for everything. And I ate a lot. I felt kinda bad and offered to pay for at least the movie, and he said something like, "No way. This is your night." He was trying to be gallant or something, which was pretty cool, I guess.

After all the glowing reports and happy teachers, I could probably do milk commercials for Carson City wearing one of those freakish milk moustaches.

I was the boy who shot his friend, and look at me now. Don't let homicide ruin your smile. Drink milk.

Mr. Cordoba was the only one who didn't congratulate me.

"I watched *Black Mask,* Mr. Caroll." Mr. Cordoba was working his way through the media center, scanning all the computers for viruses.

"Really?" I was relieved to talk about something—anything—besides my miracle grades. "And?"

"He was quite an unusual librarian."

I laughed. Most librarians probably didn't do kung fu stuff. Most librarians weren't boxers, either. "Did you like it?"

Mr. Cordoba paused. "Yes, I did."

"Good."

"So?" Mr. Cordoba peered over his glasses.

"So what?"

"I could use a recommendation for another movie."

"Sure," I said. It was nice to feel like I knew a lot about something.

"How about one of your favorites. Maybe by one of your favorite directors." Mr. Cordoba said. "One you used in your notebook."

My hands felt clammy. I hated thinking about that notebook. I hated thinking about that scene that none of the directors could get right. Whenever I thought about it too hard, I started questioning myself all over again. I couldn't have done it on purpose. Shit happens, right? Mr.

Cordoba looked up from the computer screen. He was waiting for me to say something.

"Okay. Maybe a Clint Eastwood movie? Not *Dirty Harry* or anything, even though those are pretty tight. You should see this western he directed and starred in. *Unforgiven.*"

Mr. Cordoba scribbled something down on a sticky pad. "Why do you like it?"

"Because it's everything you don't expect from a western, you know? It's about how bad somebody can feel doing what he used to do best."

Mr. Cordoba waited.

"And it has the perfect line in it." I cleared my throat and lowered my voice, trying to do Eastwood. "'It's a hell of a thing, killing a man. You take away all he's got, and all he's ever gonna have. . . .' It's a good movie."

Mr. Cordoba smiled. "Better than your Eastwood impersonation?"

"Much." I grinned. Jase would've nailed it. There wasn't anybody he couldn't impersonate.

"I'll watch it this week."

"Cool." I went back to the tables and pulled out a book to read.

"Mr. Caroll, have you thought about what you're going to do after high school?"

I looked up. "That's another two and a half years

away. That's forever."

"Two and a half years isn't that long."

I shrugged.

"You're a good student. When you want to be one."

So he had seen my grades too. I wondered if there was some kind of "underground Kyle network" that monitored everything I did. Maybe Mark was the big spy of the whole operation, and his secret 007 lover was Dr. Matthews, totally redefining the Bond chick look.

I closed my book. "I dunno. The only reason I had ever really thought about going to college was to room with Jason and try out a ramen noodle diet."

"A ramen noodle diet?"

"Well, you know. Like that fat guy did eating sub sandwiches, and the other guy did for his documentary on McDonald's. Jason and I were going to see how long we could live on ramen noodles. I was going to direct a cool documentary and win awards and stuff. That was the only reason I would really want to go to college—the ramen noodle documentary."

Mr. Cordoba arched his eyebrows. "So what's stopping you?"

"You can't do that kind of stuff alone." I picked at a sticker somebody had stuck on the table. "Anyway, it was Jason's idea. It'd be pretty shitty to steal it. He had a lot of good ones, you know." I bit my lip. "Excuse me. I didn't mean to say *shitty* in the library. Twice."

Mr. Cordoba returned to his desk and sat down. "I bet you have your own ideas as well."

"Nah, not like Jase. I mean, Jason was an animal for insane ideas." I laughed. "The only plan of his that backfired was trying to puff out pond frogs' croakers by sticking straws up their butts and blowing. We thought we were onto something until one of the frogs exploded. We were only seven at the time."

"He sounds like he was a smart guy."

"Yeah. Funny how I ended up being his best friend." All of a sudden my throat felt like it was closing up. My nose burned. I swallowed and counted to twenty. I couldn't have done it on purpose.

"You don't think you were a good friend?"

"Not like in the books." I pointed to *The Outsiders*. "Those guys stood up for each other through it all—never questioned each other."

"And that's how Jason was with you—never questioning? Standing up for you?"

"Yeah. I guess." I thought about Jason hanging out with Alex because I didn't want to go to the "cool" parties; how they called me Shadow and laughed at me and he let them. I glared at Mr. Cordoba. "Jason was a great friend. The best."

"I don't doubt he was, nor do I doubt that you *are*."

"Whatever."

"So, Mr. Caroll, you still haven't answered my question. What would you think you would like to do? After high school?"

How would Jason like to see you?

It wasn't fair. How could I move on and leave everything behind when I stole that from Jase? I shrugged. "I haven't thought about it."

"Think about it."

All I knew was that I had to stick around. I couldn't leave Chase. I couldn't leave Jason and the old man who raked the leaves off his grave. I couldn't just up and go.

At four o'clock, I grabbed my things and took off. For the first time, I felt like the library was going to smother me.

48

I heard hooting early one morning. Chase stood below my window and waved up at me. I threw on a sweatshirt and went outside to meet him.

He had on his bathrobe and slippers full of holes. His nose was bright red from the early-morning chill.

"You're supposed to hoot back."

"What?"

"You're supposed to hoot back. That way I know you've heard the signal."

"Oh. Next time, okay?"

He shook his head and sighed. "Fine."

"What's up? You doing okay?" Mr. Bishop hadn't come back to the house yet. He sometimes came to pick Chase up after school. I wondered where he was living. I wondered if he'd ever come back. But if I tried to talk to Chase about it, he'd cover his ears and turn away.

"Here." Chase handed me a card. "Happy birthday." He shivered and rubbed his shoulders.

"This is my first birthday card." I traced the orange dragon.

"That was my intention. I was going to come at midnight, but I fell asleep."

"This is perfect. Thank you."

"And this, too." He pulled a yellowed envelope out of his pocket. "I found this in Jason's room."

I looked at Jason's handwriting: *Kyle*.

"Is your mom, um, cleaning out his room?"

Chase shook his head. "No."

We sat on the porch steps, watching the last stars fade away.

"I sit there," he said. "In his room."

I nodded.

"It doesn't smell like him anymore, but I still like it." Chase leaned on me. "I like to pretend he's coming home."

"Me too."

"But he's not."

"I know." I put my arm around Chase.

He got up. "See you this afternoon."

"See you."

"Don't be late."

"Never."

"Almost never," he corrected me, then walked down the street, leaving padded footprints in the crystal frost.

Kyle

Jason's writing.

I turned the envelope over in my hands and slipped out a brochure. *Voices of Youth Filmmaker Contest.* Jason had highlighted the application due date: May 7.

I lay on the porch, my shoulder blades digging into the concrete. The first rays of sunlight crept across the street until they worked their way up the steps. Tears pooled in my ears.

"Happy birthday, man," Kohana said, coming up to me before lunch.

"Thanks. How'd you know?"

He held out the *The Carson High Tribune*. "They always print up the birthdays here, a week ahead of time."

"I never noticed."

"I have a lot of quality reading time waiting for Gram when I miss the bus."

"Yeah, I guess so." I read my name: Kyle Michael Caroll, February 2.

"Dude, so are you getting your driver's license today?"

I shook my head. I felt kind of stupid.

"So are you having a party or something?"

"Nah."

Kohana took back the paper. "Well, happy birthday." He walked down the hall toward the cafeteria. I was on my way to the library.

"Um, Kohana?"

"Yeah?"

"Do you maybe want to come over for dinner tonight? Just if you can, you know."

He grinned. "Sure."

"We can pick you up and take you home, if you need."

"Cool."

"Um, seven o'clock okay?"

"Definitely."

On the way out of the library, Mr. Cordoba handed me a small package. "Open it." I guess he read the *The Carson High Tribune* too.

The whole birthday thing is way overrated. It would be cool if we had a system where birthdays were earned. Like if you lived the year right, then you could get older by one year, or even two if you lived the year really perfect. If not, you'd end up staying the same age until you did. That would've made more sense than giving somebody a present just because they happened to get born on some particular day. Especially if that person didn't deserve it.

Mr. Cordoba leaned on the desk.

I opened up a tattered book in Spanish: *Crónica de una*

muerte anunciada. The name *Edgar* was scribbled inside.

"That's the first book I ever owned," he said.

"Your very first book?"

He leaned his elbows on the desk. "It's *Chronicle of a Death Foretold*, in Spanish."

"You read *this* as a kid?"

He laughed. "I got it when I was nineteen."

"Nineteen? You didn't have your own book until you were nineteen?"

"No, I didn't."

"What about school? Didn't they give you books?"

"I didn't go to school in Colombia."

"Really?"

"I had to work. I boxed."

I shook my head. "They let you box instead of going to school?"

"No. I boxed because my family needed money. School didn't come with a paycheck like I got from the ring."

I cradled the book in my hand. "So how'd you learn how to read?"

"When I was eighteen, I was given a few years to think about a lot of things. That's when I decided to study and learned to read. That's when I learned to make peace."

"Peace?"

Mr. Cordoba eyed my notebook. "To make peace with the past." He got up from his desk and motioned me to sit down. He sat down across from me at the table. He pointed to his scar. "This is a memory, a reminder of who I was. I take this to bed with me every night." He scanned the library. "And this is who I am."

"Who were you?" I looked at the scar.

Mr. Cordoba smiled. "A foolish young man who was given a second chance at life."

I stared at the scar on his face. I wondered if Kohana had ever taken a photo of Mr. Cordoba's scar, if he had ever captured that story.

Mr. Cordoba watched me intently, then said, "I choose not to live my life based on one moment." He rubbed his scar.

I ran my fingers over the soft edges of the book, worn like velvet. "So you didn't learn how to read until you were eighteen?"

"No. And I've been trying to catch up ever since."

"And after you learned, this was the first book you ever bought?"

"Actually, my best friend gave it to me."

"And you're giving it to me?" I blushed.

He smiled.

"I don't know what to say. About this."

" 'Thank you' will do." He got up from the table.

"Thank you, Mr. Cordoba."

"Happy birthday, Mr. Caroll." He patted my shoulder

and headed back to his office.

That afternoon, even Mark stopped by with a card. "Happy birthday, Kyle. Now that you're sixteen, gotta get you up on a motorcycle one of these days."

Mom set her jaw and scowled. The last thing she needed was for me to join a biker gang.

"Just kidding, Mrs. Caroll." Mark laughed and winked at me. The last of his Cancun sunburn had flaked off. For a while his head had looked like a blotchy billiard cue ball.

We picked Kohana up at seven o'clock. Dad grilled burgers out on the deck. Mom made sweet potato fries. Kohana had three helpings of everything. He turned red every time Mel said anything to him. It was the first time I ever saw the guy flustered.

Mom brought out a double-chocolate fudge cake with chocolate-chip ice cream, my favorite since forever. Everybody sang.

"Make a wish, Kyle," Mel said.

I closed my eyes and blew out all the candles. *I just want things to be okay again. I want Chase and the Bishops to be okay.*

Mom and Dad gave me a key chain and keys to both their cars. Mel gave me a TEAM DUDE BIG LEBOWSKI T-shirt.

Kohana pulled out his photography portfolio. He handed me a photo. "This one's for you."

It was a black-and-white of my shoes, hand-tinted orange. "This is really cool."

Mom, Dad, and Mel crowded around to look at the pictures Kohana had taken. "Those are so good, Kohana," Mel said. "I never thought those shoes of Kyle's would be photogenic." She pinched her nose, and everybody laughed.

Kohana turned magenta. "Thanks."

"They're stories," I interrupted. Then I explained Kohana's philosophy of photography.

"Maybe one day you can tell us the stories," Mom said.

"Sure, Mrs. Caroll." Kohana chewed on his lower lip and fidgeted with the zipper on his portfolio.

Mom smiled at Kohana. "Only if you'd like."

Mom, Dad, and Mel looked at every one of Kohana's pictures, then headed into the kitchen. I got up to help with the dishes. "I got 'em, Kyle," Mel said.

Kohana reorganized his portfolio, leaving a blank spot.

"What picture goes there?" I asked.

"Your shoes."

"You can keep this if you need it." I handed him the photo.

"I have a copy," he said.

"So? Why leave it blank?"

"This is like an anthology. But it can't be complete without your story. No story. No photo."

"Oh." I swallowed.

"Maybe another time."

"Yeah. Maybe."

Dad and I took Kohana home. He talked the entire way about how much he had loved dinner. Mom had made him a leftover bag so he could share with his grandma.

As he was walking into his house, he shouted, "You owe me a story!"

On the way home, Dad turned on the radio and hummed along to some jazz solo. He looked over at me and said, "Anything else you'd like to do?" He motioned to the slice of cake I'd wrapped in aluminum foil and brought with me at the last minute.

"Do you think we could stop by the cemetery?"

Dad nodded. We drove in silence and parked outside the gate. "I think it's closed."

"I know a way in."

"Do you need company?"

I shook my head. "I'd rather go alone. If that's okay."

"Sure." He lit up a cigarette and winked. "Don't tell your mother."

"I won't." I rolled my eyes. It would be easier if they just smoked together.

I slipped through the shadows of the cemetery, unwrapped the cake, and left it next to Chase's M&M's jar.

Happy birthday, man.

Thanks, Jase.

Make a wish?

Yep.

Hope it comes true.

Me, too, Jase.

"Okay." I ran up to Dad. "I'm ready."

I got into the car and Dad cranked up the heat. "It's cold outside."

"Yeah." I cleared my throat. It had felt pretty scratchy all day. "Can you maybe not tell anybody we came by?"

He turned off the radio and touched his forehead to mine, just like he used to do when I was little. I leaned into him and it felt good, like I was ten years old again.

When we got home, I hung Kohana's picture up next to Chase's Orange Dragon drawing. The walls didn't seem so empty anymore.

49

Every day I'd wake up hoping to find Mr. Bishop's car back in the driveway. It didn't make sense to me that he had left Chase and Brooke like that. Jason didn't have a choice, but Mr. Bishop did.

I walked down the winding path to Jason's grave one day and saw Mrs. Bishop on her knees. The snow had melted and the cemetery looked barren. There was a smattering of chalky conversation hearts left over from Valentine's Day. I walked away before she saw me.

I had turned sixteen. Jason never would.

Freeze frame.

The rest of February sucked. The snow was crusty and melted, black and yellow from exhaust fumes and dog piss. And all I did was write, trying to bring Jason back with every object, every scene. Once in a while I thought about Scene Three, but I was afraid it would bring me back to the way I had felt that night in the shed.

Sometimes the scenes came back so quickly, I felt like I wouldn't be able to write them down fast enough. One afternoon I sat behind the Dumpsters writing about the time Jase helped me organize a B-movie marathon in the backyard. I had gotten seven of the best B-movies to show and was ready with Grandpa's old projector. When we threaded the first film, the movie that started to play definitely wasn't *The Rocky Horror Picture Show*. We didn't get a chance to see too much before Dad ripped it out of the projector and canceled the showing until he reviewed all seven movies. All seven starred a girl named Roxy Lovelace. Apparently we had gotten the wrong shipment. I wrote the scene in a grind-house movie style—like those cheesy seventies movies with bad acting and hot chicks.

"Kyle. Hey, Kyle! *Psst!*"

Chase and Mike were standing together, peeking around the corner. "Hey, guys. Sorry. Didn't see you." I shoved the notebook into my backpack.

"You didn't hear us hoot?" Chase asked.

"I guess not."

Chase crossed his arms. "A little lackadaisical today."

"Nice word, Chase."

"Thanks. I learned it last week."

"Yeah, and he says it every day, all day long." Mike rolled his eyes. "Nobody in Mrs. Perrin's class knows what it means. I don't think she even knows what it means."

Chase glared at Mike. "It means 'lazy.'"

Mike picked at a scab. "Yeah. But who's gonna remember that?"

"I'm going to Mike's."

"Cool." I looked at the time—late for the library again.

"Anyway, I need your help with something," Chase said, turning to me.

"What's going on?"

"Well, Mom is into this heaven–eternal-life stuff, telling me Jason's with me always."

My throat felt dry. I rubbed my eyes. "What does your dad say?"

"Dad stopped going to church the day he left the house. I heard him tell Mom that there is no God."

I couldn't believe I had taken God away from Mr. Bishop too. "Have you tried praying to him? Doesn't Pastor Pretzer help you with that stuff?"

He shook his head. "I saw this thing on the Light Up Your Life channel at Mike's house, that when people die, they leave a soul print."

"A soul print?" I asked.

"There are even soul-print hunters who help people find the place where a person was at the very moment when their soul left their body."

"On *what* channel?"

"Mike has DISH."

I nodded. "I remember."

"Anyway, it's all really confusing and I can't afford a soul-print hunter. And I have something really important I need Jason to know. I need to get a message to him."

"Jase is always going to be with you, Chase. Just because he's not here"—I motioned to the air—"doesn't mean he's not here." I tapped Chase's heart.

"So do you know how I can talk to him? To feel him here?" Chase touched his heart right where I had.

I thought for a while. No clue. But I couldn't let Chase down again. "I think I might know a way."

Chase's eyes got wide. "You really know how to talk to the dead?"

I did it every day. But I didn't figure that would be a good thing to tell Chase. "Well, I wouldn't say that exactly."

Mike grinned. "Wow, Chase. This is big."

Chase nodded. "How about this Saturday? March eighteenth. Oh seven hundred hours."

"Oh seven hundred?"

"That's military time for seven A.M."

"Oh. Yeah." March 18? I wondered how it was possible that more than five months had gone by. "Oh seven hundred hours. You got it."

Chase turned to Mike. "You've got to get me an invitation to stay over Friday night."

Mike wrinkled his nose. "An invitation? Like a card or something?"

Chase rolled his eyes. "No. Just have your mom call my mom. Okay?"

"Oh. Okay."

I laughed. "Where do you live, Mike?"

Mike gave me detailed instructions on how to get to his house. Chase interrupted, giving me the GPS coordinates.

"Got it, OD?" Mike asked.

"Yeah, I got it."

"You sure?" Chase asked. "I didn't see you write down the coordinates."

It was like we were acting out some James Bond movie. "I'm sure."

"So?" Chase asked. "We're on for Saturday?"

"We're on. I'll pick you two up at seven."

"A.M?"

"Yes. A.M."

"Do I need anything?" Chase asked.

I thought for a while. "Write down the message you need to get to Jason on a piece of paper." It sounded good anyway—like I knew what I was doing.

Chase shook my hand. "I knew I could count on you, Kyle."

50

I pedaled as hard as I could, zigzagging puddles and pot-holes. Maybe Cordoba had some books on talking to the dead. Jesus, that wasn't a conversation I wanted to have with him.

How *could* Chase talk to Jason? I had five days to figure it out.

I wondered if anybody in Carson City could do a séance at the last minute. Would that kind of shit be in the yellow pages? Or maybe I could use Mel's Ouija board. But how seriously can anybody take something made by Parker Brothers? I had to find some way for Chase to send a message to Heaven.

If there even was a Heaven.

Why had I promised those things to him? Jesus.

I threw open the library doors, trying to catch my

breath. Mr. Cordoba looked up from the paper.

"Sorry." I looked at the clock on the wall and pinched my side.

Mr. Cordoba mumbled and continued reading the paper. I peeled off my sticky sweatshirt, found my seat, and brought out my notebook. The library was empty—the way I liked it. Sometimes it felt like it was there just for me. Then I closed my eyes and thought about the day we took Chase to Rancho San Rafael Park to watch the national kite festival. Colors and shapes dotted the sky like confetti. We lay on the grassy hills of the park, eating cotton candy, watching the kites cartwheel and somersault in the sky.

"KITE," I titled the scene.

Mr. Cordoba cleared his throat in the way he did when he wanted me to pay attention. Phony phlegm. Maybe one day I could write that scene. I laughed to myself, imagining a suspense scene building up to the phony phlegm sound followed by a shrill scream from a beautiful blonde. Very Hitchcock.

"I watched *Unforgiven*," Cordoba said.

"Really?" I put the notebook down. "What'd you think?"

"Interesting choice."

"It's a great western—one of the best."

"Why do you like it so much?"

I bit my lip. "It just makes sense to me. It was like the past was always with him."

"So, a man is stuck with his past?"

I thought about my old notebook, the shed, and all the ways I had tried to write the scene. Jason ended up dead every time. I nodded. "Pretty much."

"He can't choose to change?"

"He might change, but everybody else stays the same, you know. So he would have to leave everything to really change. Just like William Munny did in the end."

"Though he left, did his past change?"

"Well, no. But at least he didn't have to face it every day. It's easier to forget that way."

"And you think he'll forget his past?"

"I suppose not."

"So what has changed? What changed in him?"

"Nothing. Everything." I threw my hands up. "I don't know. It's just a movie I like, Mr. Cordoba." A slow ache settled in my heart.

Maybe I could escape to San Francisco and set up a dry-goods store just like William Munny.

Mr. Cordoba pulled out the filmmaker brochure. "This fell out of your backpack yesterday."

The edges of the brochure were curled in from the time I dropped it in the snow when I was visiting Jase. The glossy cover looked smudged and dull.

"Are you thinking about entering?" Mr. Cordoba asked.

"No." I wanted to rip it out of his hands but instead

shoved my fists into my pockets. "It's just a dumb thing somebody gave me."

"Who?"

"Jason." It slipped out. "Um, his brother found it in his room."

Mr. Cordoba raised his eyebrows. "It sounds like Jason knew you quite well."

I shrugged. "No big deal."

"Why won't you enter it?"

Because I have no right. Because I took away all Jase was and was ever gonna be. Because I don't know if I did it on purpose. But how could I explain that to Cordoba? "I need to go."

Mr. Cordoba stood in front of me, holding the brochure in his hands. "Take this. Think about it."

"I don't want it. I gotta go."

Mr. Cordoba didn't move.

"I gotta go," I repeated. My face burned. I bit down on my lip to keep from crying. My fingernails bit into my palms.

Then he grabbed me and held my shoulders. "It was an accident."

"Let me go. Let me go." My voice got lost in my sadness. I tried to pull away, tried to stop the tears, but the harder I tried, the closer he pulled me in.

"Kyle, it was an accident."

I pushed him.

"It was an accident." Mr. Cordoba pulled me tighter.

"How do you know? How do you know I didn't kill him on purpose? How do you know what happened in that shed when I don't even fucking know?"

"I know you. It was an accident."

Then it came—all of Jason flooded out of me. I couldn't push away anymore. Mr. Cordoba held me up. And I cried.

He repeated, "It was an accident."

Was that it? Did that make it okay?

Mr. Cordoba let go of me and helped me sit down. His jacket was soaked. I couldn't look him in the eyes. Couldn't stop crying.

"Kyle, I have something for you." Mr. Cordoba went back to his office and brought out my old notebook.

I pushed it away. "I can't do it. I can't think about that day anymore."

Mr. Cordoba put it in my hands. "You have one director left to write the scene."

I nodded.

"*You* write it. Face it. Find your peace."

I looked at the notebook. "What if," I whispered, choking out the words, "what if I remember, and it wasn't an accident?"

Mr. Cordoba looked really sad all of sudden. He rubbed his temples. His eyes clouded over. "Don't die with Jason."

All night I thought about how I would direct the scene. Even though Jase would never come back, it mattered. I needed to know what happened that day. Cordoba was right. I needed to make peace. I held the notebook close. One more take. It was time to remember, so I wrote:

SCENE THREE: Take Fifteen—Kyle style

FADE IN: Kyle and Jason are going through the shelves. Kyle sees his grandpa's old 8 mm film projector and takes down the box of home movies. He blows dust off the old reels and checks to see if the film is still good.

KYLE

Maybe we can set it up later, huh?

CUT TO: Jason jimmying the lock of a metal box.
Jason doesn't pay attention to Kyle.

KYLE

Whatcha got, Jase?

Jason whistles.

ZOOM IN: The gun in Jason's hand.

JASON

Check this baby out. It's pretty
tight, huh?

KYLE

Sweet, Jase. That's sweet.

CUT TO: Jason twirls gun around his thumb, a
confident smile on his face.

WIDE ANGLE of shed. Kyle's pajama pants are
stuck to his ankles. Kyle crouches down to
squeeze out the dew. He takes a deep breath

336

and stands up again. Jason still twirls the gun around his thumb.

> JASON
> (Holds the gun out to Kyle)
> What do you wanna do?

> KYLE
> (Pulls his hands back–instinctively.)
> I dunno. What are we s'posed to do with it?

> JASON
> (Pulls up T-shirt collar around his neck, like a pastor. He scowls.)
> Well, Kyle, let's see what our options are. We could A: put the gun away and continue to freeze, B: put the gun to good use; or C (and my personal favorite): rob the local convenience store, frame Mel and Brooke, move to the Cayman Islands, and never, ever have to work again.

> KYLE
> (Relaxes his shoulders and laughs.)

We don't work now, you moron. (He
looks at the gun.)

ZOOM IN: Shot of gun in Jason's hands.)

                    KYLE
You wanna shoot it or something?

                    JASON
(Shrugging, looking indifferent)
Maybe we should. I dunno. (Cocks the
gun and slips the cock back into
place.) Why does your dad have a
gun, anyway?

                    KYLE
(Grinning) Maybe Dad's a spy for the
CIA. Maybe he does undercover DEA
shit and the café is a front.

                    JASON
(Rolls his eyes and shakes his
head.) In Carson City?

                    KYLE
(Glaring at Jason) Just because you

                    338

hit puberty like three years before
me and probably every other guy our
age in the state, you don't have to
act like a jerk.

                    JASON
     (Raises his eyebrows and grins.)
     Dude, whatever. Well? What're we
     gonna do?

Kyle hesitates. He squeezes his pajama pants
again. Jason holds the gun out to him.

                    JASON
     Here, Kyle, you take it.

Kyle swallows. He takes the gun from Jason,
but it slips from his frosty hands. His
fingers are stiff. He tries to grab the gun,
to stop it from falling to the ground, so he
grips it tighter, his fingers squeezing the
trigger. There's an explosion in the shed.
Kyle looks at the gun. He touches the barrel
of the gun and jerks his hand back. He looks
up, confused, not quite understanding that the
gun has just gone off.

> ### KYLE
>
> Oh shit, Jason. Shit, shit, shit,
> shit, shit. Mom and Dad are gonna
> shit.

CUT TO: CLOSE-UP of Kyle's face. Kyle closes his
eyes and his lips move, forming the words "Please,
God. Please don't let this have happened."

CUT TO: the watch on Kyle's wrist.

ZOOM IN: The time is 9:16 a.m.

FADE OUT: Jason slumped against the workbench,
then slowly falling to the floor of the shed.
Blood pools beside his body.

> I felt a wave of relief.
> It was an accident.
> It was an accident.

I biked in the chilly spring afternoon to visit Jase. His grave
hadn't changed much. The marker had been washed
recently. All the spring mud was cleared away. I pulled the
Dimex out of my pocket and set it on his marker.

10:46.

I got out the notebook. "I was worried, you know?" I

sat and faced the marker. "But you knew all along. You knew I didn't mean to." I hugged my knees to my chest. "It's been pretty shitty thinking all this time that— Well. You know." I brushed dirt off my knees. "And no, 'shit happens' was not enough information."

I stretched back with my arms under my head, watching the clouds drift by. A cloud covered the sun, blanketing the cemetery in soft shadows. The last rays of sunlight finally broke through, warming my face.

"I'm so sorry, Jase. I'm sorry to have taken your life away like that." I wiped the tears from my eyes and sighed. It felt good to say that. Sorry. It made a difference.

How would Jason like to see you today?

I sat up. "Hey, Jase. I thought maybe I'd write the scene about what I think you'd want for me. If that's okay?"

Spring afternoons were pretty windy, and I had forgotten my jacket. I shivered. "You know, it sure would help if you had one of those standing-up gravestones, because then I could lean on something. Or even a tree."

New shoots of grass pushed through the soil, covering Jason's grave with what looked like tiny green polka dots.

"Maybe we can write this together."

HOW WOULD JASON LIKE TO SEE ME TODAY: *Scenes to write . . .*

- Getting action of any kind
- Cruising the strip up in Reno
- Getting a sweet summer job at the Rage

- Wearing out the orange shoes so I don't win his vintage comic books
- Making a movie instead of just talking about it

I read the last line over.

"See, Jase. That's kinda tricky. I'd need your mom and Chase for this movie I've been writing, and things with your family are pretty bad. Your dad left." The words hung in the air. "I'm sorry about that, too."

"Does he talk back?"

I looked up. Chase held a jar of red M&M's in his hand. "Chase! You don't usually come here during the week."

"Does he answer you?"

"Um, no. Maybe just in my head. Sometimes. I dunno." I closed the notebook and stuffed it into my backpack. "Are you alone?"

Chase shook his head. "Mom's talking to Mr. Peoples."

"Mr. Peoples?"

"The caretaker."

"The rake guy?"

"She's coming, though." He looked behind him. "I'm not allowed to go to Mike's this weekend. It's a Dad weekend. Brooke's with Mom. We alternate. So I can't talk to Jase." He shoved his hands into his pockets.

"We'll do it another day, Chase."

"When?"

"Chase, I gotta go."

Chase grabbed my hand. "But it's important."

"I know." I rubbed my neck. "But you gotta see your dad. That's important too."

"Well, they never ask me."

"Ask you what?"

"What I wanna do."

I sighed. "We'll do it another day. I've really gotta go."

"When? When will we do it?"

"Whenever you can."

"But I never can. They made this calendar of "Chase days." So every weekend I have to go to Virginia City, Ichthyosaur State Park, Sand Mountain, and the Tahoe Rim Trail either with my mom or with my dad. I'll never stay at Mike's again. They're just big bullies disguised as parents."

I squatted down next to him. "Give it time. And when you can, we'll go." Chase looked so small. I squeezed his hand. "I promise. Just say the word." I grabbed the watch and turned to go.

"But it's important. His soul print!" he called after me.

Mrs. Bishop walked up the path. I rushed past her with my head down, staring at the ground.

"Kyle?" Mrs. Bishop said.

I didn't turn around. My throat felt dry and my heart hammered in my chest. I made it to my bike and didn't stop pumping until I was home.

52

That Tuesday, I waited for Dr. Matthews in her freshly painted waiting room. It was a psychedelic green color. Retro green. Hippy green. Matthews green. Maybe it was her favorite color.

Jason's favorite color was blue. What were his other favorite things? Maybe I could write a scene.

It was an accident.

"Kyle, I'm sorry you had to wait today. Come in." Dr. Matthews peeked out of her office. Some kid pushed past her and grumbled something on the way out.

"It's okay." I was happy to be thinking about Jason's favorites. There were tons of things I could write about. I followed Dr. Matthews into her office. I threw my backpack on the lumpy college couch and sat down.

Dr. Matthews sat next to me.

"You look"—she paused, as if trying to find the right word—"happy. Yes, happy." Dr. Matthews crossed her legs.

She looked happy, too. Like a different person than the one I had first met. Everybody changes, I guessed.

"I'm okay." I thought for a second. "Maybe happy."

"How come?"

"I, um . . ." I chewed on my bottom lip. "I was thinking about that scene again, you know?"

She nodded.

"It was an accident." There. I'd said it. I waited for the world to crumble around me, but the office stayed the same; sunlight streamed through the windows.

"Can you tell me about that day?" she asked.

I told her how the gun slipped from my fingers, wet with frost. I told her how scared I was; how important it was for Jason to have fun that morning and want to hang out. It was an accident.

"Did you know that? That it was an accident?" I asked.

She nodded.

"How?"

"Intuition, I guess." She handed me a Kleenex.

"You know," I said, after I had wiped my nose, "I think Jason would want me to be okay."

"I think so, too. In fact, I think you will be okay," she said.

I shrugged. "I guess I don't have much of a choice, huh?"

Dr. Matthews smiled. "We all have choices."

"Yeah," I said. "I guess we do."

53

Weeks passed as Chase was passed back and forth between the Bishops like a Ping-Pong ball. One afternoon he and Mike came up to the Dumpsters and hooted.

I hooted back.

Chase came around and said, "Kyle, I need serious help."

Mike came and stood behind him.

"What's going on?" I asked.

Chase lowered his voice. "Have you ever planned a prison break?"

"Prison break?"

Mike bit his lower lip and looked from side to side. "Were you really in the can, Orange Dragon?"

I burst out laughing. "Where'd you learn that? Wait . . . FX?"

Mike nodded.

"No. I've never been in jail," I assured him.

Mike looked relieved.

"I told you," Chase said, elbowing Mike. Chase turned to me. "They made me go to Wild Waters last weekend. And I hate getting wet." Chase pointed to the skin peeling on his head and the splotchy calamine lotion on his back. "I got really sunburned, too."

Mike scratched his nose. "I sure would've liked to have gone to Wild Waters. All I did was go to my sister's dumb dance recital."

Chase glared. "Nobody brought the right SPF."

Mike rolled his eyes.

"Hang in there, Chase," I said.

"But what are we going to do about the wardens?"

"The wardens?"

"My parents."

I shook my head. "I don't know. But I'll be here tomorrow."

He sighed. "Yeah. See you, then, I guess. If my skin doesn't peel off beforehand."

I ruffled his hair. "I'll be here." They slumped off across the field. Mike put his arm around Chase. Mike's mom's car pulled up just as they reached the walk.

One night I lay in bed thinking about Kohana's philosophy of photography and how that helped me write the scenes

348

from Jason's life. There had to be a way to combine photography and film with Jason's stories to make something awesome. Something for Chase. Something that would never be forgotten. If Kohana's portfolio was a photo documentary, maybe I could make a short subject documentary like *Hardwood*. Something that would help me bring Jason back to everybody. I could use old home movies, invent interviews like that guy did in *Good Bye Lenin!* (I didn't figure the Bishops would be too keen on real interviews), and film all the things that meant the most to Jase. I imagined the script for those objects—what I would say. But I'd need help. Nobody can make a film alone.

The brochure for the voices of youth filmmakers documentary short competition was sitting on my desk, its pages fluttering in the wind from my open window. I got dressed, stuffed my backpack, and wheeled my bike out of the garage, cycling down the black streets until I got to Kohana's house. I owed him a story. And I needed his help.

The house was dark except for one window. Muted yellow light glowed behind translucent shades. I tapped on the glass.

The blinds opened and Kohana pressed his face against the pane. "Who's there?"

"It's me. Kyle."

He opened the window. "Your watch still broke?"

I pulled out the watch, a kite, Jason's sketchbook, the filmmaker competition brochure, and my notebook. I took off my orange shoes and put them beside the other objects. "I want to tell you a story."

We sat on the porch. And I began to talk.

I talked until the first light of dawn stole across the sky. When I finished, Kohana sat silently. He hadn't said anything all night.

He finally turned toward me. "So," he said. "When do we start filming?"

54

The next couple of weeks, Kohana and I worked nonstop before and after school to make Jason's film. Dad let me use his video camera. Kohana even came with me to Chase's school, and we got shots of the Dumpster.

The next day, Chase got picked up by his dad, but he sent a message with Mike that said, SOS. *This weekend, they're making me go to some ice-skating show up at Lawlor Events Center.*

When Kohana read the note, he said, "He has to be part of this, Kyle. We've got to get him to help."

"He's the new Bishop pawn. They don't leave him for a second."

Kohana looked disgusted. "That's too bad."

Late afternoons and into the evening, we used Mr.

Cordoba's multimedia room to edit the footage and cut old home videos into the new material we filmed. It was as if we were getting Jason's life back with every scene we shot.

Kohana knew all sorts of stuff about great camera angles. And I had learned how to make stills and cut moving film into them, creating a "frozen time" effect. The whole documentary had all of Jason's objects frozen, while I walked around them, talking. But I decided to film it so I would always be overexposed—a shadow walking through Jason's world. Over the course of the documentary, my image got clearer. But we needed Chase for the kites and the end.

Mr. Cordoba ordered film books for the library, and as soon as they arrived, he let Kohana and me check them out. I studied the pages of those books whenever I had a chance.

One afternoon, Mike came running to me as soon as he left the school building. "Chase is missing," he gasped.

"Missing?"

"Yeah. My mama was talking to his mama this morning on the phone. Mama asked me about all our favorite hiding spots." Mike wiped the tears out of his eyes. "I think he ran away."

I hugged Mike. "It'll be okay. We'll find him."

Mike shook his head. "He left me this note yesterday. I

didn't read it. It was too long." He handed me a wrinkled piece of paper with jelly stains on it. "There."

I read the note:

April 20 (COPY OF ORIGINAL LETTER DATED APRIL 20 ADDRESSED TO JASON BISHOP)

> Chase Bishop
> 6167 S. Richmond Avenue
> Carson City, NV 58367

Jason Bishop
The Great Beyond

Dear Mr. Bishop (aka Jason) (aka means Also Known As),

I am learning to write letters in class now, so I'm writing you in business letter format. First, I make a brief introduction. Then I state my business. Then I end, cordially, thanking you for your time, reminding you of my business.

How are you? Julian, Marcus, and José don't beat Mike or me up anymore because I contracted the services of Kyle as a bodyguard. We call him Orange

Dragon, or OD. Kyle might be skinny, but he can be pretty intimidating. Plus they think he's a lunatic because he hangs out behind Dumpsters. (Lunatic comes from the word *lunaticus*, meaning "moonstruck"; affected with periodic insanity, dependent on the changes of the moon. Kyle's is more of a permanent thing, but not in a bad way.)

Things at home aren't too good. Mom and Dad fight all the time. And Dad doesn't even live there. So they fight long distance. Brooke cries a lot. And Chip doesn't have much of an appetite. (Chip is my new goldfish who you haven't met yet.)

I don't think things are that great for Kyle either. (But not because of the Dumpster thing. I know that's part of his work as a bodyguard: low-profile stuff.) It's just that he's different than he used to be. He doesn't really smile anymore, and he hasn't invited me over to watch a movie marathon in ages.

I don't know if you're okay or not. I've looked, but I can't find your soul print anywhere. Even Pastor Pretzer can't help me. (Quite honestly, I'm getting a little tired of Sunday school. They made me be a shepherd again in the pageant, and told me that in Jesus's time there were no aeronautical engineers to visit Baby Jesus. I find that hard to believe, since the Chinese were flying kites in approximately 200 b.c. And if anybody would be given a kite for his birthday, it would be Jesus.) Also, Dad quit church.

I'm writing to tell you I miss you. I think I'll always miss you. I didn't know missing could be forever. Do you know a way for it to go away? This sad feeling I have? Is there a way to find you? So the missing doesn't hurt so much?

Your attention to this matter would be greatly appreciated. Thank you for your valuable time and consideration.

Best regards,
Mr. Bishop (aka Chase)

I read the letter three times. "Mike," I said, "did Chase say anything else to you? About where he wanted to be?"

Mike shook his head. "Only that he wanted to be where Jason was."

My insides turned to ice. No, I shook my head. He wouldn't do that. He would never do that.

"Orange Dragon?" Mike looked really scared.

I fought to catch my breath. "I'll find him, I promise. I'll find him, and I'll see you both here tomorrow."

Mike grabbed my hand. "He's my best friend."

"I know." I hugged Mike again, then tore off on my bike.

The cemetery was empty.

He wasn't flying kites at Mills Park.

I raced home. Running up the porch, I slammed into Mr. and Mrs. Bishop.

My throat froze again, just looking at how thin Mrs. Bishop had gotten—how sad she looked.

"Kyle," she said. "He's gone. We can't find him."

I'm sorry.

I'm sorry.

Jesus, just say it. It's all my fault. I wanted the tape to get reversed—back to the very beginning. Without me Jase would be alive. Chase would never have run away. And everybody's life would've been just right.

"Please help find my baby, Kyle. I can't lose him, too." Her last words were muffled in a sob.

I will.

I watched them head frantically back to their house, the candle lamp glowing in the window. *Jesus, please don't let her light another one.* This couldn't be happening.

Mom was talking on the phone. She motioned for me to sit down. "They've been looking all day. I need someone to stay here. Just in case Chase comes around, okay?"

"All day?" I interrupted. "Why didn't somebody tell me? Shouldn't it be on the news? Shouldn't there be police officers everywhere?"

She grabbed her car keys. "Dad and I are going with the Bishops. Mel and the cheerleaders are posting flyers all over town."

A knot formed in my throat.

"We're setting up a search-and-rescue post at the community center."

"Did he leave a note? Did he say anything?"

Mom pulled on a sweatshirt. "He said he wanted to be where he could find Jason's soul print. None of us can figure it out. Stay here. Just in case he comes over. We need you by the phone." Mom left.

"Okay." I slumped at the kitchen table.

Soul print. I sighed, relieved it wasn't what I first thought.

Where would Chase look for Jason's soul print? The neighborhood bustled with action. I stood out on the porch, then walked around to the backyard and stared at the shed.

I hooted.

Somebody's lawn mower kicked on, and the familiar smell of fresh-cut grass drifted through the neighborhood.

I hooted again. After hooting two or three times, I finally heard a soft hoot in return. I circled the shed. The cardboard Dad had used to tape up the window was gone. I hooted louder.

Chase's hoot echoed in the shed.

My heart felt lodged in my throat. Memories of that moment flashed through my mind.

I took a deep breath and climbed through the window.

The shed smelled like fertilizer and oil. It smelled like Clorox and gasoline. I inhaled again, expecting to smell Jason, death, the stench of burned matches, but all I smelled was the familiarity of the shed—a place I used to love as a kid.

My eyes took a second to adjust to the darkness. Chase sat cross-legged in the center of the shed.

"Can I sit here?" I asked.

He scooted over to make room.

I avoided crossing over the bleached spot and made my way to Chase. We sat in silence.

"I just wanted to see," he finally said.

I listened.

"Where it happened."

I nodded.

"I thought it would make it better to see. Maybe he would've left his soul print here, and I could talk to him." Chase sniffled and choked out the words. "But he isn't here, either. And I've been waiting since last night."

I swallowed. But I knew there were no words that would make it better for Chase. We were both looking for the same thing, but neither of us knew how to find it. "I'm so sorry," I finally said.

Chase looked up at me. He leaned his head on my shoulder. We sat for a long time.

"I don't think Dad's coming home," he finally said. "Do you?"

"I don't know, Chase." I squeezed his shoulder. "Maybe."

"Maybe not."

"Maybe not." I sighed.

The light outside the shed changed. I watched through the square of the window as it turned from yellow to a bright orange. "How about if I take you home? A lot of people are really worried." I held out my hand.

He hesitated, then slipped his hand into mine. He had a letter crumpled in his fist. He turned to throw it away in the garbage, and I stopped him. "Do you still want to get a message to Jason?"

Chase turned and looked me in the eyes. "More than anything in this world."

"How about Saturday? Do you think we can meet at Mike's?"

"I dunno. I think I'll be grounded."

"True."

"Maybe I can sneak out."

"And get more grounded?" I asked.

"This is really important."

"Okay. Saturday at seven A.M. I'll tap on your window." I boosted Chase out and followed close behind. We walked out the back gate. "Do you need me to go with you?" I motioned to his house.

He shook his head. "Sometimes a man has to face his fate alone."

What a kid.

He walked home, stepping carefully over the lines in the sidewalk. When he got to his front porch, he turned and waved, then disappeared inside the house.

55

"**C**'mon." I tapped on his window.

Chase peeked out. When he saw me, he grinned and ran to the backyard.

"Did you brush your teeth?" I asked.

"Oh, no!"

"I'm joking! Chase!"

Before I could catch him, he ran back into the house. He came back out. "That was close. Ready?" He grabbed my hand.

"How much time do you have?" I asked.

"About two hours."

"What happens if your mom wakes up and doesn't find you?"

"I've left a note on the kitchen table. It says I went to

do the Carson City historical walk."

"And she'll buy that?"

"Mike and I used to do it every Saturday—before the event calendar. I have the map here." He pulled out a tattered map. It had red markings and highlights all over it. "And the guided tour is in my MP3 player."

I didn't even know there was a Carson City historical walk. "Two hours is plenty of time," I said.

"Maybe next Saturday, you ought to do the historical walk with us." Chase raised his eyebrows.

"I'd like that." And I meant it. "Okay. Let's go." I handed him a helmet. "It's too far to walk. So you get to go for a ride." I hoisted Chase onto the bike.

"Does riding double comply with traffic regulations?"

I laughed. "Sure."

"Really?"

"C'mon, Chase. We don't have all day."

Chase scowled. "Okay. But just this once."

"Okay."

"But ride careful."

"I will."

"And don't tell Mike."

We rode to the graveyard. Rake guy waved at us. When he saw Chase, he came out with a couple of chocolates.

"We come here every Sunday," Chase whispered.

We found Jase's grave. Fresh lilies and daisies covered

it. I wondered if Jason had a favorite flower. I'd never really thought about it before. I didn't have a favorite flower—at least I didn't think so.

We stood there for a while, listening to the silence of the graveyard. I pulled Jason's sketchbook out of my bag and opened it up to the last page. A full-scale comic-book battle.

Finally Chase said, "That's me, isn't it?"

I explained a little. "You're Kite Rider. You're a superhero. A real live superhero."

"Only in Jason's world," he mumbled. "If that were really true, I wouldn't need a bodyguard."

I flipped through the pages and showed him Freeze Frame.

"Hey, you're a superhero too!"

"Yep. With more experience. Maybe I'm supposed to train you."

"Instead of protect me?"

"Maybe."

He grinned. "That sounds better." He rubbed the chalky drawings and smelled his fingers. "Chalk," he whispered.

"Chalk." I closed the notebook. "I just wanted to show this to you. I'm sorry I didn't earlier."

Chase smiled. "It doesn't matter. You're still going to help me talk to Jase, right?"

"Yes."

"Do you think he'll hear me? Get the message?"

"Definitely. Do you have the letter?"

"Yeah." Chase pulled a folded-up note out of his pocket.

"Good." I took a kite out of my backpack. It was one of those cheap, garbage-sack plastic kites. The AM/PM store didn't have a great kite selection.

Chase's eyes got real big. "We're gonna fly a kite. I could've brought the dragon. It's *much* nicer than this one."

"Don't worry about it. Fold your note and put a hole in it. We have to put the string through the hole."

It took Chase about fifteen minutes to find the one spot that didn't have words to put the hole in it. "I want to make sure Jason gets the complete message."

"Okay, sure." It was a good thing we had two hours.

Chase pulled the string through the hole. "That's a lot of string."

"We've got to get the kite as high up as we can—so high we might not even be able to see it."

"And this is gonna work? To get my message out?"

"Yep."

"How do you know about this?"

"I read about it somewhere."

"You read nonfiction?" Chase looked at me sideways.

"Sure, I read everything." I had lately, anyway—anything Mr. Cordoba threw my way.

Chase bit his lip.

"C'mon, Chase. It'll work. I'm gonna run up the path. The wind is pretty decent. We've got to get the kite in the air, okay?"

"Yeah, but don't run over any of the graves, Kyle. You might wake some of these dead people up."

Dead people don't wake up.

"I won't. Don't worry. You hold the kite there." I had Chase hold on. "I'm gonna get it flying, then you'll do the rest."

He nodded.

"When I say, 'Let go!' let go. But not any sooner."

"Okay."

"Ready?"

"Ready!"

I ran up the path, the string trailing behind me. "Let go! Let go!" I shouted. Chase let go just at the right time, and the wind caught the kite, pushing it high above the elm trees and graves.

"C'mon, Chase." Chase caught up to me and grabbed on to the string. "You've got to work the note up to the top of the string, okay? Jiggle it a little in the beginning, and the wind will do the rest. The kite has to fly until the note hits its base."

Chase ran up and down the path; the kite flew high between trees—a plastic red square in the sky. Its colorful tail zigzagged with gusts of wind. It was perfect April wind for flying a kite.

"Kyle, it's there. The note is there! See it?" He laughed.

"Okay. Now let the string out. Let it out until the very end."

Chase unraveled the extra string until all he had was what was looped around his hand. By then the kite was nothing but a tiny red dot in the sky.

"Come over here." We stood next to Jason's grave. "Now you've gotta think about the person you want to receive the note, okay? Think real hard about Jason."

Chase squeezed his eyes closed.

"When you're ready, let the kite go and let it fly away."

We waited. Chase clutched the kite string, taut from the tug of the almost invisible kite. "Ready?"

Chase sniffled and clutched the string.

"Jason will get your message, Chase. Just think real hard about him. Think about how happy he'll be to hear from you."

"Promise?"

"I promise."

"Boy Scout's honor?"

"Yeah. Boy Scout's honor."

"You're not a Boy Scout." Chase's lip quivered.

"But I have honor." I smiled.

"That's my line," he protested.

"I learn from the best." I winked. "Let go of the kite. It's okay."

"Okay." He inhaled and let go of the kite. He unlooped the string, and it slipped out of his hand and floated away, attached to the kite we couldn't even see anymore. Chase grabbed my hand.

He looked up at me. "I really think he got it."

"Me, too," I said. "This is for you." I handed him the sketchbook.

Chase hugged the sketchbook. "It's him. He's really here." His eyes flooded with tears. "This is the best present ever." He wrapped his small arms around my waist and hugged me. "I'm so lucky to have you."

"I'm lucky to have you, too, Chase." He hugged me harder. "Hey, listen, I was thinking that maybe you could help me with something too, something I have for Jase."

"You wrote him a note, too?"

"No. But I thought I'd leave him this." I pulled out the watch.

Chase grabbed my hand. "It's okay, you know?"

"What's okay?"

"It's okay to let it go."

I nodded and wiped the tears from my eyes. Jesus, Chase made my throat knot up.

He squeezed my hand tighter. "Come on, Kyle."

Together, we put the watch on top of Jason's grave. I

looked at the time—on the watch Chase had given me. "Jase," I whispered. "It's eight thirty-seven."

Then Chase took my hand and we walked back through the heavy silence of the graves.

56

Early on April 23, Chase, Kohana, and I got together. I took off my shoes. "One year," I said. "three hundred and sixty-five days."

"Actually three hundred and sixty-five point two-five days, Kyle," Chase corrected me.

Kohana smiled. He and Chase got along really well. I thought Chase would feel bad that I had a friend, but one day he'd said, "It's just too bad Jason wasn't friends with Kohana, too. He's really nice."

"Are you ready to film?" Kohana asked.

I took a deep breath. We'd already filmed Jason's duffel and sleeping bag. We created a movie poster/comic art montage with all of Jason's favorite comic-book artists, including Kyle Baker and Frank Miller. We had footage from old home movies that Chase had snuck out of the house: birthdays, Christmases, Little League and stuff. Chase had found the WXYZ volume of the encyclopedia in Jason's room, and we filmed that. Kohana convinced me to open up the papers and film them. Funny. Jase and I had written the same thing:

> Kyle: Ten years from now, I'll be hanging out with Jase.

> Jason: Ten years from now, I'll be hanging out with Kyle on his birthday. (Hopefully in a bar with really hot women).

My hands shook so bad, I couldn't keep the camera in focus. That day we didn't film any more. I think it made us all sad.

We had even filmed Chase and his kites—running up and down the path of the cemetery sending Jase messages. The only thing I didn't film was Jason's secret stash. I figured it was okay for some scenes to be just between Jase and me.

"Are you ready?" Kohana asked again. "Last scene."

I looked over my director's notes. Chase came over and sat next to me. "He'd like this scene. Even though it might bug him. He never lost a bet, you know."

I laughed. He hadn't. Not with me, anyway. "Ready," I said, and took another deep breath. This was the final scene. There were no more stills, no more overexposures, no more shadows. Just regular filming—moving forward.

UNTITLED: FINAL SCENE–Orange Chili Shoes
Kyle is sitting in the middle of cans of chili. He doesn't speak. He sits there, waiting for his cue.

KOHANA (VOICE-OVER)

We're rolling, Kyle.

KYLE

Ready. (Looks into the camera)
Three hundred and sixty-five point
two-five days, Jase.

Kyle takes off the shoes. Chase comes into the camera's view and hands Kyle a 1948 Captain Marvel Adventures #81.

KYLE

(Shakes his head) You keep this,
Chase.

ZOOM IN: on Kyle's face as he flips
through the pages of the comic book.

(Off camera) A bet's a bet. He'd
want you to have this.

ZOOM IN: On the comic book.

FADE OUT:

KYLE (VOICE-OVER)
It looks like that's a wrap.

Kohana, Chase, and I sat there for a while, just hanging out on the porch. "Hungry?" I finally said, holding up a chili can. Then we all cracked up. It had been a long morning.

"What if we finish editing this afternoon?" Kohana asked.

"Yeah!" Chase jumped up. "Let's go!"

"You think Mr. Cordoba would be okay with that? On a Saturday?"

"We can ask," Kohana said.

We called Mr. Cordoba.

"Can we work in the library today? To finish the movie? I asked. "I know it sounds crazy, but—"

"I'll meet you there in half an hour," Mr. Cordoba interrupted, and hung up the phone.

We hardly recognized Cordoba. He was wearing a pair

of jeans, a Juan Valdez T-shirt, and a paint-splattered baseball cap. He let us work all day, late into the afternoon.

"We're done," I finally said.

Kohana and Chase nodded.

"Let's watch it," said Chase.

"Wait." Kohana went and got Mr. Cordoba.

The four of us sat down and watched as Jason's friendship and memories came to life. When the movie ended, nobody said anything for a while. Then Chase started clapping. I thought I saw Mr. Cordoba wipe his nose with a handkerchief.

"What do you think?" Kohana asked.

Mr. Cordoba said, "I bet the judges in the film competition will love it."

Maybe they would, but that's not why I had made it.

"You did it, man." Kohana took out the DVD, slipped it into the case, and handed it to me. "What are you gonna title it?"

I turned it over in my hands and felt relieved. And sad. But I knew it was going to be okay. "*Freeze Frame.*"

"That's a perfect title," Chase whispered.

"Do you boys need a ride home?" Mr. Cordoba said, interrupting the silence of the media room.

"That'd be great, Mr. Cordoba," Kohana said.

We piled into his car. When we got to Kohana's house, he said, "We're going to Squaw next week, Kyle. Can you come?"

"I'd like to," I said.

"You asked your PO?"

"Yeah. He said it wouldn't be a problem."

"Cool." Kohana walked up the path to his house.

On the way home, Chase told Mr. Cordoba about Jason's planets being wrong on the ceiling and how the Mayas had calculated Venus's orbit for 6,000 years and were off by a day or something. Mr. Cordoba told Chase he had a great book about the Incas and their solar calendars that he would get to me to give to him. I loved listening to them, talking about ancient worlds, planets' orbits, and things that made a difference in the world.

57

When I got home, Mel was all ready for the junior prom. "Whaddya think?" She curtsied. She had on a green shiny dress that, I admit, was tight in just the right spots.

"You're real pretty, Mel."

She blushed. "Thanks."

Mom cried when Jake (a.k.a. Hoover) showed up with some massive carnation corsage dyed mint green. She took about a thousand pictures and Dad looked crabby. He did that for the intimidation effect, and since Jake said, "We'll be home by midnight," I think it worked.

Mom and Dad decided to go for a walk.

I stepped outside in the chilly evening air. The clouds had faded into streaks of pastels and purples. It was the time of day when the moon still has to share the sky with the sun.

Mrs. Bishop had already turned on her lamp, waiting for Jase to come home. I walked across the street and worked my way to the porch. I stood there in the dim evening light. My hand trembled when it reached out to ring the bell. I listened to the life unfolding inside. Chase and Brooke were fighting about something. Somebody put dishes in cupboards. What would I say?

Mrs. Bishop opened the door with a damp dish towel in her hands.

For a moment, I thought about running away, but some force kept me on that porch. Her cheeks sagged a little. She looked thin. I knew I had done that to her.

My hands shook as I gave her my DVD. "I'm so sorry," I whispered. "This was the best I could do to bring him back."

She wrapped me in her arms. "I've been waiting for you."

Acknowledgments

Thank you to the supportive communities of children's writers I've been fortunate enough to be involved with: Northern Nevada SCBWI, in particular Ellen, Suzy, Sheryle, Emily, and Katy; my writing family, the Wordslingers, Trish, Christine, Jean, Lisa, and Mandy; and the Blueboarders. Special thanks to my extraordinary family that has always encouraged me: Mom, Dad, Rick, Syd, and Kyra. And finally, I am privileged to work with two of the most amazing professionals in the business: Stephen Barbara, my intrepid agent, who believed in this project from the beginning, and Jill Santopolo, my brilliant editor, who challenged me to take this novel to a whole other level. I am so grateful.